An Angel's Touch

CUPID'S TOUCH

Pea grabbed her father's rough, callused hand and pulled. As he bent down, Pea's eyebrows rose and fell in earnest while she whispered into his ear.

He frowned.

"Do it, Papa," she demanded loudly.

Gathering what courage he could muster, Seth moved quickly toward Maeve and clasped her shoulders. He planted a gentle kiss on her cheek.

"No, Papa, on the lips. She wants a real kiss, don't you, Maeve?"

Maeve blinked rapidly, afraid to move, afraid not to. Seth tucked his thumb under her chin and tilted her face upward. She reminded herself he was only doing this to make Pea happy, not because he wanted to...or did he? She focused on his mouth, finding it impossible to meet his gaze. His tongue flicked outward, moistening his lower lip, then disappeared.

Time Heals

SUSAN COLLIER

LOVE SPELL   ◆   **NEW YORK CITY**

LOVE SPELL®

June 1995

Published by

Dorchester Publishing Co., Inc.
276 Fifth Avenue
New York, NY 10001

Copyright © 1995 by Susan Collier

Cover Art by John Ennis

Printed in the United States of America.

To Matt, who taught me to believe in miracles—
this one's for you.
Special thanks to Jean and Dee—I asked for agents
and received two angels.

Time Heals

Prologue

Montana, 1888

As the winds swept over the prairie, three sets of eyes watched Seth Caldwell shovel the dirt on top of their mother's grave.

"Bow your heads," their father commanded gruffly.

"When's Mama coming ho—"

Blossom's brother grabbed her hand to stifle her words. "Shh," Jeb admonished, while his father's deep, resounding voice filled the heat-laden afternoon.

Thunder rumbled in the endless Montana sky, and Jeb watched a streak of lightning hit the ground in the far-off distance.

"I want my mama," Blossom wailed loudly.

Jeb pulled the trembling child close to his

side, then peeked at his sister, Gracie, who, naturally, had her head bowed reverently. He knew he should be praying but he couldn't bring himself to petition a God who had taken his mother away. Besides, it wasn't as if he hadn't prayed for her before.

In the long weeks of her strange behavior, he had talked to God constantly. Now an inner voice blamed him for not being able to save her.

Jeb kicked the dust angrily. Evidently God just didn't listen to little boys. Not that he was little, of course. At age 12 he was expected to be a man and do his share of the work. Another clap of thunder made his little sister whimper. He stopped his train of thought and concentrated on getting this over with.

Replacing his worn straw hat atop his head, Seth turned to face his children. "We best be gettin' back. Chores are waiting."

His clothes were ordinary, not at all what one would expect to see when attending a funeral. But these weren't ordinary times and Seth wasn't an ordinary man. The years of hard work had taken their toll on him, and his face was a path of that labor.

Now this.

He glanced over his shoulder to make sure all three children followed him, then turned back toward the flat, desolate plains and home.

Gracie stopped suddenly, causing Jeb to bump into her. "It's too dang hot to walk," she muttered miserably.

"Go!" Jeb snapped, seeing his father look

back with a frown. He noticed that Blossom, better known as Pea, had a handful of his shirt and sucked on her thumb as if she hadn't a care. He matched his father's scowl. If Papa saw her, he'd tan her hide for sure. It had taken 'em near on two years to break that habit and here she was, doin' it again. He glanced down before admonishing her. "Babies suck their thumbs, Pea."

A pair of brilliant blue eyes peered up at him, a smile forming on the cherry lips that were clasped hard to the thumb. "Tastes good," she stated with a lisp.

"Yeah? Bet it won't taste near as good if'n Pa—" He stopped. "Well, maybe so, but don't let Papa catch you at it, okay?"

Pea gave a solemn nod.

Seth heard the fragmented pieces of conversation between his eldest and youngest, and shook his head. Duessa's body wasn't even stone cold yet and the problems had already started. What in the hell was he going to do with three kids? Being so busy trying to provide a living on this hard, unyielding land had left little time to form the type of bond his wife had with them.

Seth realized he knew nothing about children, especially one as young as Pea. It wasn't that he didn't love his kids—Seth knew he'd gladly lay down his life for any one of them— but how in God's name was he going to be both mother and father?

As he felt Pea's soft little hand slip into his

hard, calloused palm, a smile played at the corners of his mouth. Seth glanced down at his youngest daughter and felt a tug at his heartstrings.as he noted her feathery blond curls bouncing with each step she took. He purposely slowed so she wouldn't have to struggle as hard to keep up with his long strides.

When she offered a look of gratitude, his smile widened. A body couldn't help but love this one especially. One look into those cornflower blue eyes would melt the hardest of hearts. He remembered how his wife used to hide her laughter behind her hand when he tried to discipline the rambunctious toddler. He'd start out all tough around the edges, and as Pea would sneak closer, finally ending up in his lap, his anger slowly dissipated to be replaced by a strong surge of affection.

That was when Duessa would offer him that secret smile of hers, assuring him no matter what, there would always be a rainbow at the end of the storm.

But that had been before she'd stopped smiling. Before his wife had become so unhappy that she no longer laughed, no longer loved, no longer cared.

Gracie ran forward and grabbed her father's free hand, dancing around as she kept up the stride. "Papa? How much farther? How come we had to bury Mama so far away from home? Won't she git lonely, Papa?"

"She's in God's hands, child. She ain't lonely no more."

"Oh." The answering voice seemed small.

Simple, Seth thought. Simple as that. An "oh." Maybe Duessa was in a far better place than he'd been able to provide for her, but that didn't stop him from worrying. And when the children realized the finality of their mother's passing, would the explanation be enough?

Spotting the chimney of the cabin, Seth pointed a finger. "Go on now, get home. I got some plowing to do."

Jeb raised a questioning eyebrow and Seth shook his head. "You get on home too, Jeb. Watch Pea. I'll be in about sundown."

They made a pathetic sight, the three children, as they slowly walked toward home. And when the horizon had all but swallowed them up, the giant of a man hung his head and cried.

Chapter One

Montana, 1989

Maeve Fredrickson pulled another M&M from her emergency stash beneath a plush paisley pillow on the couch, popped it into her mouth, and narrowed her eyes at her half-naked cousin.

Natasha continued her tirade. "You could be getting ready too, Maevie."

The cutesy name made Maeve gag on the candy.

"It's your own fault, you know," Natasha said, turning to stare in the mirror above the fireplace mantel. Her pageboy haircut swayed gently against her jawline. The smile her reflection returned indicated her approval.

"If you'd just agree to go out with Arnie's step-brother, then you too could enjoy the fun, and just think, Maevie. . . ."

Her words faded, blending with the Western documentary blaring from the T.V., as Maeve's imagination took flight.

The sun beat relentlessly against Maeve's back. Sweat drops trickled down the sides of her face but she couldn't wipe them away. Not now. Not when there was about to be a showdown at high noon in Dodge City with the owner of the Skinny Women's Dress Emporium.

In the hot, shimmering silence, Maeve heard the creak of swinging doors when Natasha stepped outside onto the boardwalk.

She observed through narrowed eyes as, one by one, the cowhands lined up to kiss Natasha's perfectly manicured hand. Maeve planted her feet wide apart, using the movement as a ruse to get Natasha's attention.

"Natasha, it's high time you paid your dues." She watched her archenemy priss down the steps. No doubt about it, this was going to be a difficult job, them being kin and all. The thought that a whole slew of women from the Loyal Order of— no, make that the Secret Order of the Thunder Thighs, were depending on her, drove her to continue. The pressure was on and she couldn't let them down. Withdrawing her gun from the special hand-carved chocolate holster strapped to her thigh, Maeve took aim.

Natasha began the dance of dodging the bullet,

*but to no avail. The fat gun was mightier than
the dance.*

*She was quick, she was good, she was deadly.
In no time, Natasha received a shot to the hips,
the stomach, and worst of all, the rear. Twenty-
four hours was all she'd have left to enjoy her
perfect figure. After that? Fat City!*

*Maeve blew the last of the fat rays from her
smoking weapon, replaced it in the holster, licked
the chocolate from her fingers, and walked away.*

*The Secret Order of the Thunder Thighs would
be safe once again.*

". . . and if you never get up off that couch and
quit watching T.V., how are you ever gonna
meet a man? Maeve, are you listening to me?
This isn't funny, you know!" Natasha flung her
hands out in defeat.

Maeve smiled, popping another M&M in her
mouth as her cousin left the room. She felt
something hard press against the back of her
scalp.

"Stick 'em up, lady; this here's a robbery.
Hand over the loot."

Without turning around, Maeve grinned. Her
eight-year-old cousin sneaked around the corner of the couch and held out a grubby hand.

"The loot or your life," he demanded, mim-
icking the real-life cowboys galloping their way
across the television screen.

She handed over the rest of the chocolates.

"Gee, thanks, Maeve. Mama wants you in the
kitchen."

Susan Collier

Her grin disappeared. "What does she want, Freddie?"

"How should I know?" he answered with a mouth full of chocolate. "All she said was to go get Maeve."

"Thanks, pardner. And don't be telling where you got the candy! The last thing I need is Aunt Gladys on my bu—case."

Freddie nodded, tipped his genuine imitation Roy Rogers cowboy hat, then mounted his imaginary horse to ride away and create havoc on another victim.

Reluctantly, Maeve stood. She already knew what her daddy's sister was going to say. Ten seconds later, the conversation confirmed her psychic abilities.

"Maevie, honey, I wish you'd reconsider and go to the country club with us. I hate to think of you all alone on the Fourth of July."

"Don't worry so much about me, Aunt Gladys! Believe it or not, I'm kind of into this show I'm watching on the centennial anniversary of Montana's statehood." Maeve knew it was a small fib, but she most definitely had her own plans for later on, and she wasn't so sure Aunt Gladys would approve.

"You're enjoying a documentary? Come on now, dear, what will you do with yourself?"

Maeve decided it best to face her aunt's disapproval. "I'm thinking seriously about going to the Rendezvous Amusement Park. They're supposed to have a big fireworks display around ten."

18

"Not to mention all that junk food, eh, Maevie?" Gladys stopped loading the dishwasher and stared at her niece. "Sweetheart, why not go with me to my next weight-loss session? Meet the people, Maeve. Listen to their stories. You'll find, my dear, you're not the only one with sadness in your life. I know you still miss your mom and dad, but time heals all wounds . . ."

Dr. Bones stepped out of his office holding a straitjacket. "Come, Maeve."

Maeve held on to the handle of the door. "No! I won't go!"

"Yes, you will. All we're going to do is fill you full of about a thousand—no, make that ten thousand kilowatts of electricity every time you think of food. Stop being such a baby about this."

"But I like being cuddly."

"When we're through with you, you'll be the perfect weight. Ten pounds."

". . . Maeve, honey, have you heard a word I said?"

"Sure, Auntie, I heard every word," Maeve assured her.

Gladys wiped her hands dry and cupped her niece's face. "Such a pretty girl. You've got Janet's eyes, you know." She clucked her tongue. "You've also got Janet's stubborn streak. Are you sure you won't change your mind and come with us?"

Maeve shook her head in adamant refusal.

"I'd rather go to the amusement park instead."

"Promise me you won't . . . what is it you kids say?"

"Pig out?" Maeve offered helpfully.

"Yes."

"Don't you worry about me, Aunt Gladys. I'll be fine." Before her aunt could respond, Maeve pecked her on the cheek and left the room.

Whew, close call there, Maeve. Just the thought of watching Natasha dance with all those preppies makes my stomach turn.

Closing the door and twisting the lock, Maeve rummaged through her underwear drawer to retrieve another sack of M&Ms. She quickly popped one in her mouth before crossing the room.

An Elvis Presley poster hung over her bed, and Maeve propped a dimpled knee on the mattress, then stared at her idol with worshiping eyes. He'd been her first and only idol ever since she'd seen the movie *Blue Hawaii* on television at the tender age of six.

"Wella, wella now, Elvis. What do you think? The amusement park or a stuffy country club?" Her hazel eyes sparkled as Maeve smiled happily. "I knew you'd agree."

She hummed as she put on a fresh pair of size 13 jeans and an oversize T-shirt which read: "Elvis lives . . . somewhere in Jersey."

The fear of further detainment spurred Maeve to slip out of the house without saying good-bye. She hurried down the street toward the bus stop.

Angry clouds had gathered over the perfect day and she thought briefly about returning to her aunt's house for an umbrella. The sight of the approaching bus made her dismiss the idea. Maybe the rain would melt off her extra weight and Aunt Gladys would finally leave her alone.

After entering the vehicle, Maeve noticed how crowded the bus was. She figured most families would be at home doing the usual celebration things—barbecues, fireworks—things she and her parents used to do on the Fourth of July. Once again, she was reminded of how unusually close her family had been to one another.

Tears stung her eyes. It had been two years since her parents' deaths. Would she ever get over missing them so desperately? Maeve blinked quickly.

No sense crying about things that can't be changed. What I need is the angel of mercy to show a little mercy! Help me keep the memories of my parents and get over the pain of losing them.

After settling into an empty seat, Maeve heard a low sob, and the sound caused the hairs at the back of her neck to stand on end. She took an anxious peek at her fellow passengers, but no one looked the least bit upset.

Maeve shook her head and stared out the window. She'd probably heard a distant roll of thunder. But there it was again. This time she recognized the noise for what it was, a grief-stricken, masculine sob.

Again she scanned the faces of the passengers. Except for the angry young mother trying to control her son, everyone else seemed quite cheerful, almost jubilant, in fact. How odd!

The bus slowed down as it neared the large amusement park and Maeve forgot all about the weeping when she saw the Ferris wheel's array of lights beckoning her to ride.

Although she was almost 19, the fair—any fair—still had the power to start her heart racing with excitement like that of a small child.

Stepping onto the sidewalk, Maeve inhaled the scent of rain building in the air. As much as she enjoyed the heavy, musty smell, she hoped it would hold off until after the fireworks display.

After paying her admission fee, she walked through the gate. In the event the fair should close early, it would be best, Maeve felt, to start with the food vendors. No sense taking chances, she decided.

She began with a giant cob of corn dripping with butter, then methodically worked her way down the midway appeasing herself with one sample from each booth.

The foot-long hot-dog stand was her favorite. Watching the wieners turn on the skewer made Maeve's mouth water in anticipation.

Although her jeans were already tight, she willingly took a chance on busting a seam. After paying for her purchase, Maeve layered the top with onions, relish, and lots of her favorite condiment, ketchup.

Turning the bottle upside down, Maeve frowned when it gave out an airy blast instead of thick sauce. She slammed her hand against the bottom to force the last drops to the top of the bottle, then gritted her teeth and squeezed. Elvis's face was soon covered with a thick glob of red as the ketchup squirted her T-shirt instead of the hot dog.

Maeve grimaced and grabbed a stack of paper napkins. Now Aunt Gladys would have proof she had indeed "pigged out."

The thought of listening to the lecture once again caused Maeve to throw the last few bites into an already overflowing trash receptacle.

Well, Aunt Gladys, it was the craziest thing! I was standing—no, sitting, next to some kids, just resting my feet, and before I knew what happened, this kid shot me with ketchup.

What do you mean, what did I do?

I called the ketchup patrol. They lined those kids up and forced them to drink bottle after bottle of ketchup. It was a terrible sight, Aunt Gladys.

Really! I wouldn't lie!

What do you mean, I'm losing my touch?

Okay, it's like this. There was this terrible accident on the midway and what with me being a candy striper at the hospital, I felt it was my duty to apply pressure to the wound until the ambulance arrived.

What do you mean, I just deliver flowers to the patients? Should that stop me from saving someone's life?

* * *

As Maeve walked down the pathway to the Ferris wheel, the lights made her forget all about Aunt Gladys, the ketchup patrol, and rescuing people.

For as long as she could remember, at every amusement park she'd ever been to, she and her daddy rode the Ferris wheel while her mama watched and waved.

The remembrance was bittersweet, and a surge of longing filled Maeve's heart. She watched the benches sway away from the ground and circle up to reach the black of night. As much as she wanted to ride it this very minute, finances deemed one ride only, and she was determined to wait until the fireworks were sending out their brilliant array of colors.

Continuing on down the pathway, Maeve walked past the freak shows, past the roller coaster, and came to a stop at the fortune-teller's tent.

"Fortunes told. Past, present, and future," the woman called engagingly as she adjusted her heavy veil in boredom.

Maeve fished into the pocket of her jeans and handed over two dollars. The gypsy beckoned her to follow.

"Say, do you really know the future?" Maeve questioned.

"I do. Past, present, and future. Come along, child."

Maeve walked to the back of the small, dimly lit room and sat down at a card table covered in black cloth. The only object adorning the square area was a round globe of glass. Maeve grinned. "That your crystal ball?"

"That's right," the woman answered. "Now then, let me see your hand."

Maeve placed her palms between her legs. "Nope. I want the crystal ball."

The gypsy's eyes narrowed. "It'll cost you an extra buck."

Leaning over, Maeve pulled a crumpled dollar from her pocket and placed it on the table in front of her. "What all can you see in that thing?"

"The future, my dear," the woman stated in a mysterious tone.

Maeve rubbed her hands together in anticipation "So, like, is Elvis alive?"

The gypsy frowned. "*Your* future," she stated flatly.

"Oh."

As the fortune-teller's hands moved over the glass ball, Maeve stifled a giggle. It reminded her of the wicked witch in *The Wizard Of Oz* when she commanded Dorothy to sleep.

The gypsy interrupted her thoughts. "Tell me, what do you wish for?"

Dimples appeared in her cheeks as Maeve grinned. "Gee, I wish I was about a hundred years and thousands of miles away from here. See, when Aunt Gladys notices the ketchup stain on my shir—What is it? What's wrong?"

The fortune-teller's face had turned ghastly white as she gazed into the ball. Her words came out in a singsong. "You are the chosen.

You will go on a journey. A child needs you desperately and, even now, cries for you . . . listen!"

In the ensuing silence, Maeve concentrated but heard nothing. Suddenly the room was filled with the pitiful sound of a child weeping. She covered her ears against the pathetic sound. "Stop this!" Maeve pleaded. "Stop it at once!"

The fortune-teller's eyes burned with fire. "You shall seek the young child out. Three call your name and one you shall lose. He will forgive you."

Bowing her head, the gypsy closed her eyes. "Leave," she demanded quietly. "The crystal has gone black."

Maeve's eyes were wide. "Where are these people? Who are they?"

"The crystal is black. Leave . . . please leave." As she spoke, a clap of thunder rocketed the sky.

Maeve felt a cold chill travel up the length of her spine and settle on the back of her neck. When she rose, her hip bumped against the edge of the table and the crystal fell from its stand, rolling to the floor where it shattered into thousands of glimmering pieces. "I-I'm sorry," Maeve stammered.

"There is no need to be sorry. The future has been foretold, the past taken care of." The woman placed the three dollars in front of Maeve. "You are the chosen."

Maeve backed away and began to run. She didn't stop until she reached the Ferris wheel. With trembling hands, she slid the last of her money under the plastic opening and grabbed the ticket from the attendant.

A drop of rain splattered against her cheek. "Hurry," Maeve whispered to the ticket taker, ignoring his reaction to her haste. She couldn't explain the driving force inside her, couldn't explain the fog shrouding her brain.

The need to board the ride was so great she rushed ahead of a young couple and slammed the safety bar closed as she sat down in the gondola.

A streak of lightning blended with the brilliant flash of a bottle rocket high overhead. Maeve felt herself being lifted into the night air as the ride began and watched as another angry flash of lightning lit the darkness. The lightning splintered in all directions, coming closer and closer until she crouched in her seat, filled with fear.

Although she remained completely still, the gondola began to sway back and forth in violent motion. "Help me," Maeve screamed. "Get me off of here!"

The lightning complied as its icy fingers reached out to lift her from the safety of the ride and carry her high into the night.

Throwing the switch into the off position, the attendant watched the angry skies with a wary eye. This storm was unlike anything he'd ever seen before. The atmosphere was charged with electricity, charged with . . . with . . . the word *danger* came to mind.

In horror he watched as the young woman who had been so anxious to ride was thrown out of the wildly swinging gondola. A sick sensation caused him to place one hand over his mouth as he comprehended the results. There would be no need for an ambulance; surviving such a fall was impossible.

So this is what it's like to die, Maeve thought. There was no pain, just a warmth that rushed through her body, settling in her head. After that? A floating sensation. She thought about being afraid, but couldn't. The feelings were too comforting, too soothing. She tried to see, but there was nothing to see. Not in this place, this space in time.

Maeve wondered if her parents would recognize her with all the weight she'd put on since their death. The thought amused her. Of course they would. In heaven there would be no weight problems. She began to look forward to her destination when the harsh, ragged sobs she'd heard on the bus filled her very being.

He needs me, she thought.

Knowing she was crying, but helpless to stop it, Maeve felt an overwhelming desire to hold this man who suffered so desperately, close to her heart.

Her eyelids grew heavy as she felt herself being lowered.

Oh no! I'm going to hell! I'll bet it's all that food I sneaked when Aunt Gladys wasn't looking.

Time Heals

It was to be her last coherent thought as she slipped into a space where time became something to be worshiped, something to be revered. Indeed, time at last became the healer. . . .

Chapter Two

Montana, 1889

"Are you children ready?" Seth questioned, pulling his hat down low on his head to ward off the misty rain.

"Papa, why do we have to go? It's raining outside," Gracie complained, tugging on her coat uncomfortably. "This ol' thing's too small for me."

"Next time I go to town, I'll see if I can find a seamstress to make you another, Gracie. Now come along."

This day marked the first anniversary of Duessa's death. While he hadn't been able to bring himself to visit her grave site before, Seth knew he owed it to his wife's memory to take the children there. Pea's happy chatter bothered him greatly. No matter how hard he'd tried to explain, the youngster had it in her head they were going to see Duessa in person.

As if to confirm his fears, Pea explained to her cornhusk doll, "Don't you be missin' me too much, Miss Liza. We're gonna go see Mama and when I tell her how much we love her, her's gonna come straight home to us. Betcha she'll make us a new coat too. I kin tell ol' Gracie's tryin' to talk Papa into givin' me hers just so's she kin have a new one. Mama ain't gonna let that happen. Just you wait and see." Thinking of her mother's pretty face, Pea let out a squeal of delight. "Mama's comin' home, Mama's comin' home!"

Jeb brushed his cowlick into place as he walked to his father's side. "Pa, what we gonna do about Pea? She's gonna be heartsick when we git there and all she sees is a bunch of dirt covered in overgrown weeds."

"We'll handle it, boy. We've handled everything else that's come up this past year, ain't we?"

Thinking of all the burned meals, Gracie's temper tantrums, Pea's bad nightmares . . . and the sound of his father pacing the expanse of the cabin when everyone should have been asleep, Jeb frowned. Papa wouldn't want to know the truth about what he really thought, so best let this question slide by unanswered.

He watched his father hesitate before opening the door. Strange how Papa didn't seem to want to go visit the grave. So why did they have to? Gracie didn't want to walk that far, and Jeb sure didn't need reminding Mama was gone, if that was what this was all about.

"Let's go, young'uns."

The morning was hazy with the covering of fog and mist. It struck Jeb as eerie the way it hovered around their feet: as if they were walking on clouds or something. Before long, just as he'd silently predicted, Gracie started to complain about the long journey.

"My shoes are done worn plum through, Papa. These old rocks and pebbles are ahurtin' my feet." Her scowl darkened. "Don't know why we have to go anyway. Mama ain't gonna know the difference."

"That ain't true!" Pea cried. "Mama's expectin' us, 'cuz Pa said so, didn'tcha, Papa?"

Once again, Pea had confused the truth with her private fantasy, Seth realized. He stopped and knelt down in front of the little girl, mindless of the damp seeping through his trousers. "Pea, honey, your Mama isn't going to be there in person. She's an angel now."

"Ooooo! Does she have wings? Is us gonna git to see her wings? Reckon she'll let me touch 'em, Papa?"

"You ain't gonna touch 'em, 'cause you ain't gonna see her!" Gracie exploded. The light mist had finally turned to rain, and cold water dripped down the back of her neck, making her thoroughly miserable.

Standing, Seth took Pea's hand in his. "Maybe this is something I should have done a lot sooner. Gracie's right, you know," he said, looking down into Pea's trusting blue eyes. "Mama won't be there. She's in heaven and she lives with God now."

"Then I gots me a good idea," Pea stated solemnly.

"What's that?"

"I'm gonna tell God to give her back. I'll tell him we won't even touch her wings if'n he don't want us to, if he'll just let her come home."

Surely seeing the burial place would once and for all settle the matter in the child's mind, Seth thought. He cringed as a drop of rain found its way from the rim of his hat down the back of his shirt. Hadn't it been the same type of weather the day they buried Duessa?

Seth shook his head. It happened too long ago to recollect. So why could he still recall so clearly the softness of her body, the warmth of her smile?

Thunder rumbling in the sky brought him out of his reverie. "Come along, children, let's step lively or we'll be caught in the storm."

Once they reached their final destination, Seth knew he'd made a mistake. All the anger, the rage at being left with the children, seemed to build inside him. The feelings were unfair to Duessa's memory, he knew, but he couldn't help them. "Let's go ahead and say a prayer for your Mama." And me, he added silently.

Instead of doing so, Jeb bowed his head and peeked through half-closed lids. He watched as Pea backed up on tiptoe and began to search the area. The stormy look on her face matched the darkening skies and Jeb knew at any moment his little sister was about to let loose with her ear-piercing wails of distress.

Casting a glance in Gracie's direction, Jeb couldn't decide how she felt. The stony expression that had carried her through this entire first year was impenetrable.

As his father's deep voice carried over the sound of thunder, Jeb glanced up at the sky. A sharp crack of lightning, followed by yet another, momentarily caused him to cringe. It seemed as if the entire sky was filled with streaks of fire.

"Does anyone else want to add a prayer?" Seth offered. "Best hurry if you do; I don't like the looks of this storm."

"I don't like the sound of it," Gracie stated with a shiver. She watched as, in the far distance, the tops of the pines began to sway.

The small band made their way back toward the cabin. As quickly as the storm had approached, it seemed to clear, leaving behind a too-brilliant sun and hot, muggy warmth. "You ever seen anything like that, Pa?" Jeb asked.

"Can't say I honestly have . . . not in a while, anyway. You take the girls and get on home, hear me, boy? I'm going to go check on the horses and I'll be there in a while."

"Yes, sir. Come on Pea, stop dawdling. You heard Pa, let's git to the cabin."

"Me's thirsty," Pea wailed, her thumb inching its way into her mouth.

"We'll git a drink at the well," Jeb offered. "Come on, Gracie, help me talk her into hurrying."

Gracie scowled. She'd hoped someone would mention going into town, but if Papa was going to check on the horses, he'd take a while. Drat! Her plan for Pa meeting another lady wasn't going to work out this time.

"Doesn't anyone want to go see the fireworks in town?"

"What fireworks?"

"It's the Fourth of July, Jeb. Remember?"

Actually, he hadn't. But to admit such to Gracie would make her feel superior. "So?"

"Don't you want Pa to take us?"

"Pa's got too much on his mind to be attending celebrations. Guess we'll go to next year's instead."

Once they reached the well, Jeb pulled up a dipperful of water and handed it to his little sister. Strangely enough, Pea had yet to comment on Mama not appearing. "You gotta take that thumb out of there before you can drink, Pea." Glancing up at the sky, he murmured, "Clouds are gathering again."

"Ain't not!" Pea argued. "Sun's shining bright. 'Sides, Papa knows I'm scairt of the thunder and he'd come on home to make me feel better."

Jeb turned her small body around and pointed toward the east where dark, ominous clouds were building once more. "Look right over yonder, Pea." He watched in awe as one cloud, traveling with astonishing speed, flew across the sky. It almost seemed to touch down in the forest behind their cabin. As much as he wanted to go investigate, Pea had already made it quite clear her dolls were expecting a tea party this afternoon. And as usual, Pea won.

After several hours of their tea party, Pea watched Jeb's head slowly lower to his chest. His body jerked, then became still. "Jeb? You asleep?" Pea whispered and received no answer in response. She looked down at her cornhusk doll. "You go to sleep too, Liza. Pea's gonna go find Mama. She musta gotten lost when she was waitin' for us to come see her."

She stole out of the cabin while Gracie's back was turned. The woods seemed rather frightening, but she remembered how her Mama used to tell her the trees were their friends. They whispered sweet secrets at night when the gentle winds blew off the mountains. And when the rains came, they offered their branches for protection.

Popping her thumb into her mouth, Pea spoke around it. "I ain't scairt," she mumbled, walking to the forest's edge. A streak of lightning lit through the cool of the afternoon shadows. Pea removed her thumb and smoothed her dress with trembling fingers. "I ain't scairt," she repeated.

Halfway into the forest, she heard the thunder roll across the sky. Running, Pea turned back in the direction she had come. Or was it?

All the trees looked so much alike it was impossible to tell.

"Mama? You in there?" She heard the creaking of branches. "Mama, Pea's scairt. . . . Pea's real scairt, Mama, come git me!" Giant tears rolled down her pale face as she stumbled and fell.

"What in the blazes do you mean, you can't find Pea?" Seth removed his hat and stormed back and forth across the expanse of the small cabin. "She's got to be around here somewhere; she's scared to death of those woods."

"Papa, I'm sorry." Jeb's face was a mask of misery. "I musta fallen asleep or something. We was playing dolls—well, Pea was anyway—and the next thing I knowed, she was gone."

Seth looked toward his ten-year-old daughter. "What about you, Gracie? What were you doing?"

"I was thinking about doing the dishes, only I couldn't lift the bucket of water by myself."

"Thundering mules, Gracie! You either do the dishes or you don't, but you do not *think* about it!" Seth lit his pipe and threw the match toward the fireplace. "No tellin' where the child's wandered off to. Best git your jacket, boy, the wind's pickin' up."

"Yes, sir, Papa, right away." Jeb ran to obey.

Gracie picked at her finger.

"Stop that, Gracie. Now you stay here in case she returns, you understand me, girl?" The look on his face matched the deep roll of thunder shaking the house.

"Oh, Papa, don't make me stay here all alone! I'm scared of the thunder," Gracie whined.

Seth removed his rifle from the shelf. "I said to stay, understand?"

Tears filled Gracie's eyes. "Y-yes, sir, Papa."

Laying the rifle aside, Seth walked over to the weeping child. He bent and clasped her small hands with his large palms. "Gracie, ain't nothin' gonna hurt you. We've got to find Pea before the storm breaks, understand me, child?"

She nodded and Seth planted a kiss on her forehead. "That's my girl."

Pea heard the gurgling of water before she saw the creek. She walked through the brush, scratched her face on a branch, and started to wail. At that moment, her eyes caught the attention of a white object lying several feet away. She walked forward to investigate, her thumb automatically going to the warm comfort of her mouth.

A fairy! Lying fast asleep in the dirt. And what a pretty fairy she was, with her rich brown hair fanned out around her face. Pea's eyes traveled downward to the splotch of red on the fairy's camisole. Why would anyone hurt a fairy? she wondered. She had no doubt this woman was a fairy because, after all, Mama had told her of such things. When the enchantress made a whimpering sound, Pea's eyes opened wide. "Is you okay?" she whispered.

Thousands of minuscule drummers had taken residence in Maeve's head and she was certain that, any moment, her skull would split from the pain. Although her eyes were open, she had trouble comprehending the fact that a cloth of darkness was all she could see. "Help."

The single word sounded raspy, panic-stricken.

"Did them Injuns git you?" Pea questioned her curiously.

"Where am I?" Maeve croaked.

"Is you the forest fairy?"

Maeve could tell the voice belonged to a child. "Go get help . . . please." Warm tears wet the sides of her face.

"Can't. I'm lost," Pea stated matter-of-factly. The knowledge didn't upset her in the least now that she had found the fairy.

"Listen, you have to go get . . ." Maeve could feel herself sinking back into the pit of obscurity and welcomed it as a chance to escape the pain inside her head.

Pea sat down beside the fairy and listened to the *ping* of raindrops hitting the smooth rock beside her. The branches of the trees danced with the wind. Far off, she could hear her papa's voice calling, and, with a backward glance at the sleeping fairy, she ran toward the approaching crunch of footsteps.

"Blossom Caldwell, why did you run off?" Seth's words were harsh, but he wrapped his arms around her tightly, relishing the feel of his daughter against him.

"I found a fairy, Papa."

Seth knelt down and pushed back a clump of tangled curls. "You must promise me you'll never leave the house without Jeb or Gracie again." He shook her shoulders gently in chastisement. "The woods aren't safe for a little girl all alone, Pea."

A tear trickled down her dirt-streaked face. "Will the fairy be safe, Papa?"

Sweeping her off the ground, Seth headed back in the direction he had come. "Pea, I know you miss Mama, but there's no such thing as fairies." Had he been silent for a moment, he would have heard a weak cry for help. "Now then, let's get on home."

Pea popped her thumb in her mouth. "Papa? Kin fairies die?"

Seth shook his head, giving in to her childishness. "No, Pea, I don't think so."

"This fairy was hurt."

He knew he should put an end to this, but the relief of finding her was too great. Catching up with Jeb, Seth glanced warily at the darkening skies. "Rain's beginning to pick up a bit. Let's get home."

"Does fairies mind the rain, Papa?"

Jeb looked toward his little sister, cradled safely within his father's muscular arms. "You find a fairy, Pea? Did she have wings?"

"Couldn't tell. She was down by the stream; she was crying. Papa, why would a fairy cry?"

Seth frowned. "That's enough, Pea. There isn't any such thing as a fairy and I don't want to hear another word, understand?"

"But Papa—"

"Enough, Pea."

"Yes, Papa."

Maeve managed to rise into a sitting position and, from the ensuing silence, realized she was once again alone. Holding the sides of her head, she blinked to try to clear her vision. Was it her imagination, or did she see a speck of light? There seemed to be tall shapes closing in on her. "Hello? Is anyone there?"

The wind whistled eerily through the branches.

"Please, if you can hear me, answer me." She felt the cold earth through the dampness of her jeans and stood, going in the direction of the shadows. When she reached out and felt the rough bark of the tree, Maeve moaned. "Somebody, please . . . help me."

After feeding the children a supper of porridge and the last bit of bread, Seth watched his youngest child. Her face looked sad and drawn. Very unlike Blossom. "Come and sit with Papa, Pea Pot."

When she obliged, he sat down in the rocker, resting his chin on her golden curls, and began to rock gently. Pea cuddled close and he could feel her steady heartbeat beneath her tiny frame.

"Papa, you reckon Mama sent that fairy to take care of me till she finds her way back to us?"

He rocked gently, humming under his breath. "Maybe so, Pea."

"Kin you fetch her home for me tomorrow, Papa?"

"We'll see, little one. If I have time, maybe I'll go back there with you in the morning and take a look around."

Seth smiled as his daughter gave in to sleep. When her breathing became rhythmic, he carried her to the trundle bed, laid her down, and kissed her forehead. Standing, his face filled with anger. "Family meeting, kids. Get over here."

Gracie was slow to come. "We ain't had a family meeting since Mama died, Pa."

Jeb lightly punched her side.

"Oww! Stop it, Jeb! Papa, did you see that? Jeb punched me."

"Jeb, Gracie, listen to me. Blossom must never be allowed to go into the forest alone again. When I think what could have happened to her, I—well, let's just say I'm angry. Gracie, I've told you plenty of times, she's your responsibility while Jeb and I work the fields."

"But Papa, that's not fair!" Gracie cried. "Why should Jeb get to play outside and I have to stay here and watch after Pea? It just ain't fair, I tell you!"

"Nothing is fair, Gracie. Not your mother's death, not this land, not anything." Seth's words

43

came stingingly harsh, and Gracie covered her face with her hands, crying.

Seth walked to the fireplace and stared down at the dying embers. Troubled thoughts shadowed his mind.

What am I going to do? I can't raise these children alone. I just can't do it.

Jeb cleared his throat. "Say, Papa, I can help take care of Pea. I can work in the fields and watch her too."

"You can't keep one eye on the child. She'd up and wander off the first time you weren't looking. No, Gracie will have to learn to take better care of her alone." Seth hesitated, softening his tone. "Children, I know this is hard; the first year of a loved one's death always is. But somehow, some way, we'll get through it."

It took all the nerve Gracie could muster to speak up. "Papa, can't you get us a new mama? I mean, I know she wouldn't be as good as our mama, but maybe she could take care of us and fix supper and mend our clothes, and . . . and . . . well, can't you, Papa?"

"Aw, hush, stupid! Papa ain't gonna find us a new ma. Whad'ya think he's gonna do, order us one from the wish-and-want book?" Jeb demanded.

Seth's loud sigh filled the small cabin. "Jeb, don't call your sister stupid. Until we can figure out a different arrangement, Gracie, Blossom is your responsibility. Now go on, both of you get to bed. Mornin' comes way too early."

He watched as the children scurried up the

ladder to the loft. "Night, kids."

"Night, Papa."

"Night, Papa," Jeb called. "Hey, Papa?"

"What is it, son?"

"Whad'ya reckon Pea saw out there in them woods?"

Seth blew out the lantern and sighed once more. "With that child, there's not much telling. Not much telling at all."

Chapter Three

Maeve felt the cool evening air surround her. The shadowy images she had seen earlier faded once again into nonexistence. Her mouth was dry, her head pounding.

She could hear the splash of water traveling downstream over rocks and gullies. Making her way toward the sound on hands and knees, she was comforted to feel the cold liquid on her fingers. Carefully she cupped her hands, trying to assuage her unquenchable thirst. As she drank, her mouth was filled with a brackish taste. Although it was unpleasant, Maeve forced herself to swallow. In moments, the foul water rebelled against her empty stomach, pressuring its way back up.

"Help me, please, someone help me," Maeve cried out to the silent forest.

Susan Collier

She heard a scurrying noise and her heart thundered against her chest. "Is anyone there?"

A twig snapped. A drop of rain fell against her fevered face. She crawled forward, feeling the prickle of sharp twigs through her jeans until once again she was safely beneath the tree. Curling into a fetal position, Maeve tried to hold back the tears.

Gradually the need to sleep replaced her fright and, with a silent prayer on her lips, she surrendered to the sweet comfort of dreams.

After a hasty breakfast, Seth grabbed his jacket and his child's hand and led her outside. "All right, Pea, where was this fairy?"

Following his daughter through the thick brush, he tried to curb his growing impatience. Blossom had started right where she left off the night before, and Seth knew her well enough to know he'd have no respite until proving, once and for all, there was nothing in the woods except God's creations.

"She was right here, Papa, by the water."

Seth bent and gently clasped the child's face between the expanse of his thumb and fingers. "Pea, there's nothing here."

A tear trickled down Blossom's nose and dripped onto his hand. "But Papa," she pleaded, "she was here, I promise she was."

When Maeve heard the sound of voices, she licked her cracked and swollen lips. "Help me," she rasped weakly. "I'm over here." Clawing desperately at the ground in search of some-

48

thing to throw, her fingers curled around a sharp, prickly object. With all the strength she could muster, she threw the pine cone in the general direction of the voices.

Hearing the sound, Pea jerked free and ran toward a clump of pines. She neared a tree wider than herself, peering expectantly around the edge. The fairy lay on her side, collapsed against the earth. "Papa, quick, I found her! I found the fairy!"

Seth shoved his way through the half-dead branches slapping against his jacket and walked into the heavily wooded area. He saw a flash of fabric and quickly joined his daughter's side.

His heart lurched when he caught sight of the woman. Covered in dirt, her hair matted and tangled, she looked barely alive. He noticed a spot of fresh blood trickling down the side of her head but refrained from showing his increasing panic in front of Blossom. Kneeling down, he placed two fingers against her neck. When he felt a steady pulse, Seth breathed a sigh of relief.

Pea's eyes widened in fright. "Is she dead, Papa?" she whispered.

"No, Pea, she's alive."

The child squealed happily and clapped her hands together. "Kin I keep her, Papa? Huh, kin I?"

Seth's gaze traveled over the stranger's attire. His face drew into a scowl. No respectable woman would wear britches.

But his watchful eyes were drawn back to the woman's face. Even with all the dirt and filth, he had to admit she was a feast for the eyes. When her eyelids fluttered, Seth swallowed hard, then forced himself to speak. "Ma'am, can you hear me?"

Maeve couldn't understand why the man talked as if he were deep inside a tunnel. Her reply came weakly. "I hear you, I just can't see you," she explained.

"Let's get you back to the cabin," Seth muttered, more to himself than the woman, "and see what we have here." Picking her up, he cradled her against his chest. Her soft moan caused him to panic. He urged his excited daughter forward. "Go on, Pea, go straight ahead," he commanded, keeping up a rapid pace as he walked toward the cabin.

Gracie dropped her embroidery, mindless of the missed stitches, and stared openmouthed at the sight of her father carrying in a man with long hair. After obeying her father's request to pull back the covers of the bed, and upon closer inspection, she realized the stranger wasn't a man at all, but a woman dressed in men's clothing.

Gently placing the woman on the straw-tick mattress, Seth noticed the splattering of dried blood on her chemise. Although he was no expert on female clothing by any stretch of the imagination, he'd never seen women's undergarments shaped in quite this fashion.

For one thing, there was some sort of photograph beneath the covering of blood. And words? He grew more bewildered.

"Gracie, what does that say?" he questioned, pointing to the garment.

"What is it?" Gracie mumbled.

"Never mind that, tell me what the print says."

"It says 'Elvis lives . . . somewhere in Jersey.' Papa, who is Elvis and where is Jersey?" Gracie questioned.

"I don't know, Gra—"

His words were interrupted by Pea as she fidgeted beside him. "Kin I keep her, Pa? Kin I?"

When Gracie reached out and touched the sleeping woman, Pea wailed loudly. "She's my fairy, Gracie Caldwell, and you keep your hands offa her! If'n you find a fairy and catch her, then she's yours. Ain't that right, Papa? Huh? Ain't that right?" She clapped her hands together and sang, "I got a fairy, I got a fairy!"

Staring down at the woman, Seth's words were filled with confusion. "She doesn't belong to anyone, Pea. This isn't a fairy. This is a woman—of sorts."

The young lady moaned softly, causing them all to jump back a few inches. Seth sprang into action. "Pea, you go find Jeb and stay with him. Gracie and I have work to do. And Blossom," he admonished, "don't come in until I tell you to, understand?"

When Seth's brilliant blue gaze lit on his

youngest daughter, Pea's thumb edged its way to her mouth. After considering the storm brewing on her papa's face, she decided it wasn't worth the risk and brought her hand back down to her side. "Yes, Papa."

As her foot hit the threshold, Pea began to yell. "I found her, Jeb, I found the fairy and she's mine to keep forever!"

Jeb threw down his bucket and ran toward the cabin, chores forgotten.

Pea held her small hand out to stop him, filled with self-importance. "Papa said I have to stay out here with you." She offered him an impish grin. "You can't see my fairy till he tells us we can."

As soon as his daughter left the room, Seth directed Gracie to her mother's bureau, glad, now, that he hadn't done away with Duessa's clothing. "Get me one of Mama's nightshifts," he commanded. "No, wait. Fetch some water from the well and warm it."

His gaze didn't stray from the woman's features. When her lips twitched into a grimace, Seth bent forward, trying to catch the words.

"I've got to get . . . bus . . ." her words faded into a moan.

What type of woman would be concerned with her bustle at a time like this? Seth wondered. Especially one dressed in trousers? The mystery was deepening and he shook his head in wonder.

When Gracie tiptoed forward and touched

him, the action sent his heart racing. "Confound it, Gracie, stop spooking me!"

"I have the water ready, Papa," Gracie whispered in reverent fashion.

Seth's hands shook as he tried to determine the best place to start. Opting for her feet, he removed the unusual white cotton slippers with ties. Her toes drew him away from the odd shoes.

"Oh look, Papa, her nails are colored."

Glancing at his daughter, Seth's voice conveyed his disapproval. "Yes, they certainly are." He frowned as his fingers moved toward the band of Maeve's jeans. "There seems to be some type of metal clasp here and I'm not at all certain of how to remove these britches."

After pulling apart the snap, Seth tugged until the zipper gave way to his demanding pressure. "Imagine that," he mused, before catching sight of the most shocking part of her wardrobe. Her unmentionables were a mere wisp of material, barely covering the navel.

Gracie's eyes widened with interest. "What do you think happened to the rest of her bloomers, Papa?"

A hot flush crept up Seth's neck to settle on his face. "Go check on your sister, Gracie."

"But Papa, I want—"

"Now, Gracie!"

"Yes, Papa."

When the child was safely out of sight, Seth ran his thumb over the sheer material, astonished by the silky feel. "What happened indeed," he muttered. He reached back up to finger the cotton shirt. It was the most unusual type of material he'd ever seen, as it stretched in every direction before springing back to its original shape.

Reminding himself of the woman's injury, Seth lifted the shirt and searched for a wound. Seeing the scant band of material that stretched across her ample breasts, he assumed she'd been able to bandage herself before ending up alone in the woods.

Bandage herself?

None of this made any sense at all, Seth realized, growing increasingly agitated by the mysterious circumstances.

Modesty stopped him from going so far as to remove the band of material encompassing her breasts. Modesty and Gracie's return.

"Did you fetch your mother's nightdress?" Ever so gently, he lifted the woman's head and removed the stretchy camisole.

"No, Papa. You told me to warm the water."

"Yes, I did say that, didn't I? Well, best fetch it for me now, child." When she failed to do so, Seth glanced at his daughter.

Her gaze was fastened on the deep cleft of the woman's bosom.

"Avert your eyes, Gracie. Show some respect."

"But Papa, you're looking!"

Embarrassed by the truth of his daughter's statement, Seth willed his racing pulse to slow down. He found it impossible, however, to remove his gaze from the sleeping woman's creamy mounds. Just beneath the surface of her ivory skin, he watched her heart beat steadily against her chest. "God help me," he muttered, feeling an all-male response to her beauty.

"Did you say something, Pa?"

Clearing his throat, Seth nodded, his words thick as the command was uttered. "Help me get her into your ma's gown." Together they struggled to cover the woman with the night-dress. The task finally accomplished, Seth reached beneath the folds of cotton and pulled off the filthy trousers.

He left Gracie in charge of washing the dirt off the stranger's face as he went outdoors to try to gain control of his raging emotions.

How long had it been since he'd last feasted his eyes upon such an intimate part of a woman's body? Seth wondered. Obviously, from his response, too long! With the birth of Blossom, Duessa had made her feelings very clear. There would be no more sharing of their marriage bed, no more nights of passion—passion that she had been responsible for stirring alive, at one time. She'd turned from him as if his touch had become abhorrent to her. As if his feelings, his desires meant nothing. And then, when the end came, he understood that his feelings hadn't. Because had there been a shred of caring left in Duessa, she never would have taken such a risk and ridden that wild stallion.

When Pea spotted her father taking a dipper of water from the well, she came running, followed closely by Jeb. "How is she, Papa?"

Seth shook his head. "I don't know, Pea." Remembering his wife's hearty, robust figure, he realized the woman in his bed was little more than skin and bone. "No telling how long she's been wandering in the wilderness."

Jeb's eyes were keen. "Is she gonna live?"

"Of course she is, son," Seth stated with assurance. Despite the blood on her shirt, the only wound he'd found had been the scratch on her forehead. "We'll wait until she's better able to talk to us, to tell us where she's from. Then we'll return her back to her people." Wherever that might be.

Pea quickly voiced her objection. "But Papa, she's my fairy!"

Knowing it was useless to do so, Seth refrained from arguing.

Having wiped away the last of the dirt from the woman's face, Gracie took her mother's comb and began to untangle the mass of hair.

Maeve wondered why someone was trying to pull all her hair out of her head. "Ouch!" she cried, when the tugging turned too painful to bear silently.

Gracie dropped the comb. "Did I hurt you?"

As she blinked back tears of pain, Maeve tried to focus on the faint image of a small person. "I need a drink of water," she managed.

"I'll fetch you one right away." Gracie ran to the door. "Papa, come quick! She's awake!"

Bodies collided in the doorway as Jeb, Blossom, and Seth all tried to fit through the opening at one time. Pea ducked under her father's long legs and was the first to reach the bedside. "I'm Pea and I found you," she proudly announced.

Wincing from the shrill little voice, Maeve tried unsuccessfully to clear the blurred image before her eyes. "What happened? Where am I?"

"I found you in the forest. Is you the forest fairy?"

Shoving her sister aside, Gracie held the dipper to Maeve's lips, allowing her to gulp down the sweet, cool water.

"Don't drink so fast," Seth commanded. "You'll bring it back up."

At the sound of a deep, masculine voice, Maeve froze. "Who are you?"

"Seth Caldwell, ma'am. My daughter found you in the forest."

"Where am I?"

"In my home."

"No. I mean, *where* am I?"

"Sweetbriar, Montana."

Maeve fell back against the plump feather pillow. "I can't be. I was at the park riding the Ferris wheel. . . . " Her words faded as she blinked rapidly, trying to see the face of the giant hovering above her.

"Sorry, ma'am. I don't know anything about a park. As I said, my daughter found you in the woods."

Panic gripped Maeve's heart. "No. I was at the

amusement park, riding the Ferris wheel, and lightning struck. The next thing I knew I was thrown flat on my back."

Seth puzzled over the odd explanation. "I reckon you took a mighty hard bump on the head. Maybe the best thing for you to do is rest up some. I'm sure it'll all come back to you once you've had time to think about it." He could see the conversation was taking its toll by the strange look on the young lady's face. "Let's go kids; let's give the lady some peace and quiet."

"Maeve—my name is Maeve."

Seth smiled warmly while fumbling with his hat. "See there, ma'am? You're beginning to remember already."

Pea refused to leave Maeve's side and pleaded with her father to be allowed to stay. "I won't wiggle around, Papa, I'll sit real still, I promise."

Despite the circumstances, Seth couldn't suppress a laugh. "Pea, you're never still!"

Maeve interjected on the child's behalf. "Really, I don't mind at all. I'd be—well—grateful for the company."

"Rest is what you need most of all, ma'am, but if you're sure . . ."

"Oh I'm sure, really I am."

Shoving his hat on his head, Seth nodded. "Well, I got plowing to do. Gracie here'll help you if you're in need of anything. Understand, Gracie?" He raised a warning brow at his daughter. "Come on, Jeb, let's get to it."

Jeb unwillingly backed out of the door, unable to take his gaze off the strange lady in his mother's gown. Seth grabbed him by the cuff of the collar. "Watch it, boy! You nearly stepped on a chicken!"

Gracie remained motionless until her papa's voice faded. With a swift movement, she ran to the side of the bed. "If there's anything you need," she offered shyly, "don't hesitate to ask."

"Thanks," Maeve groaned. "Say, you don't happen to have any aspirin, do you?"

"Aspirin? No'm, but we've got some stew," Gracie offered, thinking the woman to be hungry.

"I know you won't believe this, but for once, I'm not the least bit hungry! Hey, how about a bathroom? Think you could help me to that?"

Pea's eyes sparkled with fascination. "You mean fairies have to bathe too?"

"Pea!" Gracie scolded. "Don't be asking such personal questions of a stranger!"

Maeve eased into a sitting position. "Don't fuss," she chided. "That's a perfectly honest question." She turned her head in the direction of the youngest child's voice. "I hate to disappoint you, but I'm not exactly a fairy."

"What if you is and you forgot you was?" Pea tearfully questioned.

Knowing her sister was about to start bawling, Gracie decided it was time to change the subject. "Would you like the chamber pot?"

"Chamber pot? What in the heck is a chamber pot?"

Leaning over, Pea whispered something into Maeve's ear and giggled.

"No way! I'm not using no bedpan! I hate those things. I can make it to the toilet just fine, thank you very much!"

Gracie's features darkened in confusion. "What's a toilet?"

Good grief! Having to define the word toilet taxed even her imagination! "It's a . . . you don't know what a toilet is?" Maeve exclaimed. "It's like a chamber pot only it's in a room! Uh . . . usually beside a tub."

"We keep our tub behind the shed."

"Well for heavens sake! Where do you go to pee, then?" Maeve questioned, hating to be blunt but knowing no other way. Her bladder felt as if it were about to burst.

Dawning recognition struck Gracie and she giggled. "Oh!"

"Yeah, oh indeed! Let's hurry, okay?" After struggling beneath the heavy covers, Maeve stood and felt a wave of dizziness wash over her. "I might need a little bit of help. I'm kinda woozy."

By leaning on Gracie and holding on to Pea's hand so the little girl wouldn't feel left out, Maeve allowed the older child to lead her forward. When the sunlight hit her face, making the images appear brighter, Maeve knew they were outside. "Hey, I needed the toilet."

"I know. I'm taking you, ma'am. It's only a few feet away from the house."

Astonished by this family's backward ways, Maeve frowned. "Do you mean to tell me you don't have any indoor plumbing?"

"What's that?" Gracie questioned.

"You know, pull the handle—flush the pot?"

Pea giggled at the grown woman's silliness. "You is really funny. How come you so funny? Is all fairies as funny as you?"

"She told you once, Pea, she ain't no fairy. Now if you'll let me lead you just a bit further, it's this way, ma'am," Gracie stated with authority.

Holding her arms out, Maeve felt for the door. After closing it, she heard the child called Pea giggle again. The sound made her smile, despite her ferocious headache. How in the heck she'd ended up on a farm, she had no idea, but at least the owners seemed friendly enough.

Jeb straightened up, wiping the sweat from his brow. "Look, Papa! They done brung that lady outside!"

"Thundering mules! I told those kids not to bother that woman." Seth turned to look. When he realized where they were going, he cleared his suddenly dry throat. "I expect the lady knows what she's doing."

"Hey, Papa? Where you reckon that lady's from?"

Seth stopped plowing and rubbed his forehead as if the question gave him a massive headache. "That's a mighty good question, son. And I reckon once the lady remembers, she'll be more'n glad to share the information with us."

The next question sent a shiver of apprehension straight through his heart.

"But what if'n she don't remember, Pa?"

Chapter Four

"Mmm, this is pretty good. What is it?" Maeve accepted another bite from the spoon Gracie held to her mouth.

"Venison stew."

Maeve gagged. "You mean it's deer meat, like in *Bambi*?"

"Papa," Pea whispered, "Gracie's talking to my fairy. That's not fair."

Wiping his mouth with his napkin, Seth covered a smile. "Pea, you can't stop someone from talking to Miss Maeve. She isn't your property. Besides, from what I can hear they're having polite dinner conversation. Now finish up your supper."

In an effort to hurry before Gracie stole her fairy, Pea shoveled the food in her mouth.

"Who is Bambi?" Gracie questioned.

"You mean to tell me you've never watched the movie *Bambi*? You know, with Thumper and Flower the skunk? Surely you've seen it," Maeve insisted with a look of disbelief.

"What's a movie?"

"Gosh, kiddo, what part of the boonies are you from? Haven't your mom and dad ever taken you to the show?"

"You talk strange," Gracie commented with a frown.

Pea hopped up on the bed, ignoring her sister's look of irritation. "Is you feeling better now?"

Maeve grinned. "I feel great. Of course, I'd feel a lot better if someone would stop playing the drums in my head, and if I could see you a bit more clearly, but I guess I can't have everything, now can I?"

Lifting Maeve's arm, Pea snuggled close against her side. "I like you even if you ain't no fairy."

"Send the children away if they're bothering you," Seth offered.

Maeve smiled in the direction of his voice. "I kinda like having someone to talk to. At home I usually take care of my cousin, Freddie. He's a mess, always pretending he's a robber, but what the hell, huh?"

The smile on Seth's face turned to a frown. "Ma'am, I'd rather you refrain from cursing in front of the children."

"What did I say?" Maeve blinked in a desperate attempt to clear her vision. From what she was able to distinguish, the man had a huge head, three eyes, and some sort of growth on his lip.

Seth removed his pipe. "Gracie, clear the dishes. Pea, you best go get ready for bed."

"But, Papa—"

"Go."

The girls answered in unison. "Yes, Papa."

Jeb lay motionless on the floor in front of the fire. If he pretended to be deeply involved in his math lesson, perhaps his presence would go undetected. This might prove to be an interesting conversation, from the incensed look on his father's face. Seth's low, rumbling voice barely reached his straining ears.

"Ma'am, we don't speak of the devil's residence in our home." When a deep blush stained Maeve's cheeks, Seth was almost sorry he'd said anything.

"I've upset you, I can tell by the tone of your voice. Hey, I'm really sorry, you know? I mean, you've been really kind about taking care of me and all, then here I go and blow it."

"I beg your pardon?"

"Blow it. You know, make a mistake." A tear slipped down her cheek. "I do a lot of that. . . . I—"

"I didn't mean to upset you, ma'am." Seth fumbled with his pipe, clearly dismayed.

"I wish I could see you all, see what you look like. This is terribly unfair." Maeve couldn't control the lump of anguish in her throat as it broke apart by way of silent tears. "I mean, I don't know what happened. One minute I'm on the Ferris wheel and the next, in the woods."

Seth leaned forward in his chair. "This Ferris wheel you refer to . . . is it part of a train? A stagecoach? Perhaps one of the horses suddenly bolted and you were thrown from the seat."

"A stagecoach? Get real! Listen, I rode the bus to the amusement park and got off," Maeve recalled. "Then I ate a hot dog—"

"You ate a dog?"

"Yeah, a hot dog."

He'd heard of certain Indian tribes who considered dog meat a delicacy, but never of a white woman who did. Unless of course, she was part Indian? No, her delicate ivory skin spoke clearly of her heritage. But dog meat? He shuddered involuntarily. "I've never been inclined to try dog meat, hot or cold," Seth admitted.

Her giggle filled the room. "It wasn't a dog!"

"But you just said—"

"I know what I said. That's what they're called. Gee, what twilight zone did I end up in? Never heard of movies, hot dogs, Ferris wheels! I can't believe this!" She squirmed uncomfortably. "By the way, I have to go to the outhouse again; could you help me?"

Jeb dropped his pencil and bolted into an upright position. The shocked look on his father's face left little doubt that the conversation had just taken an irreversible turn for the worse.

Without removing his gaze from the outspoken woman, Seth called for his daughter. "Gracie!"

Maeve knew immediately she'd somehow offended her host once more. "I did it again, didn't I?"

Running to her father's side, Gracie took one look at his face and felt definite fear travel up her spine. "What is it, Papa?"

"Help this lady use the"—he whispered into her ear.

"Yes, Papa."

Fed up with these strange people's attitudes, Maeve exploded. "Hey, I have a name, you know. Feel free to use it anytime."

When he caught sight of his son's wide-eyed expression and open mouth, Seth's brow arched upward. Just how long had the boy been sitting there listening? "Let's go outside for a spell, Jeb."

Father and son walked out of the cabin to allow Maeve a moment of privacy and Gracie reached beneath the bed for the chamber pot.

"I hate peeing into a pot!" Maeve grumbled.

Pea came running with a smile on her face. "Did you call for me?"

Maybe it was the strange nature of these kind people; maybe it was because the moon shone full in the starry sky, but all of a sudden Maeve found the situation hilarious.

67

*   *   *

When the sound of laughter reached his ears, Jeb stole a look at his father's darkened scowl. "Women," he sighed in disgust. "Right, Pa?"

Seth lit his pipe and stared up at the full, yellow moon. He sighed deeply, wishing he knew more about the female gender. The only woman he'd ever really known was Duessa and even with her wild upbringing, she'd known better than to mention personal needs in front of mixed company. Duessa, who had never eaten a dog in her entire life.

A dog.

Imagine that.

Of course once the woman caught on that her statement had a disquieting effect on Seth, she'd tried to lie her way out of the declaration.

She must be part Indian. Had to be, no matter how creamy white her skin. But which tribe? Friendly or hostile? And if she was, what would happen to his family if they came looking for her? Would they think he'd kidnapped her?

Seth knew of only one man who might possibly give him the answers he needed, and that was his old friend, One Feather Hung Low. True, One Feather's mind might not have the intellect of most grown Indians, but he'd proven himself a faithful friend just the same. The thought brought a smile to Seth's lips as he recalled the first time he'd met the Blackfoot.

On the day of Blossom's birth, One Feather had shown up on their doorstep with a bead-covered amulet in the shape of a turtle to keep the umbilical cord in, explaining through sign language that Blossom should wear it around her neck to bring her good fortune. And Duessa, who'd been deathly afraid to offend the Indian, kept it hidden until One Feather chose to visit again.

It was always a mad dash to find the jewelry and put the amulet around the squirming baby's neck in time. Only later, after a formal visit from Chief Vision In The Night, One Feather's father, did they learn the custom only applied to male children.

Duessa. What would she think of this woman? He groaned softly. Would she be relieved or upset that he'd brought her into their children's lives—into their home? The opening of the cabin door interrupted Seth's troubled thoughts.

Maeve held on to each child's hand as Gracie gave her papa a happy smile. "She insisted on using the outhouse, Papa. She said she never did have good aim."

The pipe dropped from Seth's lips. "Gracie!"

Both males watched the woman stumble forward. In an attempt to be helpful, Jeb offered to find a lantern.

"No, thanks." Maeve giggled. "I can't see a blessed thing anyway!"

Taking a controlled breath, Seth turned away.

While humming a soft lullaby, Seth gathered Pea into his arms and began to rock. He allowed her to run her fingers over his lips, his eyes, his mustache. As he watched her fight valiantly to stay awake, he continued to rock back and forth, back and forth, waiting patiently. Her soft, sugary sigh warmed his tired heart, and he smiled down at the now-sleeping cherub. When he rose, the rocker squeaked loudly, and Seth glanced over at the bed. Maeve's eyes were wide open. "I'll just put the little one to bed and perhaps we can talk. That is . . . if you're not too tired."

She nodded shyly.

The silence in the small cabin was disturbed only by the wind whispering against the branches of the tall pines behind the house. A log popped in the fireplace.

Seth walked back to the rocker, struck a match, lit his pipe, and watched the smoke curl upward. This was the first time he'd found himself alone with the curious young woman, and now he shifted uncomfortably.

Maeve's nose twitched. "That's a nice smell," she murmured, trying to break the disquieting silence.

Seth nodded, settling back against the worn wood of the chair. He crossed his long legs and resumed rocking. "Duessa always enjoyed the aroma."

"Who's Duessa?"

"My wife."

"Oh."

They spoke in unison.

"Who are you?" Seth asked.

"Where is she?" Maeve questioned.

"She died."

"I'm Maeve Fredrickson."

"Beg your pardon?"

"Huh?"

Seth's eyes narrowed at the attractive young woman. "What type of game are you playing? Do you belong to the Indians?"

"Indians! Heavens no! I guess I belong to Aunt Gladys and Uncle Fred, but then again I don't really belong to anyone, now do I? I'm my own person."

Her declaration only served to confuse Seth even more. "You speak in riddles."

"I don't mean to." Maeve sighed. "It's just that I don't understand what's happening. She rubbed her pounding temples wearily.

Standing, Seth planted both feet firmly apart. "And you think I do?"

"Well, you have to admit you have an advantage over me," Maeve stated.

He sat down. "And what would that advantage be, madam?"

"Oh gosh, here we go again! I'm not a madam. I'm simply Maeve. Maeve Fredrickson. And the advantage is that at least you can see me. I can't see anything but a blur." She hesitated. "By the way, do you happen to have three eyes?"

Seth snorted at the absurdity. "Of course I don't. Now, if you don't mind, I'd like to get back to the original subject. Where are you from?"

"Originally, Austin. Then when my folks died, I moved to Helena."

"And how did you come to be down here in the woods? Perhaps these people, Aunt Gladys and Uncle Fred, were moving?"

"No, they're still in Helena, for all I know." She grinned. "You realize, don't you, that you've just asked the million-dollar question."

"How so?"

"Hey, wait a minute! Are you sure you don't live in Helena? What if you're the one making a mistake?"

The woman had already admitted she couldn't see a thing and was now questioning *his* word? Unable to hide an involuntary smile, Seth ran his hand across his mouth. "I assure you, I'm not mistaken. We've lived in this cabin for years."

Maeve's eyes grew bright. "You live in a cabin? How neat!"

Glancing around, Seth noticed Jeb's books, still spread out in front of the fireplace, and the dishes Gracie had conveniently forgotten. "Well, it isn't what I would consider neat, but I suppose it'll do. What about you? Where do you live?"

"I live in a normal house, you know, brick

structure . . . three stories."

"Nonsense," he scoffed.

"No, really! Aunt Gladys and Uncle Fred have this three-story brick home in the hoity-toity part of Helena. Complete with a swimming pool in the backyard. Not that I use it. Shoot, I wouldn't have put on a bathing suit for nothing in the world around Natasha. She's really skinny, about a size three."

"I'm sorry to hear she's been ill."

"Oh, she's not sick. She works hard to stay that size."

As his gaze wandered over the rosy-cheeked, hazel-eyed beauty, Seth couldn't help but think she needed to add a few pounds herself before worrying about the woman named Natasha. "Is this the sister of Freddie? The one that's an outlaw?" When she grinned in his general direction, he thought how becoming her deep dimples were.

"Freddie's not an outlaw!" Maeve giggled. "He's just a kid."

"I see."

Maeve plucked at the covers, smoothing the hem. "They're really okay people. They've helped me through a rough time in my life," she admitted.

"What does this 'okay' mean?"

"You know, okay! All right, not uptight . . . well except for the weight thing and all—Oh my gosh!"

Seth bolted to her side. "What is it?"

"Golly, when Aunt Gladys realizes I'm gone,

she's going to have my picture plastered on every milk carton in Montana!"

A yawn worked its way through Maeve's lips and Seth backed away. "I'm sorry. I've tired you."

"Oh no, I mean, I've enjoyed talking to you. I just don't understand much of what you've said."

The feeling is quite mutual, Seth thought. "Perhaps in the morning things will be less confusing. I'll leave you to rest."

"Say, Seth?"

"Yes?"

"Thank you. I mean for rescuing me and all."

"You're welcome." *I think.*

When the warm, glowing embers of the fire died, leaving behind a cold, powdery ash, Maeve sat up in the bed. She could swear something had brushed her cheek, but what? A mouse perhaps? Just the thought sent a shiver up her spine.

"You're cold."

Maeve glanced to her left and saw Seth standing close by . . . watching her. Oh good grief! Had she been drooling—or even worse, snoring in her sleep?

"May I warm you?" he asked, sliding into the bed beside her.

As his strong, muscular arms encased her, Maeve sighed with contentment. A man like this wouldn't let a few extra pounds stand in the way of passion. "I-I hardly know you," she

74

*stated softly and then realized the words were a
lie. This was the man she'd dreamed about,
longed for, all her life. "Please, Seth, hold me.
Kiss me."*

*When his lips feather-brushed her own, Maeve
relished the texture, the sweetness of their taste.
"Do you find buxom women attractive, Seth? Do
you find me attractive?"*

*"You're beautiful, my dear. I've been watching
you sleep for quite some time. You remind me of
an angel."*

"Kiss me again, Seth."

"And again?"

"And again."

Turning to wrap her arms around Seth's
muscular waist, to draw him as close to her
aching body as she could, Maeve fell out of
the bed.

She awoke with a start.

When her eyelids flew open in surprise, it
didn't occur to Maeve that her vision had returned to normal. The oddities contained in the
tiny cabin were far more interesting.

Giving a perfunctory glance down at the cotton gown that seemed at least three sizes too
large, her gaze traveled upward to the rough
beams above her head. Her eyes followed the
length of the wall until she noticed the shelves
made of bare wood. An oil lamp stood front and
center, surrounded by an old white mug, a coffee mill, and a pressed-glass vase. Maeve shook

her head, not believing what her vision revealed.

Turning to her left, she saw an old-fashioned rifle propped beside the door. The stove, located to the right-hand side of the small enclosure, was coal black with strange little doors above it. On the rough wood shelves surrounding the oven were blue glass jars with rubber stoppers. All of them were filled with a different type of vegetable. She closed her eyes and shook her head once more.

On the floor lay an odd-shaped doll. It suddenly occurred to Maeve where she'd seen such objects before.

The television show "Little House On The Prairie" had contained much of what she found herself surrounded by.

Okay, I think I understand. Somehow I've managed to slip through the television screen. "Quantum Leap," move over! Here comes Maeve with a brand-new series, "Lost in Time!"

Turning quickly when she heard a soft moan, Maeve glanced at the floor. A giant of a man, lying not two feet away, rolled onto his back. Her heart pounded loudly.

It was him, the man in her foolish dream. He murmured a woman's name. His eyelids fluttered madly. Dear God, he was about to wake up!

Panicked, Maeve rushed to the door, struggled with an odd-shaped piece of wood, threw it open, and ran.

Not feeling the cold air coming off the mountains, not feeling anything except an over-whelming desire to escape this dream turned nightmare, Maeve didn't stop when she heard the man call her name. Her left foot tangled in the folds of the gown and she fell to the hard, rocky earth.

She lay motionless, covering her head with her hands protectively. Be it fantasy or night-mare, she was ready to wake up.

Chapter Five

Seth stepped gingerly over the rocks in an effort to stop Maeve. Clad in his long johns, he resembled a chicken minus feathers running around in its pen. His features drew into a grimace when he brought his big toe down on a jagged rock. "Ma'am—oww—ma'am, are you all right?"

He bent down and placed his large hands around Maeve's upper arms, forcing her to her feet.

Maeve struggled to free herself. "No, let me go, I don't want to look at you . . . let . . . me . . . go!"

"Lady, what in God's creation are you talking about?" Seth managed between clenched teeth, trying to maintain his grip on her arm.

Instead of turning in his direction, Maeve

looked up at the purple-hued mountain range partially hidden by patches of fog. "Dear God, where am I?" she whispered.

Seth forced her to face him. He searched her panic-stricken eyes. His words came tenderly. "I told you, you're in Montana. Sweetbriar, Montana."

"But I can't be," she pleaded, "there's no way. I promise you, I was at the amusement park—"

"I know, riding this thing called a Ferris wheel. Miss Maeve, can you describe this wheel?"

She noted that while his eyes were filled with compassion, Seth's grip stayed firm. She took a backward step away from this gentle giant. "What kind of people doesn't know what a Ferris wheel is? What kind of people don't take their kids to see *Bambi*? Are you a Mormon? Or is it the Amish people I'm thinking of? Oh, God," she moaned, "what does it matter? Who in the hell are you?" Her question was broken by a loud sob.

Seth released her. "I wish I could understand what you're talking about, but I can't. Won't you come back inside and let's discuss this matter in a calm and rational way?"

"Just tell me one thing," Maeve persisted. "Tell me what year this is."

Puzzled by the strange question, he answered slowly, "1889."

"Oh no. Oh no, no, no, no, nooooooo!" she wailed. Her brows drew into hopeful arches.

"What you mean to say is 1989, right?"

Seth shifted from one bare foot to the other. He wrapped his hands beneath his armpits in an effort to ward off the crisp morning chill. "No, ma'am. It's 1889. Please, won't you come back inside? I'm sure there's a reasonable explanation for your confusion."

Irritated by his calm manner, Maeve brushed his hand away and stared at the exterior of the cabin. The split-log structure had faded with years of sunshine. There were two stories, but she'd never seen an upper story shaped in such a sharp triangular design. Leading to what she assumed was the loft were planks of wood— stairs, she mused. Stairs she wouldn't trust if her life depended on it.

To the side of the house an old wagon stood surrounded by tall weeds. Thin strips of iron curled around the wooden wheels.

"No," she whispered, "it can't be." Maeve turned to face him and grabbed his brawny folded arms. "Tell me this is all a dream. Tell me I'm caught up in the pages of one of those time-travel romances, tell me I'm crazy. . . . " A single, desperate tear slid down her cheek. "Tell me I'm going to wake up."

Seth reached out to give her a sympathetic pat on the arm. "Listen, Miss Maeve, perhaps you should go back to bed and rest. In time—"

Flinging her hands up to cover her face, Maeve laughed hysterically. "What time? 1889 or 1989? My time or yours?" She lowered her trembling fingers and stared at the handsome man before her. "Where are all the cars? Where're the microwaves, the televisions, radios, the bathrooms, for Pete's sake?" Her voice faltered. "You don't understand what's happened, do you?"

He shook his head.

"I've traveled through time; somehow, dear God, I've traveled through time."

Seth knew the claim was ridiculous and bit back the impulse to say so aloud. Tucking one arm around Maeve's waist, he firmly led her toward the cabin and kept prodding the troubled young woman forward until they reached the bed. The no-nonsense look stayed until he'd tucked the covers securely around her. Then he smiled. "Are you comfortable?"

"Comfortable? Yes. All right? No." She stared into the depths of his breathtaking blue eyes and melted. "Well, for now I'm all right."

Gosh but he's a hunk. Where's the growth? Where are his three eyes? As she continued to study him, Seth walked over to the ledge and pulled down his pipe. He stuck it between his lips, then removed it when Maeve started laughing. "I'm sorry," she gasped. "I thought you had three eyes and some sort of growth on your lip. But it was only your pipe. Just your pipe!"

Seth grinned warily as Maeve continued to investigate the man before her. The long johns did very little to hide his physique, and she couldn't help but admire his muscular frame. He was the stuff her dreams were made of, and if she stretched her imagination, he did look an awful lot like Elvis . . . okay, maybe his jet-black hair was the only resemblence, but gee, this man was the type of guy that books were written about.

She noticed a deep, telling blush stain his face. "I didn't mean to stare, it's just that I . . . I—"

"Day's wasting," Seth stated abruptly when he felt himself grow hot. The woman was literally undressing him with her eyes! "I better roust Jeb out from under the covers. If you'll excuse me?"

"Huh? Oh yeah, I mean, go—don't let me stop you." Maeve watched him walk away. Fine buttocks. Firm, full, oh yeah, a wonderful butt indeed. She might be lost in never-never land, but at least she had one fine hunk of man to look at until she found her way back home.

Pea studied the sleeping fairy. She wanted very badly to waken her, but Papa had said to let her sleep. He said she was unhappy. She didn't look unhappy to her. Not with the smile that played on her lips. Pea bumped the edge of the bed. The fairy sighed and turned over. She coughed, then bent down and coughed again next to the fairy's ear. Maeve's eyelids fluttered open.

"Is you awake?"

Gracie ran to the edge of the bed and jerked Pea away. For some reason she couldn't fathom, seeing the woman dressed in Mama's nightshift bothered Gracie tremendously.

"Blossom Caldwell, you leave that lady alone or I'll tell Pa on you! Come on, you gotta help me make the beds."

When Maeve spoke, both girls froze.

"Blossom. What a pretty name."

Pea wiggled out of Gracie's grasp and ran back to the bed. She gave her fairy a happy smile. "My mama said I 'minded her of a sweet pea blossom. I fold up at night and wake up in the morning. Or something like that. I don't remember real good. How come your mama named you Maeve?"

"Temporary insanity," Maeve stated with a giggle before rolling over to stare at Pea's wide eyes and bright smile. "Gee, you're pretty too! How lucky can a gal get?"

Jealous of all the attention her little sister seemed to be commanding, when in fact Gracie knew she'd done the most to help the woman, the unhappy child spoke harshly. "Blossom, I'm telling Pa that you woke her up."

Maeve looked toward the angry little girl. "Hi, I'm Maeve."

"I know who you are."

Having dealt successfully with Freddie's pouting sessions, Maeve decided to try the same tactics. "Let's see now . . . you must be Jeb." The child's scowl deepened. "Maybe, just maybe, you're Seth?" She grinned. "Naw, Seth's hair isn't nearly as pretty and curly as yours!"

"I'm Gracie."

"Oh!" Maeve gave an understanding nod. "Well, it's very nice to meet you, Gracie."

"I got work to do," she muttered in reply. No, it just wasn't right at all the way the woman seemed so comfortable in Mama's bed. Mama's clothing.

Maeve tickled Pea's sides, scooted her off the bed, then stood on wobbly legs. "Gee, I'm feeling so much better! I'd like to help you if you'll let me."

Gracie turned around and marched toward the stove. "Don't matter none to me," she threw back over her shoulder.

Knowing when to admit defeat, Maeve stared down at Pea. "Is she always this grumpy?"

Nodding forcefully in agreement, Pea's feathery blond curls bounced. "Pa says sometimes Gracie sleeps on cockleburs. But she's always this mean."

"Always?"

"Always," the little girl repeated solemnly.

"Whad'ya say we help her get this place cleaned up? Maybe that'll make her nice. Maybe the reason she's so grumpy is because she'd rather be outside playing . . . playing . . . what *do* you kids play with?"

Pea giggled. "Gracie's too old to play. Papa said so. Her has to stay inside and learn to be a proper lady."

"Shoot-fire! A person is never too old to play! Look at me, why I'm almost ancient and I still like to play."

"But you's a fairy. Fairies 'posed to play. What's ant—antant?"

"Why, you're as cute as a bug in a rug, you

85

know that?" Maeve questioned, while swinging the child around.

Pea nodded proudly and wrapped her arms around Maeve, giving her a tight hug.

She set the child gently back on the ground. "Let's go and make grumpy Gracie smile, whad'ya say?"

As the morning wore on, the more Maeve did, the more sour Gracie's expression became. Still, even with the child's obvious animosity making Maeve uncomfortable, by the time the noonday sun was high in the sky, the cabin sparkled.

Pea tugged at Maeve's gown. "Is you gonna get back in bed?"

"Of course not, why?"

" 'Cause you still have your nightdress on."

Gracie scowled and couldn't resist the biting words. "It ain't *her* nightdress, it's Mama's."

Maeve ignored the harsh statement. "Say, Pea, do you have another sister anywhere around here?"

"No'm." She held up three tiny fingers. "I just got one."

Maeve clucked her tongue. "Gee, that's odd. I seem to remember this really sweet kid trying to untangle my hair and leading me to the bathroom when I needed help." She snapped her fingers. "I know. I bet I dreamed it."

From the corner of her eye, Maeve noticed Gracie stick out her tongue and, again, pretended not to notice. "Well, what are we gonna do for lunch? What about pizza?"

Both girls gave her an odd look. "What?"

"Pizza! You know, a little dough, a little sauce, lots of cheese . . . oh, wait." If she really had been transferred back in time, which of course was absolutely impossible, then these children wouldn't have a clue as to what pizza was. How silly of her! How silly this whole situation was!

"Pa don't like nothing but meat and potatoes for lunch!" Gracie snapped, secretly pleased by the suddenly sad expression of the stranger.

"Okay then. How about hamburgers and fries?" Gracie's look made Maeve smile. She'd managed to stump little Miss Know-It-All. A feeling of infantile satisfaction swept over her.

Within the hour, by stretching her imagination to the limit and pummeling the meat to a mushy mess, Maeve had what vaguely resembled hamburgers on the table.

Seth walked in, took one long look, and made a wry face. "Gracie, what in tarnation is this hogwash?" His displeasure increased when his daughter snickered. He picked up the thickly sliced bread. "Start explaining."

"Don't get on to Gracie. I'm the one responsible, and they're called hamburgers," Maeve defended. "Try one; you'll like it." As his eyes swept over her, Maeve felt incredibly foolish. "I, uh, didn't know what you wanted for lunch and, uh—"

"That's Gracie's responsibility, ma'am."

Eyes sparkling with unshed tears, Maeve tried to explain her reasoning for taking matters into her own hands. "I just thought that if I helped Gracie, she could go play."

"Gracie's too old to be playing," Seth answered.

The silence in the room became thick with tension.

Maeve coughed lightly in an effort to hold back her disappointment. "Well . . . I'm rather tired. I think I'll go lie down, if you'll excuse me." As she walked toward the bed, she realized there would be no respite from Seth's burning gaze. Not with everything being situated in one large room. Damn! She didn't even have the satisfaction of slamming her bedroom door to show her frustration.

The covers would have to do. Maeve pulled them over her head.

Scraping back a chair, Seth sat down. He felt terribly ill at ease, almost defeated, in fact. With a wayward glance toward the bed, he wondered what there could be about the young lady that made him want desperately to please her. To see her smile.

Somehow that smile stirred up forbidden feelings. Feelings he'd buried long before his wife died, feelings that no longer held a place in his life.

He cast a doubtful eye at the plate of food. The piece of meat had an odd, crumbly texture to it. When he cut off a chunk and haltingly raised the fork to his mouth, he realized the children were watching for his reaction. Actually, it wasn't that bad. He nodded. Quite good, he supposed, for prechewed meat. But there wasn't a lick of ham in it. None at all.

Jeb took a huge bite and stated his satisfaction with enthusiasm. "This here thing sure is tasty. Why, I ain't never tasted anything this good in all my life!"

Puzzled, Seth studied his son, wondering if he'd lost his mind. "No reason to yell, boy. I'm not deaf."

Jeb blushed.

"Reckon we better get the rest of that field plowed up quick as we can manage, Jeb. I expect I'll be going to town pretty quick."

Gracie's face lit up like the first bright star of the evening. "Oh, Papa! Can we go too?"

"No, gal, better not. Someone's got to stick around and keep watch over Miss Maeve. Could be days before she's"—out of respect for the woman, he lowered his voice a notch—"right in the head. It'll be a quick trip to town."

Taking another huge bite, Jeb chewed thoughtfully. "Think you'll find anything out about the sheep, Pa?"

"Don't rightly know, son. I suppose it won't hurt too much to ask, now will it?"

Pea scooted down from her chair and wrapped her hands around her father's strong arm. "Papa? Kin you get me some sweets?"

"Well now, that all depends on how good you've been, Pea Pot."

"I been good. I found the fairy, didn't I?"

"I wouldn't call that good," Gracie argued, playing with her food. She felt a tremendous disappointment with her father for not becoming more angry over Maeve's ruining a perfectly good piece of meat.

Pea's eyes filled with tears. "It ain't the fairy's fault she got the wrong head. Maybe it's the only one she could find."

Seth's fork slipped from his hand and clattered to the table. "Blossom Caldwell, whatever are you talking about?"

"You said she ain't got the right head, Papa." The tears streamed silently down Pea's somber face.

Seth bit his lip to keep from laughing. Not right in the head had turned to not the right head. Typical Pea Pot reaction to something he shouldn't have said, even if the statement did hold truth.

"Well now, I guess that just shows I can make a mistake, now doesn't it? Why, Miss Maeve's got a right pretty head, a pretty head indeed." He looked toward the bed where Maeve had removed the covers, but lay with her back toward them. "Excuse me, ma'am?"

Without bothering to turn toward them, her voice came softly. "Yes?"

"If you'd like to go through my wife's things and find you a dress or"—he thought of the strange bloomers—"well, just help yourself to anything you need."

Maeve breathed a sigh of relief. "There is something I'd die for," she admitted. "A nice hot bath."

Seth stood and scratched the back of his head. "A bath, you say? We don't take our baths till Saturday night. There's a creek that runs in back of the property. We usually make do with that."

There it was again. Reality. "Oh, of course! The famous Saturday night bathing parties. How silly of me."

"Well, we don't usually party when we take 'em," Seth said, "but I reckon we could if that's what you want us to do."

What Maeve wanted was for someone to wake her up. Obviously that wasn't going to happen.

Mistaking the silence for disapproval, Seth decided to concede. "Jeb and I could set the tub up for you if it means that much to you. I'll get my fiddle and—"

Her laughter covered the remainder of his sentence. "Never mind." Maeve giggled. "I can make do with the creek or go without."

Seth shrugged and turned toward his son. "Jeb, you finished with your lunch?"

In an effort to make her look in his direction, Jeb coughed lightly, then flashed a toothy grin when he saw Maeve notice him. "Man's work is never done. But that tasty lunch'll fill me with the energy I need to get it done. Thank you, Miss Maeve. Thanks a lot."

Why on earth was the boy carrying on so? Seth wondered. Irritation tugged his nerves. On the way out the door, he couldn't suppress a frown. "What's the matter with you, boy? You're acting mighty peculiar."

Jeb's reply stopped him cold. "A man's gotta do what a man's gotta do, Pa."

Seth pulled the harness from around his neck and arched his aching back. He spotted Maeve walking into the woods. So she'd decided to try the creek after all. Nothing wrong with that, he mused. The cold water always had a refreshing effect on him. And maybe that's what he needed this very minute, because the image of her creamy white body, naked in that cool, clear mountain water, played havoc with his mind. Guilt tickled his heartstrings.

Duessa, rest her soul, after the birth of Gracie, had found lovemaking to be a chore. And even with 13 years of marriage between them, she'd thought it improper to lie completely nude with him. Up until he'd seen Maeve, he'd managed to forget what a beautiful sight a woman's body could be. Running his hand over his mustache, a frown formed on his lips.

He'd also managed to tuck away such feelings.

Maeve wandered down to the edge of the creek and knelt, allowing the motion of her fingers to send a ripple over the surface. The ice-cold chill of the water made her grimace. "Now how is a body supposed to bathe in something like this? Maybe I'd better wait until Saturday."

She placed her hand beneath her thick mane of hair and touched her neck. Feeling the grit, she scowled. "No way."

Stripping off the cumbersome gown, she inched into the water. Although she was halfway across the stream, it came no deeper than her knees. Baring her teeth, Maeve forced herself to sit. The cold mingled with the warmth of her body and she shivered.

Gracie noticed Pea standing at the window, watching for Maeve's return. "Maybe she won't come back," she stated with a swift kick to the rocking chair.

Pea's eyes filled with tears. "Don't you say that, Gracie Caldwell. Her is too coming back."

Slumping down in the rocker, Gracie scuffed the toe of her boot back and forth across the floor. Ever since that mean old Maeve showed up, Pea's adoration of her older sister had gone by the wayside. "She ain't no fairy, Pea. She's just like you and me, only crazy in the head. And the way Papa looks at her. Why, he oughta be ashamed."

Although she didn't understand much of what her sister said, Pea understood the tone. "How come you don't like Miss Maeve, Gracie?"

Gracie picked at a loose thread on her dress. "She's gonna take Mama's place, just you wait and see."

"Uh-uh . . . when Mama gets home, there'll be room for everybody. Maeve can sleep with me."

"You're stupid, Pea. Mama ain't coming back. Ever."

Placing her thumb in her mouth for comfort,

93

Pea spoke around it. "Did Mama send us the fairy?"

"Of course not. And I done told you, she ain't no fairy! Mama would hate Maeve and she'd be really mad at you 'cause you like her so much." Gracie smirked. "I bet Mama would whup you for it."

"Mama said we gotta be nice to people, Gracie. "She said that's good ma—ma—"

"Manners, stupid. Besides, I heard Papa talking to that lady last night and she said she eats dogs. Hot ones too."

"Uh-uh."

"Did too! Only Injuns eat dogs. What if she tries to scalp you when you go to sleep? You better watch it, Pea, I hear them Injuns like yeller hair the best."

When Maeve walked through the door in a dull brown floor-length dress far too large even for her, Pea ran and hid behind Gracie's back.

"Gee, do I look that bad?"

One cornflower blue eye peered out from behind Gracie. "Is you gonna scalp me when I'm sleepin'?"

Maeve watched a look of satisfaction settle across Gracie's face. "No, Pea, I'm not. I only scalp mean little girls who tell their sisters lies."

She strode purposefully toward Gracie. "I don't have any idea why you've suddenly decided not to like me, but I will not allow you to frighten your sister against me."

Backing away, Gracie gulped and nodded.

"Then tell her you lied," Maeve insisted, "and

then perhaps you'd like to explain why you'd want to say such awful things."

Gracie remained silent.

"Go on, tell her!"

The cabin door swung open. "Oh, Papa, she's being mean to me!" Gracie cried, running to the safety of her father's side.

"What in tarnation's going on here?" Seth fumed.

In an effort to control her anger, Maeve curled her hands into tight fists, keeping them stiffly at her sides. She faced him without hesitation. "Your child has suddenly decided to take an outright disliking to me. She's telling Pea terrible lies and refuses to explain why she'd do such a thing."

Seth removed his hat and ran a hand over his weary eyes. "What is this about?"

"Go on, tell him what you told Pea. If you don't, I'm going to."

Gracie mumbled incoherent words.

Anger built like a roll of thunder. Seth stared at his daughter. "You said *what*?"

Tears fell from Gracie's downcast eyes. "I-I told Pea she would scalp her."

Bending down, Seth placed his hands on his daughter's shoulders and searched her face for understanding. "Why would you say such a thing, Gracie?"

"I want her to go home," Gracie wailed. "You don't need her, Papa. I can take care of the house, I can watch Pea." She buried her face in her father's stomach. "Make her leave, please, Papa. Make her leave."

Seth turned to Maeve, pleading with his eyes for understanding. "What is this, Gracie? Is this the same little girl who wanted me to find another wife not so many days ago?"

"That was then," Gracie whimpered. "I was wrong. You don't need her, Papa. You need me."

He sighed. Whatever would Maeve think? Would she realize this was probably nothing more than Gracie's delayed reaction to her mother's death? He certainly hoped so.

"Gracie, listen to me. This poor lady has no idea where she belongs. She's confused, she's—well, she's got a few problems. We need to give her mind time to heal."

Maeve brushed past Seth and stormed out the door, muttering under her breath. She rushed down the path beside the outhouse to a small shed, her eyes brimming with tears. What if Gracie made Seth change his mind about allowing her to stay? Where would she go? What would she do?

There had to be a reason for the child's sudden turn, but what? "Maybe she just plain hates me."

"That's not so. Gracie's simply having a bit of trouble adjusting to someone other than her mother wearing her mother's clothing. Taking her mother's place in our lives."

Turning, Maeve saw Seth standing a few feet away from her. Wanting nothing more than to escape his presence, she pulled open the door to the shed. Her nostrils filled with a sweet, smoky smell.

"Ma'am," he stated calmly, "that's the smoke-house."

"I know that," she snapped. "I was going in there to smoke."

"You were what?"

"Okay," Maeve conceded at the look of shock stamped across his face. "So I don't smoke. I don't know what I'm doing! How do you expect me to know that when I don't even know how I got here?"

Chapter Six

In the silence of the night, so far disturbed only by the swishing of the trees outside the cabin, Maeve heard a whimper. Already restless, she rolled over and raised her head to listen. Seth's gentle snores were all she could hear and she lay back down.

Again, the whimper.

"I want my mama." Pea's words were muffled by racking sobs.

Maeve waited a moment to see if Seth would awaken. When he failed to, she shoved back the heavy quilt and tiptoed to the little girl's side. "What's the matter, honey? Did you have a bad dream?"

Pea lifted her arms to Maeve. "I miss my mama."

Cradling the child in her arms, Maeve carried

Pea back to the rocking chair and sat down. She stroked back the loose strands of hair. "I know you do."

"Why did Papa put her in the dirt?"

Hoping that her silence would soothe the child back to sleep, Maeve didn't answer. How could she? How could anybody explain death to a four-year-old?

"Why, Maeve? Why did Papa put her in a box and put dirt on her?" Pea repeated.

Maeve's heartstrings tugged at the sight of the small child's wide-eyed expression. "I'm sorry you miss her so much, Pea."

Pea snuggled into the warmth of Maeve's chest and heaved a sigh that lifted her body. "I want her."

"I know you do, but she lives in heaven now."

Clasping Maeve's face with her hands, Pea pulled until their foreheads touched. "How come Mama left me? Was I a bad girl?"

"Oh, Pea! Of course not. It's just that sometimes someone is so special God knows they can't continue to live on this earth. So he takes them up to heaven with him."

"Is I special?"

"You most certainly are," Maeve stated with a hug.

"Then I want to go see my mama. I wants to kiss her good night."

Maeve sighed. She was so intent on providing solace to Pea, she didn't hear the creaking in the loft as Gracie slid from her bed and rested her head at the edge, listening. "Okay, here's what you have to do then, Pea. Close your eyes."

Pea squeezed them tightly shut.

"Now then, I want you to see your mama with your heart and not your eyes."

The child rose from the comfort of Maeve's chest and stuck her thumb in her mouth. "Can't."

"Sure you can. Close those pretty blue peepers and think of how your mama looked, can you do that?"

Pea nodded.

In the darkness of the loft, Gracie did the same.

"Okay now, do you see her face?" Maeve questioned gently. Again, she was answered with a nod. "I want you to pucker up those lips and kiss her from your heart."

Eyes still squeezed tightly shut, Pea's lips formed an O. Maeve reached down and brushed the child's lips with her own.

"I feel it, Maeve, I feel it!"

"Why don't you try to go back to sleep?"

"Can't."

"Try, Pea. Try really hard."

"Kin you tell me a story?"

Slowly Maeve rocked. "Once upon a time there was this little girl. She decided to go and visit the king."

"What was the king's name, Maeve?"

"Huh? Oh, uh . . . King Elvis. Anyway, this little girl traveled far, far away from home until she reached the king's castle—uh, Graceland.

101

And when she got there, what do you think she saw?"

"The king?"

"That's right," Maeve said with a smile, gently stroking Pea's feathery curls. "And the king was wearing . . . let's see . . . blue suede shoes. Well now, this little girl had never seen blue suede shoes before and she ran toward the king, stepping all over his feet in her excitement. King Elvis picked her up, gave her a hug, and told her, "Don't you step on my blue suede shoes." He liked what he said so much that he turned it into a song and made lots and lots of money."

Pea breathed heavily through a stuffy nose.

"Are you asleep, Pea?" Receiving no answer, Maeve rocked the child for a few more minutes, reveling in the girl's sweet, innocent warmth, then carried her back to bed. She planted a kiss on Pea's forehead before tiptoeing back to her own bed, which now seemed far too big and lonely.

"Was this King Elvis happy when he made all that money?"

Maeve felt her face grow hot with embarrassment. "Seth, I didn't know you were awake. I was just—just . . ."

"I know, and thank you, Maeve." Seth sat up. "The children are having a difficult time adjusting."

"When did your wife die?"

"We buried her exactly one year ago to the day you arrived."

In the solitude of the night, his obvious pain filled her heart with sympathy. "I'm sorry. I know what it's like to lose someone you love."

"You seem to know a lot of things." Standing, Seth pulled the blanket around him and felt along the ledge of the fireplace for his pipe.

Maeve brushed back her hair with one hand. "Yeah, I know everything except how I got here." She watched as he struck a match and held it to his pipe. His features were momentarily visible and she thought how handsome he looked in his disheveled state.

"Perhaps you're asking yourself the wrong questions," Seth offered, stoking the fire to life. "Instead of asking how you got here, maybe you should ask why." He straightened and turned to face her, his silhouette glowing orange as the flames lapped at the logs behind him. For a moment, their gazes met and held. Something unnamed stirred deep inside him.

"I never looked at it like that," Maeve admitted, her voice slightly husky. Suddenly she had a hard time swallowing.

He shrugged. "Just a suggestion."

As he sat down in the rocker, Maeve bit her lip. Almost embarrassed to ask, but unable to keep from it, she spoke with ragged emotion. "Why do you think I came here?"

Seth puffed on his pipe, deep in thought. "Maybe it is magic. I remember thinking how difficult it's been to take on the responsibility of

103

raising the children by myself. How in the past year I've prayed for a helpmate.

"You see, Duessa did a wonderful job with them for a long, long time. I suppose I never gave their care much thought. So perhaps someone, somewhere, sent you."

Maeve giggled. "Don't tell me you think I'm some sort of angel or something."

The sound of her laughter was pleasing to Seth's ears. He rocked back and forth for a few moments before answering. "I know that you appeared when I needed you most. Do angels do that sort of thing?"

Examining his words, Maeve pondered over the possibility before smiling. There was no way anyone back home would consider her an angel. But there was a peace to his words and she gathered comfort from them. Besides, his reasoning made more sense than her own.

Time travel, slipping though a television set, fantasies . . . they all left far too much to be desired. So if this man wanted to think her some sort of angel, who was she to argue? She swallowed the unexplained lump in her throat. "I only wish Gracie could see my arrival the same way," Maeve admitted.

"Gracie is . . . well, Gracie. She never really had the opportunity to be a child. When she was born, her mother had already started turning inside herself. She had no choice but to mature early on."

"And so you treated her like a grown-up."

Seth nodded. "I suppose we did."

"Maybe," Maeve offered, "maybe she just needs someone to teach her how to be a child. If you let me stay—"

"Let you stay? Where else would you go?"

"Well, you do have a good point. Anyway, if I stay, maybe I can take over the responsibilities of the house. If Gracie's free to do nothing, she'll have to learn to play, won't she?"

His response was filled with mirth. "Just so long as you don't cook any more prechewed meat and never, I repeat, never, try to feed me dog—hot or cold!"

Maeve burst out laughing. "I told you, it isn't really dog meat! It's wien—" Her face grew hot. "It's just a kind of meat."

Tamping his pipe, Seth smiled. "Good night, Miss Maeve."

"Good night, Seth."

Gathering what clothes she could find, despite Gracie's obvious disapproval, Maeve walked down to the stream with a washboard stacked on top of the garments. After settling on the hard ground, she stared at the contraption, not at all certain of how to proceed.

Gracie had followed her from the house, and now she grabbed the washboard out of Maeve's hands. "Here, let me show you." She took one of Pea's dresses, dipped it in the stream, and began to rub the material back and forth across the raised surface of the board. A smug look of confidence crossed her face.

After watching for a few minutes, Maeve took the board out of her hands. *Okay, Miss smarty-pants, if you can do it, so can I!*

She sent Gracie downstream to search for Pea, who had wandered away to look for fairy dust.

Scraping her knuckles against the washboard for the third time, Maeve realized there was nothing fun about this particular chore. What she would give for a washing machine and dryer! A microwave to cook popcorn in. Bread in wrappers so she wouldn't have to bake it from scratch.

Monotony took over the backbreaking task, and Maeve arched her neck, trying to relieve the dull ache that had settled there.

The sky was perfectly blue, except for a few puffy white clouds floating across the sky in lazy fashion. She heard Gracie's giggle, then a screech from Pea, and smiled. So the child really did know how to laugh, after all.

A gentle breeze kicked up, playing along the surface of the water. The motion sent ripples over the rocks. Looking down, Maeve became puzzled by a strange phenomenon. Facing her was a small circle of water so still, it resembled glass. She blinked to clear her vision. The face that peered back at her was definitely not her own. It was the face of a woman. A woman Maeve didn't know.

Glancing over her shoulder, she expected to see the stranger standing behind her, but there was no one to be found.

Again Maeve studied the face. It was pleasantly plump with lines creased around the edges of the eyes. It was a face that clearly showed the hardships of all life had offered her.

For a moment, time seemed to stand still, as did Maeve's heart. Words echoing through the water sent her into shock.

"Hello, Maeve. Don't be afraid."

"Wait a minute! Water doesn't talk, not in my time—not in any time," Maeve stammered.

"I wanted to thank you for coming. I sent for you, you know. To take care of my children, to care for our Seth."

"Who are you? What do you mean, 'our' Seth?"

Duessa smiled. "Don't you see? I'm an angel now. I can do things like this—with permission, of course. And since Seth has always belonged to you, the time was right for me to guide you. You see, my child, I only borrowed him until you could join him."

"Give me a break!" Maeve exclaimed. "You really expect me to believe that?" She frowned. "Besides, angels don't appear in water; they fly . . . don't they?"

"I'm quite serious about this, Maeve. It's the same with my children. Though I loved them deeply, I knew my time on earth would be short. So now the responsibility of raising them goes to you."

Struggling to her feet, Maeve cocked her head

to one side and pounded her temple. "Well, that's it, I've managed to lose what little sense I had." She started to walk away and then, as if to prove she'd been seeing things, looked back down into the water.

The woman's smile was warm, gentle. "Oh, Maeve?"

"Yeah?"

"Seth is a good man, despite our problems."

"What problems? What problems? I'm standing here talking to a pool of water that tells me it's—she's?—an angel and I ask what problems?"

"In time, Seth will be willing to share with you. Until then, be patient."

The apparition began to fade. Maeve panicked. "Wait a minute! Where are you? I mean, I know you're in the water, but then again, how can that be? I mean, people can't talk underwater!"

"Quite simply, I'm where I longed to be. I must go now, Maeve. Thank you."

"No! Wait a minute! Don't be thanking me—send me home!"

"I can't do that, Maeve. Your time for living has just begun. I'll be watching you. Take care, my friend . . . take care." The voice shimmered, hovered, then vanished along with the image.

Mindless of the cold water, Maeve forged ahead, the hem of her dress dragging in the stream. "Come back!" she called. "Please come back." Her plea echoed in the silent forest.

Somewhere a bird trilled. A pine cone fell, and all was still.

When the sound of the children's laughter reached her ears, Maeve panicked. "Gracie! Pea! Come quick!"

Both girls came running. "What is it?" Gracie asked. "What's wrong?"

Maeve grabbed her shoulders. "Your mother. What did she look like?"

The description Gracie offered matched the face Maeve had seen. "Why?" she demanded. "And let go of my shoulders. You're hurting me."

Trembling, Maeve knelt down and pulled Gracie close, despite the child's stiffened body. "You wouldn't believe me if I told you, kiddo."

"Probably not," Gracie snapped, jerking away.

"Hey, Gracie?"

"What?"

A struggle ensued as Maeve tried to hug her again. Maeve won. "I want you to know that I'm gonna like you no matter how you feel about me. And it's all going to be okay." The dubious look she received in response to her soulful declaration matched perfectly the condition of Maeve's heart.

Trying not to appear conspicuous, Maeve found inane reasons to leave the cabin at various times of the day, going back to the stream of water. But the reflection didn't reappear. The

109

harder she tried to put things into some sort of perspective, the harder it became. Maeve simply couldn't find it in her imagination to believe Seth's wife had paid her a visit. That would be harder to accept than any of the rest of this crazy situation. Much harder.

If Seth noticed Maeve's odd behavior, he made no mention of it, for finally the fields were prepared for planting. In the mood to celebrate the joyous occasion, right after the supper dishes had been cleared from the table, Seth pulled down his fiddle and played a lively tune. The girls giggled, clapping their hands while Jeb did a fast-moving jig.

When Maeve wiped her hands on her apron, Jeb caught her eye. "Come on, Miss Maeve. Dance!" His face was the picture of radiance.

"Oh gosh, Jeb, I can't dance. Especially not to that!"

"Pa, play 'The Meadow Whispers Sweetly.' "

Seth nodded his approval and began to play a slower melody. Jeb extended his arm and Maeve took it, feeling very self-conscious. Placing her hand on the young boy's shoulder, she watched his feet, following his every step. White teeth flashed against a mass of freckles as Jeb beamed up at her proudly.

When she happened to glance in Seth's direction, she noticed him watching her and received a friendly wink. But she also saw something else on his face, some unreadable expression that caused her to blush even as she tried to understand it.

What she did comprehend was the fact that when he looked at her this way, she felt alive. More alive than she had ever felt before. The feeling, so sweet and tender, caused her to pause. As his deep blue, laughing eyes met hers, she could feel herself drowning in a sea of tranquillity. Of desire.

The music stopped.

Her heart began to sing a song as old as time, yet wonderfully new to her. Maeve recognized the tune instantly.

It was the melody of love.

In the middle of the night, Maeve opened her eyes and sat up in bed, instantly awake and aware. What had she really seen this afternoon? How could she explain it?

Was it a ghost? Hardly.

Was it a premonition? Doubtful.

Maybe the sun had gotten to her. Of course! That's what happened! Heatstroke! From all that sun and scrubbing.

Still, she mused, what if I wasn't mistaken and saw what I thought I saw? A dreadful thought shadowed her mind. What if Gracie mentioned it to her Papa? How would she even begin to explain?

Oh, pardon me, Seth. I thought I told you. Yes, your dead wife appeared in the form of an angel this afternoon. Of course, she wasn't flying around or anything. No, she was in the stream and yes, she seemed very happy. As a matter of fact, she literally gave me your children . . . and,

111

uh, by the way . . . we have her permission to fall in love.

And what would his response be to that little tidbit of information?

Chapter Seven

When the rain came, it came in sheets off the mountains, soaking everything it touched in a matter of seconds. Thunder rolled and shook the glass panes in the cabin windows. Maeve shivered as she helped Pea take a fresh batch of bread from the oven.

Seth came running in from the barn, soaking wet, a happy smile plastered on his face. "Nothing like a good soaking rain to get those fields ready. A man couldn't have better luck!" He shook the moisture from his hat and hung it on the peg. From the sight of the flour on his youngest daughter's nose, he guessed she'd been helping Maeve bake again.

He noticed Jeb lying by the fire working on his math. The child seemed much more understanding of the subject now that Maeve had tutored him so many times during the evening hours. Finally he turned to the young woman responsible for this newfound feeling of contentment. Should he tell her of his feelings? After all, she barely knew him. What if a heartfelt statement scared her? He settled for a question. "Got any coffee?"

As she walked toward the stove, Maeve's foot caught in the hem of her skirt, and she would have tripped had it not been for Seth's quick action. He pulled her back to her feet, holding her close—too close—to his body. "Are you all right, Miss Maeve?"

"I th-think so." Mercy, did he feel good! "It's these clothes; they're miles too big for me and way too long, as you can see. . . . " She knew she was rambling, but his close proximity flustered her completely.

His gaze captured her, enthralled her. His words were a letdown.

"Feel free to hem them, or take a seam— whatever it is you women do."

She laughed. "Me? Sew? You have to be kidding."

He smiled down at her. "What did you do for clothes then? I mean before you came to us? Perhaps you're from a wealthy family. A family that can afford store-bought."

"Hardly anybody makes their own clothes. It's too easy just to charge them."

"This hoity-toity must be some kind of town," he mused, realizing he should release her immediately, but reluctant to do so.

"Huh?"

"I believe that's what you called the area you're from, isn't it? Hoity-toity town?"

Maeve thought for a moment, trying to recall her words. When she did, she couldn't stop herself from giggling. "No, I said Aunt Gladys and Uncle Fred come from a hoity-toity section of town. Not hoity-toity town!"

"Oh."

"Well, getting back to our original conversation, if I needed something, I usually just charged it."

Seth released her, a frown where a smile had been moments ago. "I don't believe in charging things. A man should only buy what he can pay for with cash."

"I forgot . . . you don't know anything about charge cards, do you? See, in 1989, everybody charges on these plastic cards and you don't worry about paying for it until the bill comes due. Then when that happens, you make a little payment here, a little payment there—it's really pretty simple."

"And what happens if you can't make these 'little payments' when the bill comes due?"

Maeve laughed. "Then you're in lots of trouble!"

"Seems simpler to me to just wait and purchase items when you can pay for them." He took a sip from the steaming coffee Maeve offered.

"Yeah, but see, this way you don't have to wait. If you need it, you just go buy it."

Susan Collier

Seth lit his pipe and mused over her explanation. "But how do you know if you really need an item if you don't go without it to find out?"

Pea tugged at her Papa's damp britches. "Papa?"

"Pea, I'm talking to Miss Maeve. It isn't nice to interrupt."

"But Papa—"

"Pea!"

"But Papa," she pleaded. When she saw she had her father's complete attention, Pea smiled. "Kin you git one of them charges and git me some candy from town? I done been without it for an awful long time and I know I need it!"

Throwing back his head, Seth roared with laughter. "You do, huh?" He picked her up and tickled beneath her chin. "I bet your Papa can manage to get you candy without one of those cards. What do you think?"

Pea squeezed her father in her best bear hug. "You is the very bestest papa there ever was!"

He growled into her neck, nuzzling it gently. "And you're the bestest little Pea Pot there ever was."

Maeve stood silently by, watching him with his youngest child. It was a sight that warmed her to the tips of her toes. The feeling fled when grumpy Gracie joined them.

"Papa, if you have enough money to buy Pea candy, can you buy me that china doll at Wil-

116

lard's Mercantile? Now that's what I really need."

Seth glared at Maeve in mock anger, barely able to contain his smile. "You've started something, you know."

She placed her hand to her heart and smiled innocently. "Who, me?" After taking a sip of coffee, Maeve continued. "I must say, the way you put things makes a lot of sense. I guess I never realized just how different things are. I mean, you folks don't worry about cholesterol and eating red meat three times a day—"

"What else would we eat?" Seth questioned, clearly confused. "And what's cholesterol?"

"Well it's, uh . . . it's bad for you, okay? Clogs up those arteries and all. Funny thing is, everyone seems so healthy—without all the exercise machines and the aerobics and all that stuff."

"Exercise machines? Aerobics?"

"Well sure. People have to get enough exercise to burn up calories—Seth, you're not understanding a word of this, are you?"

"Actually no," he admitted. "But I sure am enjoying listening to you try to explain it."

"Let's suffice it to say things are just real different between my time period and yours."

"Better or worse?"

She ducked her head shyly. "I'm beginning to think much better indeed."

Gracie interrupted once more. "About that doll, Papa, are you gonna get it for me?"

Hesitating for just a moment, Seth saw a

way to work the child's request to all of their
advantages. "I'll tell you what, Gracie, you
help Miss Maeve size those dresses and I'll
see about it."

"I can't do that, Papa."

"Why not?"

"Them's Mama's dresses. She wouldn't like us
cutting up her clothes."

"Your mama would be more than happy to
share, Gracie," Seth gently admonished.

"Well, I won't do it and you can't make me!"

"Gracie!" Seth stared after his fleeing daughter.

The warm tingle Maeve had experienced
earlier was replaced with cold, harsh reality.
"Don't," she whispered, when Seth rose to
fetch his daughter. "I'm a failure. A complete
and total failure. The child hates me and re-
sents me wearing these." She held the dull
gray skirt up. "I can hardly blame her, you
know. It must be pretty tough with all those
painful memories bottled up inside her. If
only she'd trust me enough to talk to me, to
share her pain."

Seth's gaze fastened on Maeve's bare ankles
and feet. Her toes wiggled as if they had a life
of their own, and indeed, as she continued
talking, they kept rhythm with the intense
words.

"I don't mean to complain about things,
okay, Seth? I mean, at least I have clothes
to wear. But all I seem to be doing is remind-

ing Gracie of her mother. I wish I had, I
wish . . ."

"Go on," Seth prodded gently.

Maeve lowered her gaze to the floor. "I wish
I had a pair of jeans."

"Jean's what?"

"No, blue jeans."

Seth laughed. "Jean is blue?"

She snapped her fingers. "Hey, what did you
do with the jeans I had on?"

"That's what they were?" He studied her
hopeful expression, wishing he didn't have to
confess. "I'm sorry, Miss Maeve, I broke the fas-
tener when I removed them."

Her face turned a brilliant scarlet. Wonderful.
Now he knew about every bulge on her body.
Every little bit of cellulite plastered to her
thighs. "You took them off? I'd hoped that, well,
maybe one of the girls did."

"I assure you my intentions were honorable,"
Seth defended himself quickly.

"Oh, well, if it was done honorably," Maeve
said with a giggle and crossed the room to
pat his shoulder. She felt the muscles beneath
his skin stiffen at her touch while a current
of desire, so strong it made her gasp, filled
her.

Trying to appear nonchalant, she continued
as if this sort of electricity ran through her
every day. "Actually, I can't see you doing
anything dishonorable if your life depended
on it. You've been nothing but honorable and
yet here I stand complaining. I guess a lot of

it has to do with these drab colors. I don't wear browns and grays very well. They don't suit my personality."

"No, they certainly don't," Seth agreed. "You should be dressed in the brightest of colors, laughing sunshine, the light blue of the morning sky, the red of a robin."

It was the nicest compliment Maeve had ever received, and, watching Seth's face color, she knew it was quite probably the mushiest thing he'd ever said. "Well now, about those dishes. I guess I'd better go draw water."

Seth moved toward the door. "Stay. I'll go."

When he left the room, Maeve placed her hand over her pounding heart. How could she continue living in such close proximity with a man who turned her knees to Jello? Her blood to fire?

Seth stormed down to the well and slammed his fist against the handle. "Laughing sunshine, blue of morning, indeed. What in the thundering blazes came over me? The woman is crazy, completely insane, and there I sat, making an ass of myself." He lowered the bucket. "Well, Seth, it just goes to prove one thing, my man. The sooner you leave for Elkhorn, the quicker you can get this silly woman out of your system."

But the lie brought a frown to his lips. He'd never be able to forget the woman who'd brought laughter back into his life, feeling back into his heart.

The idea of waking up in the morning without

her smiling face did nothing to lift his suddenly dark mood.

"Remember, man, she's crazy. Charge indeed! For a moment there, she had me believing her strange story. But to use a playing card to pay for a purchase? Pure nonsense," he scoffed.

Maeve watched him from the window, saw him pound his fist on the handle before lowering the bucket far too fast.

Why did I feel the need to touch him? I hardly know the man. I've made him uncomfortable by treating him like a . . . She did her Groucho Marx imitation. "I know what I'd like to treat him like!"

Pea pulled at her skirt. "Who is you talking to, Maeve? And how come you did your eyebrows like that? You looked silly." She ended the statement with a giggle.

Lowering her voice to a growl, Maeve arched her fingers and came stealthily toward Pea. "Silly, you say? Silly?" When Pea began to run, Maeve chased her around the wooden table.

Seth returned with the bucket of water and found himself amid the squeals of delight and giggles. In retreat from Pea, Maeve backed into him, splashing water down his legs and onto her skirt.

Horrified, Pea's hand slipped up to cover her mouth. "Oh, Papa! You all wet!"

"And you, Pea Pot, are all dry." His eyes

sparkled. "Doesn't seem very fair to me; what about you, Miss Maeve?"

Maeve clucked. "No, not fair at all."

Before she could run, Seth grabbed Blossom and poured a small amount of water down her back.

The ear-splitting scream caused Jeb and Gracie to come running. Before the evening drew to a close, everyone had an equal amount of drenching and fun.

Later, after tucking the children in bed, Seth lit his pipe. "I'm not very sleepy. I believe I'll go for a walk. Would you care to join me?"

Does Superman wear a cape? "Why sure, that'd be real nice." Maeve's cheeks were as warm as if she were running a fever. But the fever was inside her, racing through her veins, causing her heart to do strange things against her chest.

The night seemed alive with the twinkling of thousands of stars overhead. A full moon peeked through the branches of the tall pines. Shivering against the cool wind coming off the mountains, Maeve wrapped her arms around her rib cage.

"Perhaps you need a cloak."

"Oh, no," she protested, afraid that if she hesitated for the slightest of moments, Seth would leave her behind.

He shrugged, noticing that despite her denial, she still kept her arms wrapped close to her chest. Seth walked to the edge of the forest and stopped suddenly, turning to face her.

122

Studying the slight tilt of her nose, the fullness of her lips, he swallowed down a sudden impulse to kiss her. And if the light of the moon was responsible for warming her features, then surely she was responsible for warming his heart.

Maeve's breath caught in the base of her throat at the seriousness of his expression.

This is it. He's gonna tell me to leave.

"Miss Maeve, we need to talk."

Chapter Eight

"Wait a second," Maeve interrupted. "Seth, would you do me a favor?"

He nodded slowly, searching her face.

"I already feel very out of place, and every time you refer to me as Miss Maeve, it just reminds me how misplaced I really am."

His concern seemed genuine. "I hope you realize by now I wouldn't do or say anything to make matters worse for you. I can only imagine how difficult it must be, thinking you belong in another time."

Maeve grabbed his arm. "Whoa! What did you just say?"

"I said—"

"I know what you said. You still don't believe me, do you?"

"You have to admit the story you would have

125

me consider is rather, shall we say, different?"

Swallowing back a surge of anger that threatened to release itself in the form of tears, Maeve felt her eyes fill. "Hey, bud, try living it from this end. How do you think I feel? I get thrust back in time where dishwashers and cars are a thing of the past—I mean future. I see visions in water, I have to wear dresses that drive me nuts—" She stopped, unable to continue for the racking sobs that claimed her words.

Seth tucked his thumb beneath her chin and forced her to meet his gaze. "Maeve, I'm sorry. I'm very sorry."

His breath fanned softly against her cheek.

"I can't believe the things you've told me, but I can believe you. Does that make sense?"

Half laughing, half sobbing, she nodded. "About as much sense as any of the rest of what's happened does."

Reaching into his pocket, Seth withdrew a crumpled handkerchief. "Here . . . blow hard."

Maeve giggled. "I'm not your kid, Seth. I know how to blow my nose!"

"Do you also know how to care for children alone?"

The sudden switch in conversation caught Maeve off guard. "Why?"

"As I stated to the children, I need to go to Elkhorn. It's about three day's journey, and although I don't like the thought of leaving all of you behind, it would be easier if I made the trip alone." Seth refrained from adding the fact that if she were with him, he'd be unable to inves-

126

tigate her sudden appearance in his life.

"I've baby-sat before, so I can handle it."

"I'm afraid I don't understand. That is to say, I—What does this word 'baby-sat' mean?"

Feeling rather foolish, Maeve tried to explain. "Baby-sitting is when parents leave their kid in your care while they go to the show or out to eat or whatever."

Confusion filled him as he fumbled with his pipe. Seth's brows drew together when he contemplated her words. "But wouldn't the children enjoy being outdoors and eating?"

Here we go again, Maeve thought. "No, I don't mean that. What I mean is sometimes a husband and wife like to have some time alone. You know, to court? So they hire someone to watch their kids while they do it."

Seth nearly swallowed his tongue. "Do it?" he croaked.

Maybe some things crossed the span of time!

Obviously he understood that bit of slang well enough! Maeve bit her lip to keep from laughing. "Not do 'it' . . . but . . . go out." Knowing she was about to get caught up in another long explanation, she sighed. "Look, Seth, I'll be happy to take care of the kids while you're gone."

"Thank you."

As they walked further into the woods, Maeve could tell her escort seemed more pensive than usual. Something troubled him tonight, and from the sad look on his face, she could wager a guess as to what. "You're thinking about your wife, aren't you? Seth, will you tell me about her?"

For a moment, a shadow seemed to cross over his features. It wasn't something he wanted to talk about, wanted to remember. But the sincerity in her tone made him answer. "Duessa was . . . Duessa was . . . something special. At least when we first met she was. Always smiling, always laughing." He stopped and turned to face Maeve. "A lot like you. But that was before."

"Before?" Maeve prodded.

"Before she became so unhappy. To make you understand, I'll have to start at the beginning. It's a rather long story, I'm afraid. One that will probably bore you."

"I won't grow bored," Maeve promised quickly.

Seth remained silent until they came upon a clearing. His words were slow to come, as if he were reluctant to bring the painful memories to the surface.

With a deliberate sigh, he motioned for her to sit down on a wide rock beside the stream. As he paced back and forth in a restless manner, he twisted the stem of his pipe with his hands.

"When I first met Duessa, I was a miner. She was my boss's daughter . . . and a sight for sore eyes. Part Gypsy, she was unlike any other woman I'd ever known. She used to dress in bright colors—perhaps to display her lively soul. And I found that for a man accustomed to working hard for what he got, I won her affection relatively easily.

"Two weeks after we met, I asked for her hand in marriage. Duessa agreed. We were both so young. . . . I don't think either of us realized what we were getting into; we just knew we loved one another deeply."

An inexplicable twinge of jealousy crept into her words as Maeve murmured a response. "How nice for you both."

"It was for a while," he agreed. "Until she became pregnant with Gracie. Because by then, you see, I'd grown tired of the mining accidents, the long hours, the terrible conditions.

"In an effort to better our lives, I moved us to this valley. I thought that by removing ourselves from the decadence of big-town life, I could somehow protect my wife, my children. It turned out to be the biggest mistake I've ever made." Seth glanced up at the star-filled sky, lost in the past.

"The mountains had a way of closing in on Duessa. She longed for what we'd left behind. I kept promising her things would be different once we made our fortune in cattle, but as you know, the winter of eighty-six proved that impossible."

Racking her brain for history lessons learned in high school, Maeve frowned. 1886. Something devastating had happened, what was it? The information stayed just out of reach. "I'm sorry, Seth, please be patient with me. I want to understand, I really do, but you'll have to explain what happened."

"It was the worst winter Montana has ever

seen," Seth mused, dredging up the painful recollections. "First came the snow. No one worried, for in Montana the winters always bring snow. But with the ground completely hidden, warm winds blew in off the mountains. The devil's breath, some said." He shuddered. "Whatever it was, it melted the snow. The streams and the rivers began to flood the land. When the temperatures dropped once more; we thought it was a blessing from heaven. It turned out to be hell. Because then came the blizzards. Blizzards that destroyed my cattle, ruined my dreams for a secure future and Duessa's happiness."

Maeve cleared her throat. "You can't be held responsible for what nature does, Seth."

He nodded. "I know that. Deep inside, I know that." When he turned to meet her sad expression, her look of sympathy made it easier for him to continue. "I think a lot of Duessa's problems stemmed from cabin fever. We were snowed in for months and months. When she became pregnant with Blossom during that period, she was convinced the baby she carried brought the bad luck, and nothing I could do or say seemed to change those feelings."

The words hurt Maeve to the core. How could anyone think such a precious child could be bad luck? Her eyes filled with tears and she blinked quickly to stop them from falling. Seth seemed not to notice. He was miles away, reliving that tormented time.

"After Blossom's birth, Duessa worked hard

to hide her troubled feelings. I didn't find out how deep those feelings ran until I tried to—"

When his hesitation became unbearable, Maeve prodded him to continue. "Until you tried to what, Seth?"

He turned away from her curious gaze. "Until I tried to return to our marriage bed," he confessed.

"I see," she uttered quietly.

Whirling around, he stormed forward and grabbed her arms, propelling her off the rock. "Do you?" he questioned harshly. "Do you? Because I didn't. Not even then. No . . . not even then." A bitter laugh escaped his lips. "I noticed that Duessa never seemed to smile anymore, never laugh. She became burdened by the simplest of tasks. Tasks which I thoughtlessly turned over to Gracie in an effort to ease her plight.

"It wasn't until the day of the accident, the day I told her about what I'd done, that I realized I'd taken a rare and beautiful flower and crushed it with my thoughtless actions." He took a deep breath before continuing the painful story. "We argued. Duessa ran out of the house, toward the stallion I was in the process of breaking. She wouldn't listen to my warnings, paid me no attention when I yelled for her to stop, that the horse was dangerous. I don't even know if she heard me; her wrath was so great . . ."

Seth allowed his hands to fall back to his sides, lost in his own private misery, his feelings of failure and the memory of his wife lying in a puddle of her own blood. The sound of the gun echoing off the canyon walls when he shot the animal who had killed the woman he loved.

The desire to reach out to him, to hold him ever so close, was almost more than Maeve could bear. She wanted nothing more than to kiss away his torture, relieve him of his guilt. Instead, she allowed him his distance. "What could you have possibly done that was so bad, Seth?"

"I took the money she'd planned on leaving us with and used it for my own gain."

"But your gain would also be your family's gain," Maeve argued.

"Duessa didn't see it that way."

His crushed expression scorched Maeve's heart. Because his pain had become her own, she tried to lighten the moment. "So tell me, what frivolity did you spend the money on?"

"Frivolity? I didn't spend it on anything frivolous, I assure you. I used our savings to purchase sheep."

"You didn't!"

"I did," Seth admitted, disheartened by her obvious disapproval.

"Oh, how awful! How terrible! You actually took your money and purchased something that might help to better your financial situation!"

It took a moment for her words to sink in. Seth blinked. "You mean—"

"I mean you only did what any other man would do. You searched for a way to provide a better future for your family." Maeve grabbed his rough, callused hands and gently admonished, "Seth, she wasn't in her right mind at that point. I doubt very seriously that anything you could've done would have changed Duessa's state of mind."

Relief flooded his heart. "Do you really think so?"

"I know so," Maeve reaffirmed, applying gentle pressure to his fingers. "I bet there were plenty of times you made Duessa very happy. You need to hold on to those memories and forget the bad. I assure you she has." She squeezed his hands tightly and smiled up at him.

At that moment, Seth wanted to kiss her so intensely that he could taste the sweetness of her lips on his tongue. Instead he returned the smile. What had he ever done to deserve the presence of such an angel? Such a wise and special woman? And what would she do when she regained her memory? Would she move on?

Thankfully, Maeve's question drove the thoughts from his mind.

"When will you be leaving for Elkhorn?"

"Tomorrow. I need to check on the whereabouts of my sheep, pick up seed, and buy supplies."

"Oh." A sense of dread filled her. Though she often baby-sat for Aunt Gladys and Uncle Fred, her cousin was a willing victim and they usually enjoyed their time alone by popping popcorn and watching scary movies. What in the world was she going to do with these three children?

Jeb and Pea would be no problem, but what about Gracie, who seemed to delight in causing her unnecessary grief?

"Is there anything I can get you in town, Maeve?"

As the cold earth penetrated the ruffles of her skirt, causing chill bumps to form on her legs, Maeve nodded enthusiastically. "Yes! I want a pair of jeans—I usually buy Gloria Vanderbilt, but any brand will do."

He smiled. "You're referring to the britches you were wearing on the day of your accident, right?"

"That's right."

"I've been doing some thinking about those britches"—*And what was in them!*—"I believe they're a newfangled fashion. We refer to them as dungarees."

A loud squeal split the night. "You mean you can get 'em?"

"I think so. If I can, what size do you wear?"

A deathly quiet silence descended upon them. "Maeve?"

If he thinks I'm admitting my size, he can forget it! "On second thought," Maeve stated with a sick smile, "how about some material?"

The morning dawned bright and clear. Seth rose early to get most of the chores done before the rest of the household stirred.

While milking the cow, he thought about the trip ahead. What in the blazes was he going to do if someone had reported Maeve's disappearance? Could he, in all actuality, give up the kindest, most warmhearted lady he'd ever met? The answer lay heavy on his heart.

But there could be no choice. Seth had always prided himself on doing the proper thing, and the proper thing, of course, was to return her to her family.

He promised himself it wouldn't happen without a fight. A fight to keep what he'd come to think of as his own personal gift from heaven.

His mind turned to more mundane things. Mentally he prepared a list of supplies. Suddenly his imagination soared over the menial task and Seth imagined himself walking into the dry goods store and asking for the brightest material available to match his woman's smile.

My woman? The words sent a shudder throughout his system. *I better return her to where she belongs and quickly!*

Seth's lips curved into a smile. He imagined Pea's giggle of delight when he brought home the much-talked-about sweets. Gracie's look of surprise when he gave her the china doll. And for Jeb, of course, there would be new books for him to study by. Perhaps a new pencil and tablet.

And the fabric for Maeve. By closing his eyes, he could see her touching the material, a bright smile on her lips. Reaching out to stroke his cheek in gratitude. Then later, after the children were peacefully asleep, she would come to him, wrap her arms around him, and —

"Pa? Did you hear me?" Jeb touched his father's shoulder, watching the secret smile disappear.

Seth turned to face his son, feeling guilty and confused. "I'm sorry, boy, I don't guess I did."

"Pea is crying for you, Pa. She wants to make sure you don't leave until she kisses you."

Kisses. Ah yes, that's what Maeve would do.

A look of wonder crossed over Jeb's features. As far back as he could recollect, his Pa had never been one to give in to daydreams, but Jeb could swear that was what his Pa had been caught up in. "Pa? Whad'ya want me to tell Pea?"

"Tell her I'll be in as soon as I'm done milking." Seth went back to his chores with a resigned attitude. *Foolishness. Pure foolishness!* Maeve wasn't going to kiss him and she wasn't going to smile and she wasn't going to understand if he kissed her!

Maeve cast a dubious glance at the mode of transportation that Seth hitched the horses to. "This ol' thing doesn't look like it's gonna make it out of the forest, let alone to town. What happens if it breaks down on you, Seth?"

Making certain the brake was set, Seth grinned. "The worst that can happen is one of the wheels will come loose, and I have the materials to remedy that!" He glanced down as Pea grabbed his legs.

"Papa, you gonna miss me?"

"Sure am, Blossom."

"Does you want me to come and keep you happy?"

Sweeping her off the ground, Seth gave his daughter a tight hug. "Maeve wants you to stay here so she'll be happy, don't you, Maeve?"

Their gazes met and held. Maeve felt a shiver of delight wrap around the very fiber of her being. "Yes, I want you to stay . . . Pea."

Finally there was no reason for Seth to delay his parting any longer. The children lined up, the girls waiting for a good-bye kiss, Jeb waiting for the moment he would become the man of the house. Maeve remained a few steps away, unsure where she fit in.

Seth kissed and hugged Gracie, admonishing her to be on her very best behavior.

Burying her head in her Daddy's shoulder, Pea pleaded with him to allow her to go. Seth shook his head, kissed the sunshine of his life, and stood.

Jeb held out his hand, wanting desperately to appear grown-up. "Pa, don't worry about a thing. I'll care for the women and do the chores just as if you were here."

"Jeb, you know where the shotgun is. Don't hesitate to use it. Remember, boy, you're in charge."

"I can handle it, Pa, I promise," Jeb stated grimly.

Without warning, Seth pulled Jeb close and hugged him. "When did you turn from a boy to a man, son?"

The blush crept up Jeb's neck to cover his face. "Awwww, Pa!"

Glancing in Maeve's direction, he tipped his hat, not realizing how disappointing his action was to her. "Well, that's it, then."

Pea grabbed her father's rough, callused hand and pulled. As he bent down, Pea's eyebrows rose and fell in earnest while whispering into his ear.

He frowned.

"Do it, Papa," she demanded loudly.

Gathering what courage he could muster, Seth moved quickly toward Maeve and clasped her shoulders. He planted a gentle kiss on her cheek.

"No, Papa, on the lips. Her wants a real kiss, don't you, Maeve?"

Maeve blinked rapidly, afraid to move, afraid not to. Seth tucked his thumb under her chin and tilted her face upward. She reminded herself he was only doing this to make Pea happy, not because he wanted to . . . or did he? She focused on his mouth, finding it impossible to meet his gaze. His tongue flicked outward, moistening his lower lip, then disappeared. Her heart did strange things as Maeve stood on her toes to make it easier for him.

Seth saw desire flood her features. He could almost taste the sweetness of her before he pressed his mouth to hers. When her lips parted, he couldn't contain a soft groan. Trying to appear calm, he placed his arm around her waist and drew her closer, responding to a need as natural and primal as time itself.

The moment embedded itself deeply in Maeve's heart. How long had she prayed for this? A moment when she could press her mouth to some gorgeous hunk of a man? All those nights practicing kisses with her pillow, pretending it was Elvis, being satisfied with dreams—how shallow and childish that all seemed!

She could taste his tobacco, taste his experience, and then . . . it was over. Her knees nearly buckled beneath the covering of her skirt, and for the first time since arriving in never-never land, Maeve found herself grateful for the garment's pesky length.

As Seth climbed aboard the wagon, reined the horses in the opposite direction, and waved good-bye, she held the kiss on her lips with two fingers. Pressing, keeping it there long enough to last until the next time. And wondering. Wondering if, indeed, there would be a next time.

"Gosh, I hope Papa makes it okay." Gracie grinned maliciously and, misreading the look of worry on Maeve's face, continued. "There's all sorts of wild animals out there—bear, coyote, not to mention Indians."

Maeve caught on quickly to what the child hoped to accomplish. "Yeah, I know. Gee, just think, if he doesn't make it *I'm* in charge! Scared, Gracie?"

"He'll come back!" she snapped. "Don't you worry about that. My Papa ain't afraid of nothin'!"

*   *   *

139

In the heat of the lazy afternoon, with nothing left to do, Maeve suggested a rousing game of Cowboys and Indians. She was answered with three incredulous faces.

"Us can't play *that* Maeve! What if'n some Injun sees us?"

"Oh come on, Pea, there aren't any Indians around here! Gracie just has you spooked. Come on, y'all can be the cowboys and I'll be the Indian."

Jeb cast a doubtful eye in her direction but followed her outside, curious to see what this game involved.

As soon as she hit the front porch, Maeve shamelessly tucked her long skirt between her legs and let out a loud whoop. Throwing back her head, she did her best Indian imitation.

Pea giggled, chasing Maeve around the yard. It wasn't long before Gracie joined in, unable to resist such fun.

Watching from the depths of the silent forest, two slightly crossed eyes struggled to focus on the woman making tribal sounds. He had searched for what seemed to be many moons for the woman who had fallen from the clouds. His sigh broke the silence, and although his inner thoughts made very little sense, he was used to that.

Woman now belong to old friend who have many children. Woman much pretty, woman show ankles. Woman show pretty ankles! Youngest of children laugh like music from the winds.

Sound make me want to laugh. One Feather no laugh. One Feather must watch friend's farm while friend is gone. One Feather be wary of woman who make no enemy and walks on cloud.

Chapter Nine

Cradled in between the mountains, Elkhorn was a town built out of necessity for the miners and their families.

Seth tipped his hat to the family in the passing wagon. From the amount of supplies stacked in every cranny of the wagon, their journey into town had been successful.

The youngest child, a girl about Blossom's age, smiled shyly, and Seth felt his heartstrings tug. He missed his family and wondered how they were faring during the time spent alone.

After the wagon had passed, Seth drew his horses onto the much-used trail. Looking forward, he could see the rooftop of Fraternity Hall, a building that easily housed half a dozen organizations. If he turned to look over his shoulder, he saw the bluish-purple mountains fading in the distance. A distance which beckoned him to hurry home.

He drew the horses to a stop when he reached the graveyard, astonished by the number of new markers. The intricate carvings on the fancy headstones stated that the graves belonged to young children. Shaking his head in wonder, Seth tried to ignore the uneasy feeling settling over him and flicked the reins in an effort to jolt the horses forward.

As he reached the center of town, two scantily clad women peered over the balcony of the first of many saloons in town. One smiled, beckoning him to stop. Seth tugged his hat low over his burning face and looked away, fixing his gaze on the road ahead.

Having slept in the wilderness, he would've liked nothing more than a glass of strong ale, but Seth had more important things to do. He reined the horses to a stop in front of the sheriff's office.

After slapping the trail dust off his britches, Seth entered the small wooden building that contained two cells—both occupied—and saw no sign of the sheriff. Peering at the walls, he carefully searched the posters adorning them, praying Maeve's face wouldn't be among them. He wasn't disappointed. Just as he was about to leave, the sheriff entered.

"Well howdy! What can I do for you this fine day?"

Seth paused. He knew he had a moral obligation to speak to the sheriff about Maeve's unexplained appearance, but what would he do if Sheriff Barnibus had information? Could he really turn her over so easily?

Feeling guilty for even considering his own feelings above Maeve's welfare, he cleared his suddenly dry throat and spoke. "You, uh, heard anything about anyone missing a daughter or a wife?" The thought turned his heart cold. He'd never questioned Maeve about her marital status. What if she belonged to another man? She couldn't. In all the wild stories she'd shared, information like that was bound to come out.

Sheriff Barnibus slowly lowered his portly frame into the chair beside his desk with a groan. "Can't say as I have. Why? You found someone?"

Seth fumbled with his hat. "I, uh, it's for a friend of mine. He, um, found a gal down by the, uh, stream. . . . " *Thunder! Why did I have to admit where?* "Uh, close to Sweetbriar. Told him I'd do some checking for him while I was in town."

A sly grin formed on the sheriff's thick lips. "Purty gal?"

"What difference does that make?" Seth questioned, clearly confused.

The sheriff's bawdy laughter rang off the sides of the small enclosure. "Well now, if she's purty, maybe your friend ain't in such a hurry to rid himself of her. If she's ugly, Sweet Sal down at the Goldminer's Saloon is lookin' for a few more whores."

Seth shuddered at the thought of someone as

sweet and pure as Maeve trying to survive in a town laden with disease, homicide, and saloons. "My friend is doing the Christian thing by giving the young woman a place to live until her rightful family claims her."

The sheriff contemplated the man standing before him as he leaned back in his chair and tipped the front legs off the floor. "Well now, maybe you ought to check down to the hall. If'n it's a Christian thing."

"Perhaps I will," Seth stated as he replaced his hat.

"Careful who you come in contact with, mister. Done been several outbreaks of diphtheria. Got to be a real epidemic 'round these parts."

Anxious to be done with his business and on his way home, Seth didn't pursue the remark. "Thanks, I will."

"Warning you seemed like the *Christian* thing to do," the sheriff stated mockingly.

Seth stepped out onto the boardwalk and breathed a sigh of relief, delighted no one had reported his Maeve missing. At least the Lord couldn't count this trip against him now that he'd done his duty by asking.

Guilt tickled his heart. He probably should take the matter one step further and make the short journey down the street to Fraternity Hall. Instead, he turned in the opposite direction and headed for Willard's Mercantile.

"Good morning to you, Mr. Caldwell. 'Tis been a while." Fanny Willard smiled at her latest customer while ringing up the purchases of another.

The store bustled with activity as miners searched for new clothing and supplies. Seth felt sorely out of place among the racks of hand-crafted goods. He looked around, wondering where he should start.

A dress captured his eye. The material was a sunshine yellow with layer upon layer of lace beneath the flowing skirt. Tucked at the waist, the dress had miniature pearl buttons lined fashionably down the deep cut of the bodice.

Seth thought of Maeve's shoulder-length brown tresses tumbling down to rest upon the fabric. Her smile when she saw the dress. There would be sparks of happiness in the twinkle that stayed continuously in her eyes. And her dimples when she smiled. Oh, what those dimples could do to a man! He imagined her breasts molded together by the tightness of the bodice. The cleavage that would so obviously show in a dress such as this. His throat constricted with a sudden surge of desire.

" 'Tis right you should be lookin' at the dress now, Mr. Caldwell. That lovely wife of yours would be pleased to have such a fine garment. And how is the missus doing?"

Tearing his gaze away, Seth was embarrassed to be caught looking at feminine fancies. "Duessa passed away."

Fanny clutched at her heart and clucked sorrowfully. "To be sure?"

He wanted to snap, "Of course I'm sure!" but

buried his frustration with a sigh. "She hadn't been in the best of health for quite some time."

"How sad, Mr. Caldwell. How did she finally succumb?" the woman inquired gently.

No, Seth thought. I see no reason at all to share the details with this woman. There are some things better left unstated. "I prefer not to talk about it," he finally answered.

Fanny placed her hand on Seth's arm. "I understand, Mr. Caldwell. Now then, back to this lovely dress. I dinna think it comes in a size small enough for your daughter. Shall I check for you?"

"No, no. Don't bother."

"What else can I be helpin' ye with on this fine day the Lord's seen fit to give us?"

Striding toward the main section of the store, Seth mentally reviewed his list. "I'll need a bag of flour, sugar, and let's see—" *How am I going to know if I'm carrying enough gold to pay for all this?*—"seed, candy, books for Jeb, pencils, a doll—a china doll," he withdrew the bundle of coins and placed them in Fanny's hands. "Just tell me when it's gone."

He left the woman to figure his bill and wandered down the aisles of goods, searching for dungarees. Although he didn't approve of women wearing trousers, if Maeve wanted them so desperately, he would do his best to provide them. It was the least he could do in exchange for her taking care of the children.

When he found them stacked one atop the other, his brows furrowed. *What size should I get her?* Footsteps coming up behind him made him drop the pants nervously.

Fanny retrieved them with a smile. "Have you ever seen the likes? I told Mr. Willard they would never sell, but he insisted we try. The miners seem to be rather enthused by the rough fabric. What size would you be wanting?"

"I really don't know," Seth answered honestly. The dungarees seemed the same as Maeve's own pair, though the fabric was much coarser. Also the strange contraption that seemed to glue itself together up the front was missing, replaced by buttons. "They're . . . they're not for me."

"Ah, I see. Your son, perhaps?"

As much as he wanted to please Maeve, he couldn't bring himself to tell the shopkeeper they were for a woman, and Seth raised his hands helplessly. "Let's forget the dungarees."

She frowned. "Are you sure, Mr. Caldwell?"

"Yes, I'm sure."

Walking back toward the front of the store, Seth glanced at the dress once again. He stopped. "Mrs. Willard, do you have that dress with a waist size such as this?" He held his hands apart, realized he was imagining Duessa's waist, and smiled before bringing them closer together. "I mean like this? It's for my— my fiancee."

For a split second, he wondered when he'd begun to imagine them being married. And now that the words were out, he breathed a sigh of relief at admitting the truth of his feelings. A wave of happiness washed over him, leaving Seth smiling.

Fanny beamed. "Why, Mr. Caldwell, congratulations! Do tell me all about the bride."

If he could protect Duessa's memory, thus giving her dignity in death, surely he could do the same for Maeve. Carefully, he chose his words. "She's not from around these parts." There! The nosy shopkeeper would have to be satisfied with that.

"And how long have you known her?"

Obviously she wasn't. "I feel as if I've known her all my life, Mrs. Willard, and I'm sure you can understand that I'm in a bit of a hurry to return home, so if you don't mind?" He raised a questioning brow in hopes of gaining control over the situation.

Fanny beamed. "That's lovely, Mr. Caldwell. Congratulations once again. Tell me, when is the wedding to take place?"

As soon as I tell her my intentions! "We haven't set a date yet."

"Why, my dear man, should you not consider it too presumptuous of me, might I be makin' a suggestion?"

He smiled. "All suggestions are welcomed, I assure you."

Fanny leaned closer. "Rumor has it, Mr. Caldwell, rumor has it that the town of Elkhorn is about to experience a revival! Yes"—she beamed—"'tis true! And it'll not be soon enough for me, I can tell you that. Why the riffraff we are surrounding ourselves with is decadent!"

Not at all interested in the day-to-day affairs of city life, Seth prodded her to continue so he could get on about his business.

"Rumor has it that in September, we shall be graced with the presence of Rev. Spruster! And for the entire month, can you imagine that? He's supposed to carry on his revival from Fraternity Hall." She lowered her voice a notch. "And when he comes, I shall personally help him carry these . . . these . . . painted little tarts out of town on their ear!" Folding her arms beneath her ample bosom, she narrowed her eyes. "If you be askin' it of me, 'tis those horrible painted women that brought the plague to our town. And children, precious, innocent little children, are dying off a dozen at a time."

Seth didn't know what to say. He wondered if Fanny would be so willing to share her religious fervor with him if she knew he harbored an unmarried woman beneath his roof, allowing the woman to sleep in his bed. For in his heart, he knew what he did was indeed a sin. Even if he hadn't lain with her, God knew he'd imagined it. And didn't the Good Book preach about things such as that?

Following the shopkeeper back to the counter, Seth stared at the supplies he'd requested while she went in search of the dress. Hopefully everything he'd asked for was there. Because now all he could think of was getting back to the woman under his roof and somehow finding the proper way to propose! It was time to make an honest woman of Maeve and up to him to do so.

Fanny returned from the stockroom smiling. "Now then, Mr. Caldwell. I've managed to find the dress in the size you've requested. Should it not fit, bring the garment back into town next trip. I'll see to it Mr. Willard gives you credit, but I do so hope it fits. Why, I doubt you'd find a finer dress anywhere—"

"I doubt I could, Mrs. Willard. Now then, what is the total amount due?"

She figured the total at the bottom of his bill and slid it across the counter. Seth stared at the paper until the silence between them became uncomfortable.

"Anything wrong, Mr. Caldwell?"

"No, of course not. This, er, figure, does it include everything I asked for?"

"Everything but the schoolbooks, Mr. Caldwell. I'm afraid we're out of those. Ever since we got the new teacher, we've run short of school supplies. I can order one for you and have it in a month, if you like."

"No, that won't be necessary." He placed a pouch of gold on her counter. "Just take out what I owe you, Mrs. Willard."

When he received several pieces back in change, Seth breathed a sigh of relief.

After loading the wagon, Seth walked slowly down the main street, watching the assortment of people. Rounding the corner, he nearly bumped into a gentleman dressed in black. "Excuse me," Seth stated.

"Could be that's the luckiest mistake you've made today," the gentleman replied, offering a slightly evil smile. "My good man, do you know who I am?"

Seth shook his head.

"I'm Dr. Elliot Periwinkle. Do you suffer from malaise? Are your cattle wormy? Does the little woman run out of energy before the day is finished?" The words were delivered in a singsong voice as the man clapped a hand around Seth's shoulder. "I happen to have an elixir, the finest elixir money can buy. Makes a man feel manly, a woman feel womanly, if you understand my meaning, eh, good fellow?" He jabbed his elbow lightly into Seth's rib cage, barely pausing for a breath when he changed subjects. "Perhaps a book would suit your needs. I happen to have in my possession a certain book that is now the rage back east."

The words caught Seth's attention. "A book? What kind of book?"

"A book that was written by a man of wisdom, a man of insight, a man . . . who knew what he was doing! This book has changed many lives, all for the better, I might add, and it's in great demand."

Seth felt the change in his pocket. "A book of wisdom?"

"Wisdom indeed, my good man." Periwinkle searched through the disheveled mess in his wagon until he produced a copy of the novel.

"See for yourself." He handed Seth a thin book.

Seth stared at the cover, taking what he could only hope was an appropriate amount of time, then flipped through the pages. "I left my reading glasses at home. Can you tell me the title?"

Periwinkle's tone lowered as his eyebrows rose and fell. *"The ABCs of Miss Maribell's Secret Garden."*

Grinning, Seth rubbed his finger over the leather-bound cover. "Blossom will love it."

"You, my good man, are lucky indeed! This book was meant for sharing."

Seth reached into his pocket and handed over some change. "Will this cover the cost?"

"Oh, my, yes! And for you, sir, I shall throw in a bottle of tonic."

"Best bargain I've gotten all day," Seth exclaimed happily. Tucking the book beneath his arm and the bottle of tonic in his jacket pocket, he strolled back the way he'd come until he reached the Elkhorn Shipping Company.

The fact that his shipment of sheep was months overdue made him ignore the wagons lined up to receive their supplies.

Seth recalled a time in his life when he'd been in the same position many of these men were in. Because they were common miners, they held no prominence and would have to patiently wait their turn until the proprietor decided to deal with them. Or until one of the many bosses from the mines decided to come out of the saloon and handle the situation himself.

154

Since Elkhorn was built more out of need than desire, it had always struck Seth as unfair that the mining companies would put up with such shabby treatment of their workers. Unless a person had a pocketful of gold and could manage a way to buy their way to prominence, the miners were treated unjustly once the gold ran out.

However, many of the townspeople were bitter and blamed the mining companies for the loss of lives, fires, and general decadence they found themselves in the midst of.

"Can I help you, sir?"

Seth's attention was jolted back. "Yes, the name is Seth Caldwell, and I was due to receive a shipment of lambs in the early spring of this year. Needless to say, they haven't arrived."

The clerk scratched the back of his head in puzzlement. "It'll take a few minutes to go through the purchase orders."

"Take your time," Seth offered and walked to the front entrance.

For Seth, the memories of mining were bittersweet. Back then, the worth of a man wasn't measured by whether he was smart or dumb, but by how much gold he could obtain in one day. The more he procured, the more highly he was thought of. Seth had been considered a top-notch worker.

What would Maeve's reaction be when she realized he couldn't read? Would she label him dim-witted, as his parents had done?

"Mr. Caldwell, I found your order."

Turning, Seth shrugged off the depressing thoughts.

"Due to the bad winter, the shipment was delayed. We have an expected arrival date of August fifteenth. Shall I send a messenger down your way when they arrive?"

"I'll be glad to pay the man who can deliver them to me," Seth offered.

"I'll personally see to it," the clerk promised.

Having attended to all of his business, Seth shrugged off his weariness, happily securing his purchases for the long trip home.

As the sun began to set he headed out of town, filled with anticipation. The anticipation of a warm welcome from a certain soon-to-be new member of his family.

Chapter Ten

Maeve sat on the wooden porch and watched the gentle night breeze play among the tall pine boughs. Where is he? she wondered. And what is he doing right now? The stars twinkled like tiny fireflies in the endless sky. Maeve brushed her hand beneath her heavy mane of hair, lifting it up off her neck. The cool breeze felt wonderful.

During Seth's absence, she'd tried hard to gain perspective on what had brought her to this place in time. It was difficult to do, since common sense dictated her adventure was impossible. But impossible or not, she was here and it seemed she was here to stay.

Her mind mulled over the dozens of time-travel books she'd read. They were her favorite kind of books; the idea of stepping into some sort of time warp had always appealed to her sense of adventure. But the situation she found herself in contrasted sharply with the wonderful heroines in the pages of books.

For one thing, most of them ended up landing in the hero's bed to be discovered by him. Not only had she been discovered by Pea, she'd landed in the dirt. Figures, Maeve mused.

And didn't there always seem to be a definite reason for the heroine to step back in time? So far, the only reason Maeve could figure she'd been needed was to baby-sit. Some drama!

Of course, before the reason came the threat to the hero's welfare. But here, in the serenity of the woods, there was no threat. Only a sense of peace which Maeve had always longed for and been unable to find since the death of her parents.

Then there was a nasty little difference called love. Usually, by page 20, the hero was so in awe of his find that he fell madly in love with her, thus ensuring a lifetime of happiness.

All Maeve had received were strange looks and questions. Endless questions. So things were a little bit out of kilter. So she'd been the one to fall in love first. Did that mean she could hold on to the hope that Seth's love was sure to come?

Nonsense!

This is real life. Not the pages of a book. And in real life, no matter how strange, things just don't happen so neatly.

Gracie's deep, throaty cough drew her away

from her troubled thoughts. All day long the child had coughed, and Maeve had hoped that, with the coming of night, the cool air would put a stop to it. If anything, her condition had worsened.

Standing, she pressed her forehead against the rough wooden post and sighed. Taking care of three children without the help of television to occupy them had been harder than she'd imagined. Jeb was no problem, and he'd gone out of his way to be helpful. She was amazed at the amount of work the child accomplished in any given day. But hard work didn't seem to bother Jeb. As a matter of fact, he seemed very proud of what he could accomplish during the course of the day.

Pea was a delight, always finding ways to make Maeve laugh at her antics. She found good in every situation, which was something very rare for her age, or so Maeve believed.

And Gracie. Poor, whiny Gracie. She'd managed to complain for 25 of the 24 hours of each passing day. The food was overcooked, the washing not clean. Her mama would have done this, her mama would have done that! If mama was mentioned one more time, Maeve thought she'd scream!

Her thoughts turned back to Seth. *Is he camped out beneath the brilliant stars? Is he thinking of me?* She closed her eyes and conjured up the image of his face. The beautiful blue of his eyes, those thick brows, that secret smile and aristocratic nose.

God, he was something to behold! Watching him try to act tough made Maeve want to giggle. He was exactly like a Tootsie Roll—a little bit hard on the outside but once you got past the tough exterior, my, how sweet! She heaved a heartfelt sigh.

This land is lonesome. Lonesome and endless. He's out there somewhere, lying beneath those stars and thinking of me, I just know it.

The trees whispered in agreement and Maeve smiled. Scraping her lower lip between her teeth, she could almost taste the sweetness mingled with the bitterness of tobacco when he'd kissed her. At Pea's insistence, she added truthfully. Would he ever kiss her at his own insistence or was that to be something she simply wished for?

"Maeve?"

She knew which child it was without having to turn around by the ragged cough that followed. With the gentle rustle of the branches, Maeve felt the need to whisper as the pines were now doing. "What is it, Gracie?"

"Maeve, I don't feel good at all." Again the rasping cough.

Pressing her hand against the child's forehead, Maeve couldn't swallow her concern. "My gosh, Gracie, you're burning up with fever. Where do you keep the aspirin?"

Barely able to get the words out between coughs, Gracie questioned, "Where's what?"

Reality hit with a thud in the pit of Maeve's stomach. "I keep forgetting what time I'm in.

Tell me, Gracie, what did your mama used to do when y'all got sick?"

"Where's mama?" the child asked in confusion.

Even in the surrounding darkness, Maeve could clearly see her glassy-eyed expression. "Oh, baby, don't you remember what your mama used to do for you? This is really important, Gracie—come on, let's get you inside out of this night air." Placing her hand on Gracie's back, Maeve led the child inside, fearful of the heat radiating from the youngster's skin.

"Jeb," she whispered harshly and received no reply. "Come on, Gracie, go get into my bed."

"Where's my mama and who are you?" Gracie demanded, having no recollection of the woman now ordering her around.

"Hell's bells, I'm the good luck fairy! Now come on, get into the bed," Maeve pleaded.

After she'd tucked Gracie beneath the heavy covers, Maeve ran to the stairs leading to the loft. "Jeb, can you hear me?"

Jeb sat up slowly, still half-asleep. "Yes'm, I hear you."

Maeve breathed a sigh of relief. "Jeb, Gracie's got a really high fever and I don't know what to do about it."

Jeb's eyes widened. "Uh-oh. Last month we went to help the Campbells build their barn. Her youngest daughter was sick with the fever, Maeve. Gracie spent the entire time playing with her. You don't think Gracie's gonna d—"

"Hush! I won't even hear that word spoken in

161

this house," Maeve quickly interjected. "Now tell me, what did your mama used to do when one of you kids got sick?"

Jeb's eyes widened. "Gee, Maeve, I can't recollect, I mean—"

"Come on, Jeb, this is important," she pleaded. Suddenly she remembered an old-fashioned saying. "Feed the fever and starve the cold? No, starve the fever and feed the cold—only she doesn't have a cold . . . oh, Jeb, please!" Tears filled her eyes. "Wait! Run fetch some water from the creek, will you, Jeb? Do it as quickly as possible."

Jeb stood, scratching his stomach and yawning. "But Maeve, can't I git it from the well?"

"No! Do as I say, Jeb. Move!"

The intensity of her tone made the boy come to life. "I'll fetch it as quick as I can, Maeve."

But Maeve had already turned her attention back to Gracie as another cough seemed to steal the child's breath.

Pea heard the commotion through her sleepy state. "Maeve, is Gracie sick? Is her gonna die, Maeve?"

"She's not feeling too good right now, Pea, and no, she isn't going to die."

"Annie Campbell died," Pea announced solemnly.

The thought was too much to bear. "Go help your brother, okay?" Stripping the damp nightshirt from Gracie's body, Maeve was alarmed to feel the fever still rising. "Hurry, Jeb," she pleaded through clenched teeth when a shiver racked the child's body.

Returning with the pail, Jeb watched as Maeve began to tear the long skirt she wore into strips of material. Dipping them into the bucket, she placed each strip on Gracie's pulse points, watching with alarm as they dried far too quickly beneath the scorching heat. She watched helplessly as another cough took control. "Gracie? Listen, sweetie, everything is gonna be all right, you hear me?"

Pea tugged at Maeve's arm. "Is her gonna die, Maeve?" she repeated.

Knowing she had to pause long enough to comfort the frightened child, Maeve glanced down at the wide eyes peering up at her in trust. "Oh, honey, she's just really sick, you know?"

"I got sick once. Mama gave me some awful-tastin' stuff."

Maeve nearly cried with relief. She knelt down beside Pea and gently clasped her shoulders. "Where is it, do you know, Pea? Where does your mama keep her awful-tasting stuff?"

"Her keeps it in the pantry."

"If I carry you, will you show me which bottle it is?" Maeve questioned as a spark of hope lifted her heart. The child solemnly nodded, and, carrying her into the kitchen, Maeve prayed the medicine would do the trick. It simply had to.

Her heart sank at the sight of the tonic bottle. Reading the contents, Maeve found it to be nothing more than a combination of sugar and alcohol. She heard Gracie's feeble cry. "I'm coming, hon, hang on a second." Struck by a sudden inspiration, Maeve took the bottle back to the bed and tipped it, soaking yet another rag, before placing it over Gracie's chest. By now, the ill child's body trembled uncontrollably. Maeve struggled with the covers until she had Gracie wrapped in a semishroud.

Pea screamed at the sight.

"What is it, Pea?"

"You wrapped her like Papa did Mama! You killed her, Maeve, you done killed her!"

Maeve nearly cried. "No, baby. Honest I haven't."

The little girl kicked the side of the bed in anger. "Then you undo her, Maeve! Undo her now!"

Jeb grabbed his sister's hand and pulled her away. "I'm sorry, Maeve, but that's the way Papa wrapped Mama before burying her. I guess it scairt her."

After unwrapping Gracie, Maeve pointed to the gentle rise and fall of the sleeping child's chest. "See, Pea? She's still alive, I promise."

Satisfied, Pea snuggled against her brother and gave Maeve a wary look as she stuck her thumb in her mouth.

Waiting until Jeb led Blossom up to the loft, Maeve placed her ear against Gracie's chest. She heard an ominous rattle. The rattle of death. "No," she whispered, "I won't let you take her. I'll fight you if it's the last thing I do." She carefully lay down beside Gracie and wrapped her arms around the small body. In her mind's eye, she could see the gypsy from the amusement park. Her words came back to haunt Maeve.

You shall seek the young child out. Three call your name and one you shall lose. He will forgive you.

A tingle of fear wrapped itself around Maeve's heart. "No!" she sobbed. "You can't have her, she belongs to me now." Stifling the broken cries with her fist, Maeve bit hard on her hand. "You've taken my parents; you've taken everything I ever loved. I will not let you take my child!"

And as the sun crept over the horizon in brilliant shades of red and orange, Maeve knew she'd found what time had stolen. She'd found a family of her own.

Seth rose at dawn and grimaced as he tried to swallow. His throat felt raw and irritated. Anxious to get home, he ignored the slight chill that swept over his body and hitched the horses to the wagon. Securing his supplies one last time against the rough road ahead, he hopped aboard and took off in the direction of his loved ones.

As he gently prodded the horses forward, Seth became aware he was no longer alone. Tightening his grip on the rifle that lay beside him, he peered through the dim light of the early morning.

The birds, who had begun to sing, stopped as

if they too knew they were no longer alone. Seth's heart thudded against his chest. He caught a quick flash of movement to his right. "Hello? Is anyone out there?" The horse whickered softly at the sound of his master's voice.

Seth flicked the reins again, picking up the pace. A jar rattled against the side of the wagon as it went over a bump. He felt the hair rise at the back of his neck.

Rounding the corner, he noticed the trees weren't quite as thick in this particular section. Surely anyone who had been following him would either be forced to stay in the shelter of the trees or show himself.

A rabbit skittered across the path.

Although the morning was yet to become uncomfortably hot, beads of sweat now clung to Seth's forehead. Clearing his vision with a blink, he began to shiver uncontrollably as the fever came upon him.

Trees meshed together as limbs became talons reaching out, trying to stop the journey Seth knew he had to continue. Something was wrong. Terribly wrong. A wave of dizziness overtook Seth and he fell back against the seat, his rifle slipping to the floor.

The eyes that had been watching Seth's journey for the past few miles now stared as the horses came to a stop. Slipping down off his albino pony, One Feather settled into a crouch, waiting patiently for his friend to waken.

Last night, One Feather had had a vision. The vision showed him the bird of death circling his friend, Good Heart. It'd been so strong that One Feather had had no other choice but to go in search of him.

When the sun crept high into the sky, it occurred to One Feather that Good Heart had been sleeping for a long time. He watched the horse's tail twitch, then became mesmerized by particles of dust floating in a strong shaft of sunlight which filtered through the opening of two branches.

The realization that he was thirsty broke through One Feather's reverie in the late afternoon. Good Heart was still slumbering. As the sun began its descent, One Feather heard his friend cry out. Still in a crouched position, One Feather backed away, watching the journey of the forest animals as they went toward the water.

Harsh, ragged coughs sent him scurrying back to Good Heart's side, his own thirst forgotten.

Chapter Eleven

Placing his hand on his friend's brow, One Feather knew the Sun Goddess had touched Good Heart, leaving her burning fury in his body. If he didn't find a way to cool the fever, the Sun Goddess would send her eagle to steal Good Heart's spirit.

Having watched the ceremonies of the medicine man, One Feather lifted Seth's limp body from the wagon and carried him toward the stream. There he placed his friend in the water, trying to wash away the goddess's touch.

After building a fire, One Feather pulled from his pouch a piece of coal and placed it in the center of the fiery depths. When the outside turned white with ash, One Feather took a piece of sacred sweet grass and burned it, cleansing his hands with the smoke. As he did this, he sang the song of all the men who had walked before him to the valley of darkness, pleading with them to turn their backs on his friend's spirit.

When the grass was prepared to One Feather's satisfaction, he made an application of herbs and spittle. Taking out a buffalo-horn tube, One Feather placed the tip in his mouth and sucked up some of the substance before placing the edge of the tube against Good Heart's forehead.

It was hard to imagine what evil had possessed his friend, but One Feather was willing to take the chance of ingesting it in order to save him. Fervently praying the gods would forgive him for trying to impersonate the tribal medicine man, he saw a hawk—or was it an eagle? It was hard to tell with the condition of his eyes. No matter, there would be no time to lose now. Not with the bird circling to lay claim to his white friend's spirit.

One Feather placed his lips on the tube and began to suck out the evil that was causing the fever. He spat on the ground, dismayed when nothing appeared. When the medicine man had performed such spectacular feats, he usually had something visible to show, but One Feather had nothing but his breath. Still, he covered the area with a fine layer of dirt so the spirit couldn't escape.

In his delirium, Good Heart's arm shot out and came to rest upon the spirit's grave. One Feather gasped as he flung his friend away, rolling him once again to the stream before washing away the remaining evil.

As darkness fell, One Feather placed a hand across Good Heart's brow and watched for signs of the spirit's return. The heat in his friend's body rose again, but this time it was followed by racking coughs, then tremors. One Feather knew he must find a way to return the white man to Woman Who Walks On Cloud, then get the real shaman from his tribe.

After tethering his pony to the back of the wagon, One Feather lifted his friend into the seat and covered him with a blanket.

Seth muttered indistinguishable words, trapped in the prison of his raging fever.

Clicking softly, One Feather reined the horses toward home.

Maeve watched Gracie struggle for breath and worried what would happen if the child reached a point where she no longer possessed the strength to draw in air. Through the long night as the fever rose and chills racked Gracie's body, Maeve added more blankets to the growing mound.

Bathing Gracie's face with cool water, Maeve observed the way her chest rose and fell. The cough came from deep within. Too deep for Maeve to know what to do. The sudden change from a light cough to a heavy one bothered her considerably. Never had she seen an illness take control so quickly, so completely. When the child spoke, Maeve's first inclination was to stop her, but from the look of anguish on Gracie's face, Maeve realized there were things she needed to say.

"I never hated you, Maeve. I love you."

"I know that, baby."

"It was seeing you in Mama's clothes that I didn't like. I kept thinkin' maybe Pa would forget all about her."

"Oh, Gracie, honey, we never forget those we love."

"I'll never forget you, Maeve. But Mama wants me to go with her now, and I don't know what to do." A tear trickled down the child's flushed face.

Swallowing back tears of her own, Maeve tried to offer consolation. "Whatever you decide, I'll understand, sweetheart. But Gr-Gracie, I'll miss you so much if you go."

"Can you see Mama, Maeve? She's right over there, standing with her arms out to me."

Turning in the direction Gracie pointed, Maeve could almost imagine she did see Duessa. Common sense told her it was nothing more than shadows being cast across the room by the flickering flames of the fire. "Sleep now, darling Gracie. Try to get some rest."

The child nodded and Maeve stayed beside her until a peacefulness overtook the ravaged expression Gracie had earlier worn.

When the light of day crept into the windows, Maeve expelled a sigh of relief. With the coming of morning, sickness never seemed quite as serious.

Without having to be told, Jeb took Pea by the hand and led her outside as he went about his chores. He instinctively knew something was terribly wrong with his sister. Something so wrong, he doubted God himself could save her.

Pulling the stool over to the cow, Jeb sat down to milk. Pea stood watching in silence. "What's the matter, Pea Pot?" Jeb questioned.

Pea gathered the edge of her dress in her hand, twisting the material. "Mama ain't coming home, is she, Jeb?"

"Naw, she ain't, Pea."

"Is Gracie gonna be goin' where Mama went, Jeb?"

Jeb swallowed a sob of despair. As ornery as his sister was, he didn't want to lose her. "Don't know, Pea."

Wandering over to the door, Pea looked out at the morning light. "If'n Gracie does go where Mama went, she ain't gonna come back either, is she?"

"Well now, Pea, here's what I think. If'n Gracie does go to be with Mama, we got to be happy for her 'cause it's where she'll want to go. And we ain't gotta worry much, 'cause Mama'll take good care of her." He swiped a tear away with the back of his hand.

"Whatcha cryin' for, Jeb?"

"I ain't cryin'," he denied harshly. "I got somethin' in my eye."

Pea's eyes were solemn circles of understanding. "Yeah, I get things in my eyes too sometimes. But mostly when my insides is so full they gotta get out."

Jeb grabbed the pail of milk and his little sister's hand. "Come on, Pea Pot, let's take this milk inside and check on Gracie."

One Feather's spirit was tired. But the circling of the hawk told him he must continue his journey to save his friend from the bird's sharp talons.

Just over the rise, One Feather could see smoke curling from Good Heart's chimney. Leaping down from the wagon, he untied his horse and let out a chilling scream to scare the horses into motion. He watched the wagon bump and jostle its way down the incline.

Jeb opened the door to the cabin when he heard the hoofbeats of running horses. His spirits rose. Papa would know what to do about Gracie. Papa knew everything!

Seth wiped his feverish face and sat up in the wagon. How had he made it home so quickly? He vaguely remembered waking up that morning, or was it yesterday morning? He had a slight recollection of being carried to a stream, but by whom? Looking around, he saw nothing but the trees blanketing the forest.

At Jeb's excited announcement of his father's arrival, Maeve jumped up from the chair, ignoring her body's cry of protest. Running to the door, she watched the man she loved step down from the wagon. In moments she was at his side, wrapping her arms around his neck in a gesture of relief. "Oh Seth! I didn't think you'd make it home in time. Gracie's real sick, Seth, and I didn't know what to do for her—"

"What's the matter with my daughter? What have you done to her?" Seth's raging fever made him feel weak and he struggled to remain standing.

"Why, I haven't done anything!" Maeve searched his face, confused by his reaction. "Right after you left, she developed a terrible cough and started running a fever—"

Seth roughly pushed her aside and made his way to the cabin door.

Maeve watched him go, her heart refusing to believe he would hold her responsible.

Walking over to join her, Jeb patted Maeve's back, trying to erase the grief-stricken look on her face. "Don't mind Papa, Maeve, he's probably just tired."

Tears filled her eyes. "He blames me. I should have done more. I should have gone for help."

"You did what you could, Miss Maeve, and Papa will see that once he's checked on Gracie." He halted his conversation as his father stormed toward them.

"What's wrong with her? When did this start?"

His anger confused Maeve. Had the coughing started the day he left or the day after? She remained silent, trying to remember, since it seemed so important.

Her silence seemed to infuriate Seth. He grabbed her shoulders, shaking her entire body with furious strength. "Answer me, woman! Tell me what you've done!"

Maeve stifled a moan of pain at his cruel grasp. "I promise you I did nothing," she pleaded. "I tried to help her, Seth, but it's impossible without medicine. I-I didn't know what else to do for her, which way to turn."

Jeb spoke up in Maeve's behalf. "Papa, she tried, honest she did."

The strength left as quickly as it had come upon Seth. Shoulders slumped, he looked at Maeve, seeing not her, but his dead wife. "Why, Duessa? What did she ever do?"

"Duessa?" Maeve whispered.

His face twisted in fury as he came toward her once again. "You broke the children's hearts. You never even tried to be happy, did you, Duessa? I could kill you for the hell you've put us through."

"Papa, no!" Jeb cried as he watched Seth's hands circle Maeve's neck.

Maeve realized as she trembled with fear that his eyes were filled with a maniacal glint. This man before her wasn't her gentle giant; he was a stranger. A stranger filled with violent anger. And his hands were hot, burning against the cool of her skin.

"Listen to me, Seth. I am not Duessa, remember? I'm Maeve, the forest fairy," she added, clawing at his hands.

His fingers tightened.

"You're sick," Maeve said gently. "You have the fever, Seth. Won't you let me help you? Oh,

God, please let me help you." Her plea meant nothing to him.

Jeb tackled his father's legs, pulling him away from Maeve. "Listen to her, Papa!"

Seth turned on Jeb and the words he spoke filled Maeve with despair. "You! I left you in charge. I should have known better." He raised his hand to slap his son and Maeve gasped.

"Don't!" she shouted. "Don't hit him, Seth."

When she tried to step between them, Jeb pushed her aside before balling up his fist and striking a blow to his father's stomach.

Tears streamed down Jeb's cheeks at the sight of his father crumpling to the ground.

"Help me, Jeb!" Maeve cried. "Help me get him inside. He's sick, don't you see?"

She opened the door to a room and found herself surrounded by the skeletons of those she loved. Their white bones rattled eerily as they came toward her. A hand reached out and touched her face, making Maeve scream with fear.

"Maeve." Jeb jostled her shoulder. "Maeve, wake up."

Opening her eyes, Maeve noticed that darkness had fallen, and she struggled to see the outline of Jeb's body, clothed in his long johns.

"You fell asleep, Maeve. You told me to wake you up if you did," he explained.

She rose from the rocking chair and wiped the sleep from her eyes before looking toward the bed. "How is he, Jeb?"

"Still real hot, Maeve. He keeps talking about Mama."

Maeve placed her hand on Seth's forehead. His skin still felt like fire. Beside him, for the first time since coming down with this unnamed illness, Gracie slept peacefully.

Reaching for the covers, Maeve then pulled them over Seth's body. He coughed as if his insides were trying to escape. Maeve winced at the sound.

When Seth opened his eyes to see her hovering over him, he offered a weak smile. "I'm sorry about all of this; I'm sure you never bargained for such a plate of trouble."

Did that mean he'd forgiven her for allowing Gracie to get sick? "Nonsense," she scoffed. "Do you feel any better?"

He shrugged. "How's Gracie?"

"She's sleeping peacefully." Indeed, the child seemed to be. The covers on her side of the bed were so still it looked as if she'd quit breathing. A sudden chill swept down Maeve's spine. Trying to appear nonchalant, Maeve smiled at Seth, brushing back a strand of hair. "Go back to sleep, Seth."

He closed his eyes and nodded wearily. "The wagon—"

"Jeb and I will unload the wagon," she said soothingly. "Don't worry about a thing." Bending, she placed a soft kiss upon his forehead and noted his fever remained high. Her gaze never left Gracie's too-still form.

After ascertaining Seth had indeed fallen back asleep, she moved toward Gracie. Her efforts were interrupted by Pea's tugging of her wrinkled dress.

"Maeve? I don't feel so good."

Maeve's heart sank as she turned to cradle the small child in her arms. The fever. A sort of desperation swept over her. *What in God's name am I going to do?* Pea coughed and drew Maeve's attention back toward her. She managed a smile before asking, "Where's Jeb, sweetie?"

"Him's sleepin' by the fire."

Sure enough, the young boy had fallen into an exhausted sleep.

Maeve held Pea tight against her heart, carrying her to the rocking chair. As she sank down on it, the hard wood felt like a mountain of soft cushions as it supported her aching back. She began to hum softly.

Twice, during the darkest hours of the long night, Seth shouted out for Duessa, crying in anguish over the haunting memory of her ride to death.

As the sun blushed the early morning sky, Maeve placed Pea on a pallet by the fire. She shook Jeb's shoulder gently. "Jeb, honey, wake up."

The young boy who'd tried so hard to prove himself a man sat up and wiped the sleep from his eyes like a small child. "What is it, Maeve?"

Kneeling down beside him, she tried to control the tears streaming silently down her face. "Honey, does Seth own a shovel?"

Jeb's eyes grew round as saucers. "Who, Maeve?"

She reached out and drew him to her, needing this moment of human consolation. "It's Gracie."

He allowed his head to stay in the comfort of her bosom while hot tears rushed to his eyes. Unable to contain his grief, Jeb wept bitterly, his body heaving with giant sobs.

"Shh, Jeb," Maeve whispered. "We mustn't let your father know. Not until he's strong enough to take the news, all right?" She placed a hard kiss upon the boy's head, smelling the still-innocent aroma of him. God, how she wished she could keep him this innocent.

Jeb struggled to erase the tearstains from his cheeks. "I'll go dig the grave."

Maeve stopped him. "No, honey. Just tell me where the shovel is and I'll take care of everything."

"It's a man's job, Miss Maeve. And with Pa being sick, I'm the man of the house." He bit his lip to keep from crying once more. "According to Pa, I didn't do a very good job of it last time, did I?"

Forcing him to meet her gaze, Maeve spoke as sternly as she dared. "You listen to me, Jeb. No one can be held responsible for what happened to Gracie. No more than any one of you is responsible for your mother's death, do you understand me? It wasn't Seth talking, it was the fever."

"Pa never says something unless he means it," Jeb sobbed.

"No, Jeb. You're wrong. I promise you you're wrong." She stroked his head until the boy seemed to gain an inner strength.

"I'm gonna come help you, Maeve."

"I'd rather you stay here and watch over Pea and Seth. If you need me, I'll be out back."

"Maeve?"

"Yes, Jeb?"

"Would you bury her next to Ma? Gracie was afraid of the dark. Maybe being next to Ma and all—" He choked on his sorrow.

"I'll do it, Jeb."

"And Maeve?"

"Yes, Jeb?"

"Gracie weren't such a bad girl. She tried, you know?"

"I know, Jeb." Moving toward the bed, Maeve cradled the dead child against her before carrying her into the kitchen. Using the table as a bed, she dipped a cloth into a nearby basin of water and began to wash the dirt from Gracie's peaceful face. "Are you with your mama, sweetie? Did you tell her I tried to save you? I mean, really tried?" Maeve let the tears flow unchecked. They were broken by a smile. "I doubt it. You didn't like me too much, did you, Gracie? But I hope you understood that even though you proved to be a handful at times, I loved you anyway."

Jeb came to stand beside her. "Miss Maeve, I'm gonna go unload the wagon. Both Pa and

Pea seem to be resting pretty peaceful right now."

"Yes, do that, Jeb. I promised your Pa we would. As soon as I've taken care of Gracie, I'll come help you."

Struggling to lift the last shovelful of dirt from the depths of the grave, Maeve heard her name being called. She glanced up to see Jeb peering down at her. "What is it?" she questioned, grateful for a break.

A spray of freckles stood out against his pale face. "I done found this doll in the wagon. I figure Pa got it for Gracie."

Maeve nodded. "Then Gracie shall have it."

"But Miss Maeve," Jeb sobbed, "she ain't never gonna know that Pa bought it for her."

Maeve left the grave and circled the slender boy's frame with her arms. "Listen to me, Jeb. Do you see that sunrise?"

Jeb looked up toward the mountains and nodded.

"Okay, if God can make something that beautiful, don't you think he's capable of telling Gracie all about the doll?"

"I reckon." Jeb sighed.

Maeve grabbed his shoulders, forcing him to meet her gaze. "No reckoning, Jeb." She touched his chest with her finger. "You've got to believe right here . . . in your heart."

"Yes'm."

The weariness of the past two days made Maeve dizzy. She was so tired. So very, very tired. "Let's get your sister."

Inside, the cabin was quiet except for Seth's ragged breathing. Maeve reached out and wiped the sweat from his brow. Forgive me, Seth, she said inwardly; forgive me for letting Gracie die.

Maeve tucked the doll in Gracie's folded arms and wrapped the softest blanket she could find around the child's stiff body. Jeb walked silently beside her.

When she placed the small form in the grave, Maeve openly wept. How could she put all that dirt on top of such a little girl? A girl who'd deserved more, a child who never understood that Maeve really did love her? As Gracie's face disappeared beneath the dirt, Maeve cried harder.

Jeb finally reached out and took the tool from her hands, finishing what Maeve could no longer bring herself to do. When the task was completed, the boy placed the shovel on the ground. "Reckon we ought to pray, Maeve?"

She shook her head, unable to speak. How could she pray to a God that, once again, had cheated her of a relationship with another being? No—she just couldn't. Maeve cleared her throat. "Y-you do it, Jeb."

And in a child's simplistic way, Jeb was able to express all that Maeve's heart held locked deep inside her.

"Dear God, this here is Jeb. Now we ain't gonna pretend with you that we understand how come you decided to up and take my sister, but we know that you're a whole lot smarter

183

than we are. After all, God, I figure if'n you can make something as purty as that there mountain, then you can make a spot for my sister up there beside our Ma.

"Take good care of her, Lord, 'cause even as mean as she was, I loved her a lot." He glanced over at Maeve, whose tears were falling freely. "Reckon that's all that needs sayin'?"

"I think so, Jeb, I think so," Maeve whispered. But as she bowed her head once more, Maeve couldn't help but add a prayer of her own. If Seth was taken from this earth, God might as well take her too. There was no way she'd make it without him. No way at all.

The realization that she might not have a choice hit hard. Would he forgive her for the death of his child? Could he?

Could she forgive herself?

Chapter Twelve

After two nights of virtually no sleep, Maeve had reached the brink of exhaustion. When she heard the cabin door open, she didn't bother to turn around, but instead focused on Seth's fevered face.

"Jeb, honey, could you dump this water and fetch me another pail? I'm ready to give Pea her sponge bath."

A harsh, guttural sound made her whirl around.

Oh, Indians, how nice!

What??

No . . . calm down, my mind is just playing tricks on me, that's all. I'm going to blink my eyes and they'll be gone.

She blinked.

They remained.

As Maeve stood frozen, not in fear, she told herself, but in fascination with this latest incident, the elder of the two braves stepped forward. She studied him as if he were a picture from a history book.

He wasn't tall exactly, but somehow his stature made her think him tall. Eyes that were beady and black and framed by deep wrinkles against a leathery face stared toward her, unblinking. His hair, kissed silver by age, was long and stringy. Clothed in dusty buckskin, the Indian crossed his arms against his massive chest, his pride evident by the haughty loftiness he exuded.

Maeve's gaze darted back to Seth. "Uhhhh . . . Seth, dear . . . wake up. We have company." Her soft utterance held more than a plea; the words captured her growing sense of panic. She backed away and edged around to the other side of the bed. "I no speak Indian."

The elder's expression remained impassive.

"This isn't a real good time for a visit. Seth is sick, you see, and while I'm sure he'll be pleased to know you stopped by, it would be better if you left now, so, uh, go, okay?" She motioned with both hands toward the door. "Go on, you can come back later and we'll have a real nice visit."

In response, the Indian rattled something in his hand, then threw two black stones on top of Seth. He began to hum softly.

"Mmmm-hmmm, that's a real catchy tune. But another time, okay? You take your stones and go on home now, all right? Please?"

One Feather came forward and lifted Seth from beneath the covers while Healing Touch carried Pea.

He walked to the center of the room and gently laid his good friend on the floor beside his daughter, positioning his head toward the east. Afterward, he joined in with Healing Touch's chant and began to shuffle around Seth's body as the shaman's volume increased. "Heya-heya-heya-heya-heya-heya . . ."

Maeve stifled the urge to scream. Instead she snapped at the warrior, "Look, they're sick. Do you understand me? Really sick!" She marched forward and stopped in front of the Indian, resisting the urge to straighten the silly feather in his headband. "I want you both out of here right this very minute." Placing her hands on her hips, she narrowed her eyes. "Go!"

"Miss Maeve," Jeb whispered from the direction of the door. "It's the medicine man. One Feather Hung Low must have sent for him."

"Look, Jeb, this dancing stuff is just a bunch of hocus-pocus, okay? Tell them to go home."

Jeb crossed the room, making certain he kept his head bowed in reverent fashion until he reached Maeve's side. "It's not wise to rile the medicine man," he warned from the corner of his mouth.

Maeve watched with fascination as the so-called medicine man reached into his pouch. "Watch!" She snickered. "Betcha he pulls out a rabbit!"

Healing Touch scowled. This person One Feather insisted on referring to as Woman Who Walks On Cloud had the mouth of a squawking hen. Before he could go any further with the ritual, he would have to take drastic steps to silence her. He withdrew dried chicken beaks from his pouch and threw them into the pile of burning herbs. After they had scorched, the wizened man removed a thong with a bear claw attached. In a fluid motion, he proceeded to swing the claw back and forth . . . back and forth.

Maeve felt herself falling under his spell. Her eyelids grew heavy; she swayed in rhythm with the movement of the leather strip.

The semblance of a smile flickered on Healing Touch's lips. Now he could concentrate. Now he could heal.

The sweet, smoky smell of burning herbs broke through Seth's fever-induced state. In his mind's eye he watched himself soar high above the clouds to touch the hand of the Great Spirit. Below them was nothing but vast, open prairie, its silvery grasses blowing gently in the breeze.

The Great Spirit held up his hand to silence the wind. "Long have you searched for that which would make your soul complete, Good Heart. I command the God of Sky Fire to bring her to you."

When she appeared with a harsh clap of lightning, Seth spoke her name. It came not from his lips, but his heart. And realization dawned. For she'd been a part of him since the beginning of time, the beginning of his existence. He touched her shoulder. She turned to him and smiled as if she'd been waiting forever for that part of her which was incomplete to be made whole. The tears she wept turned to drops of sparkling joy.

And her rapture became his.

Hand in hand, they observed the Great Spirit as he plucked Seth's soul from his chest. From Maeve's heart, he withdrew her essence.

They watched in awe as spirit and soul soared with the eagles, danced among the glistening stars, and united as one before floating gently back to the shimmering grasses below.

And the Great Spirit's eyes spoke with flashing fire. "Long have you searched to find what your heart has yearned for. The rain which shall fall from your eyes will serve to make this bond between you strong. May the wind carry you softly for many moons, for you shall be as one until the rivers run dry, the ocean no longer ebbs, and time ceases to exist. And when the dirt covers your bones, your souls will once again unite to live among the stars. As I have spoken, so shall it be."

The wind whispered its contentment like two lovers time had separated and brought back together.

Drifting into a trance, Maeve watched her soul fly high among the stars.

Of course I'm not flying. Fat people don't fly, they sink! This has to be an optical—mindical?—illusion.

Susan Collier

Below her, a soft carpet of grass swayed in a gentle breeze, revealing an enormous gathering of chicken beaks. The earth disappeared as she puzzled over the oddity. When a voice spoke with such tenderness, it brought tears of joy to her heart.

"Long before the earth was formed, you were but a star among the heavens, discontent with your solitude. Mother Wind blew you on a journey that would carry you far, far away. But still you searched for completion. While you found joy in your surroundings, the light inside you slowly diminished until your soul cried out in anguish. But I, the Great Spirit, heard your feeble cries. Because you so mourned, I allowed the God of Sky Fire to carry you back among the stars. Watch!"

Maeve watched as a flicker of light soared up to touch the heavens and knew it was her soul, reaching out, yearning for something unnamed. The speck of light touched a star and became a radiant glow.

"You chose wisely, Woman Who Walks On Cloud, for your spirit guided you to Good Heart."

Suddenly, Maeve realized she was no longer alone. Beside her stood Seth and beside him, Blossom and Jeb. As he took her hand in his, they watched their souls whirl and twirl, then combine to shine brightly in the darkness. The feeling seemed so complete, so filling, that her joy overflowed and tears of happiness fell from her eyes.

The Great Spirit collected a single teardrop and placed it deep inside Seth's chest. "Let the water

190

which falls from Woman Who Walks On Cloud's eyes be nourishment as her happiness becomes your contentment.

"Though the wind will blow you apart, the tears she has shed will become like a bond between you. And neither rain, nor wind, nor fire from the sky will break this union.

"No longer will you search, Woman Who Walks On Cloud, for your search is over. You have joined with the one who was chosen for you long, long ago. And now you will have the joy and the family your soul has yearned for. As the Great Spirit has spoken, so shall it be."

A deep sense of sorrow filled Maeve as she watched the Great Spirit disappear. There were so many questions she wanted to ask, so many truths she needed to know. But suddenly the experience seemed to be over, and Maeve felt a heaviness to the air as the sweet smell of burning herbs tickled her nostrils. Aware that she was back in the cabin, Maeve blinked slowly.

The medicine man carefully returned his belongings to his leather pouch as One Feather extinguished the small mound of burning herbs.

"Oh, wow! How did you do that? Do you realize how much money something like that would be worth in my time?"

Healing Touch scowled. Should he be called back to the home of One Feather's friend, many chicken beaks would have to be offered. He grunted his displeasure, folded his arms, and turned.

Susan Collier

Reality seeped back into Maeve's consciousness. She moved quickly toward Seth and Blossom, kneeling down beside them. The sight of
their naked bodies glistening with sweat made
her want to shout for joy. The fever had broken.

Glancing back over her shoulder, Maeve
started to utter her undying gratitude, but the
Indians had departed as silently as they had
come.

Blanket in hand, Jeb reached down to cover
his father while Maeve carried Pea back to the
comfort of the bed.

The child uttered a soft, contented sigh as she
opened her eyes, smiled up at Maeve, and went
back to sleep.

While Jeb placed a pillow beneath his papa's
head, his gaze met hers.

"What happened, Jeb? What did they actually
do?" Maeve questioned softly.

Shoving his hands deep into his pockets, Jeb
shrugged. "I don't know, Miss Maeve. You were
here, you watched them. What do you think?"

She smiled as memories of her odd dream
flickered in her mind. "I think everything's going to be just fine, Jeb. Just fine."

"Maybe for you, Maeve, but I let Pa down. I
failed the test." Tears filled his eyes.

"What test, Jeb?"

"I ain't near the man Pa thinks I am, and I
ain't never gonna be, either."

The lighthearted feeling dissipated with Jeb's
broken confession. His sobs slashed the strings
of Maeve's happiness apart. She watched help-

lessly as he ran from the cabin. The sound of his weeping made her own eyes fill with tears, because deep inside, she knew she was responsible for letting Seth down, and now she must face him with the truth.

Chapter Thirteen

"Jeb, wait!" Maeve cried as the boy disappeared into the forest. She glanced up at the dusky evening sky. With darkness falling, could he find his way back home? And what about the Indians? Although they'd done a good thing, how could she be certain they wouldn't demand payment for their services—like taking Jeb?

"Let him go," Seth rasped.

Maeve turned. "But, Seth, it'll be dark soon and—"

"He'll be fine, Maeve. He just needs some time alone to work things out in his mind."

Don't we all? Maeve wanted to ask, her brain still reeling with the after effects of the strange spell the medicine man had cast. Instead, she bit back the words and walked over to the bed, sitting down beside Seth. Tenderly, she brushed

Susan Collier

back a strand of his jet-black hair.

Capturing her hand, Seth brought her fingers to his lips. "I had the strangest dream," he murmured.

The warmth of his lips moving against her skin sent an odd shiver of excitement up Maeve's spine. She placed her palm against his whiskered cheek. "You've been sick, Seth. For three days you've barely been conscious."

As if he'd just now become aware of a presence beside him, Seth turned to see Blossom's slight form, deep in slumber. "And Pea?"

"She's had the fever too," Maeve admitted. "Indians came. Jeb referred to one of them as someone named One Feather. He said the brave was your friend."

Even as weak as he felt, Seth couldn't contain a smile as he imagined what Maeve's reaction must have been. He listened while she described what had taken place.

"You should have seen the other one, Seth! He was huge—well, maybe not that huge, but pretty big. The first thing he did was throw a couple of stones on you and for a second there, I thought he'd lost his mind. And then he started this fire." Maeve paused, pointing to a soot-covered spot on the floor. "And then . . ." Her words faded. How could she describe what happened next? She wasn't positive herself.

"And then," Seth prodded, bringing her hand back to his lips.

"And then . . . well, I don't really know," she admitted. "I think I was dreaming, but the

dream seemed so real and there was this man
who called himself the Great Spirit, and—"

"And he combined our spirits and souls for
all eternity," Seth finished. He reached up and
clasped Maeve's arms, bringing her down for a
kiss.

First he kissed her brows. "I felt as if we'd
joined together somehow." He kissed the tip of
her nose. "As if we'd known one another forever." He kissed her lips, applying soft pressure
with his tongue until she understood and allowed him access to the sweet warmth of her
mouth. "As if we belong together."

"B-but h-how did you know that?" she stammered.

He shook his head slightly. "I'm not sure."

Her eyes grew wide. "It *was* just a dream,
wasn't it?" As Seth continued to stroke her hair,
her back, the length of her arms, a flash of hot
desire silenced her words. When he drew her
back to him for yet another kiss, Maeve felt de-
liciously bold as their tongues sparred for position. The deep groan she uttered came not
from discomfort, but from greed. Greed to consume him. To have him run his fingers through
her hair, over her aching breasts, to touch that
part of her growing wet and warm for him. To
have him fill this sudden empty feeling inside
her.

If they had shared more than a dream, then
perhaps now Seth read her thoughts. His fingers ran through her hair, then caressed the
lobe of her ear with a touch so light Maeve

could have sworn he used a feather.

Then, as his fingers traced the outline of her jaw and traveled lightly over the swell of her cleavage before dipping into the valley between her breasts, the hot desire became raging lust. Straining forward, she watched the spark in his deep blue eyes turn to restless passion.

Almost hesitant, as if he were waiting for her permission, Seth trailed his hand over her breast, caressing the peak until it became pebble-hard.

She caught the edge of her bottom lip between her teeth to try to contain the gasp of pleasure his touch provoked.

Watching her reaction carefully, Seth unbuttoned the first button on her borrowed dress. Then the second. And the third, until finally her aching breasts were free of the restricting fabric. He groaned with delight over the fact that nothing, not even a chemise, stood between his hand and her beautiful ivory mounds.

Capturing one aroused pebble between his finger and thumb, he squeezed gently, feeling her lean into him. With his other hand, he traced the outline of her needful eyes, the length of her nose, the fullness of her lips.

Maeve captured one finger between her teeth and bit playfully. She felt sexy, she felt seductive, she felt . . . Pea move in the bed beside Seth.

In a panic, she began to fumble with the buttons of her blouse and, for a moment, captured

Seth's hand between herself, the fabric, and her breasts.

As Pea moaned Gracie's name, Seth rested his head against the pillow, rubbing his eyes with a weariness that came from deep inside. "Where is Gracie?"

Oh, God! How could she have forgotten for even a moment? Pain flooded Maeve's heart as she stared into Seth's inquisitive eyes. "I-I—" She gulped back tears. "Seth, Gracie got really sick. Worse even than you and Pea. I tried to help her, but I . . . c-couldn't." Her voice broke.

Seth closed his eyes against the anguish. Tears slipped past his lashes to dampen his pillow. "She's dead, isn't she, Maeve?"

Unable to speak, Maeve nodded. A sob escaped her lips.

Silence cloaked him, though rivulets of tears streamed down his face in torrents of grief. With a hoarseness that stemmed from pain far worse than his sore throat, he groaned. "Ahh, God, why do things happen the way they do, Maeve? What did Gracie ever do to deserve such a life?"

She wished she held the answers he needed to hear. But there were still so many times when she questioned the death of her own loved ones, so many times when she simply couldn't understand. "I'm sorry, Seth." And, taking him in her arms, she allowed him to grieve.

As the days slipped by in a haze of work and worry, Maeve tried to pay close attention to Jeb while still caring for Blossom and Seth. She knew Jeb's heart was broken and nothing she could say or do would fix it. He needed his father, and his father just wasn't strong enough quite yet.

Meeting Jeb as he came from the barn, Maeve wrapped one of Duessa's cloaks tightly around her to ward off the chill of the rain-soaked day. "Jeb, let's you and I go for a walk, shall we?"

"I got more chores to git done, Miss Maeve."

"When did I go back to being Miss Maeve instead of simply Maeve, Jeb?"

He shrugged.

"Will you forget the damn chores and walk with me?" she snapped. The boy's eyes widened at her oath. Maeve grabbed his arm. "I'm sorry, I know that wasn't very ladylike, was it?"

A shadow of a smile flickered on Jeb's freckled face. "You ain't much like any lady I've ever met," he admitted wryly.

Maeve started walking and ignored the fact that she had to half drag the unwilling child along. "Your father is getting stronger with each passing day," she said in an effort to entice him into conversation. "Guess you're pretty glad about that, huh?"

"Yep."

She stopped suddenly, turning so that he would have to face her. As she studied his drawn brows, his weary expression, her heart went out to him. Damn it, this simply wasn't fair. He was just a boy, a freckle-faced, innocent little boy. And the harshness of his life had forced him to grow up before his mind could adjust. "Can I share something with you, Jeb?"

Eyes cast downward, he nodded.

"I lost a couple of people I loved very much about two years before I came to be here. My mom and dad. I know how bad it hurts; I know how much you want to change things, but you can't, darlin', you just can't. Gracie's gone and all the wishing in the world isn't going to bring her back."

"I shoulda—"

"You shoulda what, Jeb?" Maeve demanded harshly. "There was nothing you could do. Nothing I could do."

Suddenly, the child threw himself into Maeve's arms and began to weep bitter tears. As his shoulders heaved up and down in silent anguish, Maeve stroked his hair. "There, there, little one. It's okay to cry, Jeb. It's really okay."

"No, it ain't!" Jeb yelled harshly, though he made no move to pull away from her comforting embrace. "A real man don't cry like a baby."

"A real man cries exactly like a baby, because it takes a real man to feel things so deeply," Maeve reasoned quietly. "Don't ever try to hide your tears from those you love, Jeb. They'll turn as bitter inside you as an unripened apple. And twice as hard. Soon you'll be blaming everyone else for your sorrow."

Ever so softly, Maeve admitted a truth that had been tucked so far deep inside her it was a wonder the words found a way to surface. "Let me tell you something, Jeb. When I moved in

201

with my aunt and uncle, I tried to hide my tears, tried to pretend it didn't matter that I no longer had a home, no longer had a family. And the more I tried to hide it, the harder I became to live with. I found fault in everything, even the way my aunt cleaned her house—and you know I'm not that picky!"

Jeb managed a small giggle and Maeve smiled as he held on to her even tighter. "What I'm trying to say, Jeb, is that when you love someone and they go away, it hurts. But to try to hide those tears hurts even worse, okay?"

Nodding, he began to sob again with gut-wrenching agony. Maeve tucked her thumb under his chin and tugged slightly so that he would be forced to meet her gaze. "What is it, Jeb? Tell me what you're feeling."

"Aww, Maeve! It dawned on me that everything I've ever loved has gone away. And I wonder sometimes if you'll leave me too, 'cause I love you, Maeve. I really, really love you. And I don't want you to leave us. I want you to stay forever."

Though she wanted desperately to reassure him, Maeve remained silent. Until she knew the truth, she wouldn't lie to the child. And the truth right now was that she didn't know how long she'd be able to stay with them before time stole her back. Although her words seemed woefully inadequate, it was the best she could offer. "Jeb, I don't want to leave you. I'd like nothing more than to stay right here and watch you turn into the fine young man I know you'll become. I promise you I'm going to do my best to make that happen, but I can't promise it will." The uttered words became like a prayer upon her lips as she whispered silently, "Please let me stay, God, please let me stay."

"Jeb."

Maeve whirled around to see Seth standing a few feet away. She bit back her disapproval of his being outside when Jeb turned from her and ran into his father's open arms.

"Don't you know, son, that there's nothing you could ever do to make me stop loving you? I don't blame you for Gracie's death, and believe me, you didn't let me down," Seth admonished while stroking his son's hair.

Wanting to give them their much-needed privacy, Maeve smiled at the tender scene and gave a slight nod of approval before turning and walking away. As she strolled further into the forest, she could hear Seth's soft words of comfort fading on the night air.

She relied on the light of the full moon to guide her back to the stream. Once there, Maeve sat down and gazed at the shimmering glow upon the water. Behind her, a nightingale sang a sorrowful song. The pines swayed gently as if they were keeping time to the tune. Feeling a restless ache deep in her soul, she closed her eyes and listened to nature's soothing sounds.

"It's going to be all right," a voice announced from the depths of the glistening water.

Maeve leaned forward. Sure enough, the apparition was back. "You!" she spat. "Who in the hell are you to tell me anything? You could have stopped Gracie from dying, Duessa. If you were a real angel, you could have stopped it."

The woman's face seemed sad. "What I did, I had to do. As will you, when the time comes. You see, Maeve, sometimes we're forced to do things we don't necessarily want to do, but we know we must."

"Yeah, right!" Maeve snapped. "And you just had to hurt them, didn't you, Duessa? You had to put them through even more pain by allowing Gracie to die."

"I have no control over who will die and who will live, Maeve."

"You shouldn't have welcomed her. She wouldn't have gone without a fight had you not been there to welcome her!" Maeve shouted. "You stole her from me."

"But I've given you Seth and my other two children. To keep forever . . . if that is what you wish."

Covering her face with her hands, Maeve began to cry ever so softly. She was so confused, so very confused. "I don't know what I wish anymore," she admitted. "I just don't know. I don't understand any of this."

"You can't understand love, Maeve. All you can do is accept it, then return it with all your heart. That's what you're doing, and as I stated before, everything will work out for the best."

"Is she with you?" Maeve questioned softly. "Is Gracie with you?"

The waters swirled gently before parting to

reveal Gracie's face, glowing with happiness. "She has not passed through a complete journey to the angelic side yet," Duessa explained. "The company she is in at this moment is far more glorious than you can ever imagine, and there are many instructions she needs to be given.

"She cannot hear you, nor can she see you. But know that she is happy. That I will be with her always."

The swirling water closed to reveal only Duessa's face once more. "Do not try to understand. Instead, be happy, Maeve. Be content with those gifts you have been given."

"Are you saying Gracie had to be sacrificed for my happiness? Is that what you're trying to tell me? Because I won't have it, you know. I won't let a child sacrifice her life for me."

"It wasn't something for you to allow. What has happened cannot be changed. Now go to him, Maeve; he needs you. And listen to your heart. Just listen to your heart."

As Maeve pondered the advice, the nightingale began to trill a hauntingly sweet melody.

How could she fulfill this desperate need for Seth's touch? The memory of his kiss became as real as if he were there, pressing his lips to hers.

While she ached to go to him, common sense prevailed. After all that had happened, how could she be certain he felt the same? Too bad she couldn't go to the shaman and have him mix up another batch of the aromatic potion that had sent her reeling to . . . to where? Where had she been? And how on earth had Seth managed to have a similar experience? Wherever this magical place was, their souls had been free to fly, free to express all that was within them.

Was Seth going through this torment? Did he desire to hold her as she did him? To express his love through action?

There seemed to be only one way to find out.

Chapter Fourteen

Seth watched his son make his way back toward the cabin. He hoped the talk they'd shared had helped. Memories of his own childhood came back to haunt him. How many times had he felt the need to prove himself a man to his father? How many times had he walked away, knowing he'd failed?

Bound and determined never to let his son experience what he had gone through, Seth could only pray Jeb would take their talk to heart. Perhaps after the anguish of losing Gracie diminished, Jeb would come to realize the truth. Nothing and no one could have stopped the inevitable.

Though he hadn't meant to eavesdrop, Seth had heard most of the conversation between his son and Maeve. Why hadn't she assured Jeb she'd stay? Was she planning to leave them? Maybe she'd grown weary of all the obstacles life had recently dealt them.

A driving need to talk to her kept Seth from giving in to his weakened condition. Walking through the forest, he listened to the nightingale cry a lonesome song. The sound echoed what he felt deep inside. She couldn't leave them. Not now, not when he'd finally found that bit of happiness which had, in the past, eluded him.

Walking back the way she'd come, Maeve was keenly aware of every sound in the forest. She heard a soft crackle, followed by the sharp snap of branches. Her heart raced against her chest. Was it those crazy Indians? And if it were, would the shaman be willing to give her a potion to make Seth fall madly in love with her?

Did she have enough guts to ask?

The footsteps were definitely coming closer. Panic set in. Hell, no, she wasn't brave enough! Turning in the opposite direction, Maeve began to work her way through the thick brush. When her skirt caught on a root, she gave the material a swift jerk, hoping to free the fabric, but only tangling the hem even further.

She sensed someone behind her.

The crisp air stung her lungs as she took quick, panic-stricken gulps of air. They were going to kill her. But not before they scalped her. Jeb was right: she shouldn't have riled the medicine man.

"Can I lend a hand?"

Time Heals

Seth's voice lent instant relief to the hysteria racing through Maeve's system. "Oh God, you scared me!" she announced, placing her hand over her pounding heart. "I thought you were the Indians coming to capture me!"

Seth worked the material of her skirt until finally she was free. "Looks to me like the only thing that held you captive was a tree root. It's probably a good thing I bought that other dress for you. Tell me, did you like it?"

"What dress?" Maeve questioned, genuinely puzzled.

"The yellow dress I purchased for you in town. I took one look at it and knew it would look lovely on you."

"Seth, we didn't find a dress when we unloaded the wagon."

"That's odd, isn't it? I wonder what happened?"

He looked so disappointed, Maeve sought to reassure him. "Never you mind, I'm sure it'll turn up somewhere! Meanwhile, look . . . you're my hero. You've rescued me from that horrible root!" She fluttered her lashes in a playful manner. "I shall be forever indebted to you, kind sir."

Seth bowed slightly. "My pleasure, ma'am."

Doubts flickered like tiny fireflies across Maeve's expression as she met his gaze. "Seth," she began, struggling to find the words, "I'm very sorry about everything. I wish I could have sa—"

"Shh," he silenced her, placing a finger

against her lips. As their eyes met and held, words seemed inadequate. Overwhelmed by the desire to soothe away her anguish, Seth moaned as he pulled her against him. Burying his face in her hair, he closed his eyes. "Don't leave us, Maeve."

His words captivated her. "You—you really don't want me to, do you?"

Holding her away from him so that she had no choice but to read the truth in his eyes, Seth answered honestly. "I couldn't live without you."

Consoled, Maeve hugged him before resting her head once more against the comfort of his massive chest. She could hear the steady beating of his heart. "I feel the same," she whispered. "How can we make sure nothing happens to separate us, Seth? The thought of going back to that dreary existence I called life scares me. The thought of losing you terrifies me." She expelled a deep sigh. "Just hold me, Seth, hold me so tight that nothing can ever tear us apart."

Wrapping his arms around her, Seth crushed her to him, breathing deeply of her sweet, sweet innocence. He brushed his cheek against her silky hair, reveling in the feel of her. "Nothing will ever come between us," he promised.

Except my weight. Maeve winced. Seth was busy running his hands lightly over her back, down the length of her waist. She remembered from the many nights she'd stayed awake reading the sexy love scenes in romance books that the hero always managed to span the heroine's waist with his hands. Seth could do that too . . . if he had Michael Jordan's hands! She tried to remember just how long Seth's fingers were. Not long enough, she sighed, feeling him encompass only her hips.

Great. My hips. Miss buffalo hips. He's gonna see me naked and worry about whether I'm going to crush him. Oh no! What if I do? What if . . . what if he's so disgusted by my weight he can't perform in a manly manner?

She felt him placing feather-soft kisses along the length of her neck and sighed, miserably happy.

I need to put a stop to this. I need to go on a crash diet and eat nothing but lettuce for the next year.

As Seth pulled Maeve against the length of his body, he felt a slight stiffening in her spine, indicating her nervousness. He tugged her chin upward so that she could receive his kiss. "I hope you know, Maeve, I wouldn't do anything to force you into a situation you're not ready for."

Oh, force me, force me! Maeve pleaded inwardly as she draped her arms around his neck. Doing a mental body check, she returned his kiss, parting her lips slightly to receive the wet warmth of his tongue. He tasted better than a three-layer cake, better than chocolate. She sighed her contentment and, as if her body had a mind of its own, pressed wantonly against his groin. The hard feel of him sent a shiver of delight throughout her body, causing her to boldly thrust her tongue into the recesses of his mouth.

Okay, let's see. I won't have any panty lines because I don't have panties. All I have are those stupid bloomers which are way too big. No bra indention—bras haven't been invented yet.

I borrowed his razor yesterday and shaved my underarms and legs, so we're okay there. If I remember not to lie on my side, he can't feel my poochie tummy, so I'll have to remember to lie flat.

Nooooo!

I can't do that! Everything'll spread out! Maybe if I take a deep breath and suck it all in . . . but it was becoming harder and harder to concentrate on anything except the driving need inside her as Seth's kiss intensified and Maeve responded. Maybe she'd be lucky—maybe love really would turn out to be blind; ohhh, but blind men could still feel. . . .

Burying her face into Seth's neck, Maeve tried to ignore all the doubts threatening the profound pleasure he had managed to stroke to life inside her.

The knowledge that he dealt with an inexperienced woman caused Seth to go slowly even though he wanted nothing more than to be inside her, to join together and become one. To hear her moan with pleasure.

Taking her by the hand, Seth led Maeve through the forest to a clearing by the stream.

Maeve knew the area well. It was right beside

the spot where Duessa kept appearing. *Great! This is all I need: his first wife, in the form of an angel, watching every move we make!*

She hated to stop him, for the place where he was most intent on kissing, that little spot right there, was extremely sensitive. "Uh, Seth?"

"Hmmm?" Seth answered as he nibbled at her earlobe.

"Do you think we could go someplace a little more private?"

He drew back in confusion. "I can assure you there's no one around for miles and miles."

Oh boy! Now was definitely not the time to tell him about Duessa's appearances. No, not now, not as he captured her mouth with his, not as he stroked the slow heat inside her to a raging inferno. No, most assuredly not now.

"C-can we go somewhere else?" Maeve stammered and, instead of meeting his intense gaze, played with the buttons of his shirt.

Seth captured her hand and circled her palm with the tip of his tongue. "I've told you before, darling, if you're not ready for this, I won't for—"

"Oh, I'm ready all right," she quickly assured. Had she been too quick? Would he think she was nothing but a cheap floozy? "It's just that, just that—Seth, please! You're making my knees turn mushy!"

Seth stopped licking the valley between her luscious breasts and tried hard to ignore the ache deep inside him. "I give in. Where would you like to go?"

"How about the cabin?" Maeve squeaked. "No, wait! Not the cabin! The children are in the cabin." She shivered at the withdrawal of this warmth that had been pressing against her in such an intimate manner.

With a snap of his fingers, Seth took her hand an led her through the brush—reminding her to duck under a low-hanging branch—and back toward the cabin. "I have just the place. We can be alone—well, almost alone." His eyes twinkled as he smiled down at her. "How do you feel about the barn?"

"The barn?" Eww, she thought. The smells . . . the dark! "The barn is just fine."

A definite sense of urgency made them rush toward the small shelter, and both were out of breath as they reached the door. Much to Maeve's delight, she couldn't see her hand in front of her face, much less her partner. Until Seth lit the lantern and turned to face her with an expression of passion that needed no words. His eyes. His wonderful, expressive, deep-blue eyes. She caught her lip between her teeth. God, he was beautiful. Absolutely beautiful. And as he closed the distance between them, Maeve felt a small tremor of hope. Maybe he wouldn't be disappointed after all.

"Are you certain you're ready for this, Maeve?"

In response, she kissed him long, hard, and deep while fumbling with the buttons of his shirt. Suddenly she couldn't wait to feel his bare flesh against her own.

Seth slowly unbuttoned each of the million—he felt certain—buttons lining the back of her shirt. When he reached the band of her gathered skirt, he slid his hand between flesh and fabric to massage her lower back. As she arched her neck in bliss, he smiled. "Does that feel nice?"

"Oh, yes! So, so nice." She was drowning, drowning in a river of emotion. And when he lowered her skirt it felt right, it felt natural, to step out of the yards of material as if she'd done this all her life. When he pushed aside the fabric to expose her breasts, then cupped their fullness with his warm palms before bringing the tips to a hard crest, she had to lean into him, had to have that pressure to stop the ache deep inside.

Sweeping her into his arms, Seth stepped over the bundle of clothing lying in the middle of the barn. He walked forward until he felt satisfied with a clean pile of hay. There, he lay her gently down and stood back to gaze at her magnificent beauty. She was a portrait in motion, with ivory skin a satiny white, reminding him of her purity. Her twin mounds were just the right size, their tips dusky pink and small. As desire swelled, Seth realized it'd been a long time since he'd seen a woman shaped so beautifully. "You're such a delicate thing," he murmured huskily.

Maeve cringed as heat flooded her face. Tears of distress pooled in her eyes and began to flow down her cheeks in silent anguish. How could anyone be so cruel? She wanted to scream, she wanted to cry, she wanted nothing more than to hide herself away from his scrutinizing gaze.

Watching her joyous expression turn to one of pain, Seth furrowed his brows in bewilderment. "Maeve? Are you all right?"

"Oh, sure I am!" Maeve yelled as she jumped to her feet and rushed toward the bundle of clothing.

"Maeve, wait!"

She paused, tears still falling. "What?" she managed huskily.

"Maeve, look at me," Seth demanded.

"I can't," she cried. There was no way she could bring herself to witness his disapproval, his disappointment. "I'd rather you slapped me, Seth. It wouldn't have hurt near as much as that horrid remark."

Grabbing her arms, Seth forced her to her feet.

"What are you talking about? Tell me what I said, my love, and I'll make it right." Gently he turned her around so that she now faced him. He tilted her chin. "Please, Maeve, I wouldn't hurt you for anything, you have to know—Why, you're crying!"

"Of course I'm crying! I always cry when someone makes fun of my weight."

"I wasn't making fun of you, Maeve. I think you're beautiful."

"I'm hardly beautiful. I'm fat, I'm ghostly white, and I have this little bitty dimple on my left inner thigh!"

"Where?" Seth demanded.

"Here," Maeve snapped, pointing out the obvious.

On bended knee, Seth kissed the dimple.

On knees the consistency of pudding, Maeve allowed him to continue in an upward journey.

He pressed his cheek against her soft silken nest of hair. "You're hardly fat, my dear. As a matter of fact, you're nothing but skin and bone. Here . . . feel," he insisted, running her hand over a protruding hip bone.

Hip bone? I have a hip bone? Dear Lord, she could feel it. A bone! An honest to goodness bone! "Oh Seth, you feel it so much better than I do," Maeve confessed as he formed a large V with his hands over her stomach and pressed his fingers into her hips. "Much, much better." She sighed.

Fingers, arms, hands, and legs tangled in a furious motion as heady lust exploded into action. Rolling, tumbling, grasping all the right parts, Maeve was dismayed to find herself eye-to-eye with Seth and on top of his muscular frame. "Am I hurting you?" she demanded.

"Ahh," Seth groaned. "Just keep on hurting me, keep on moving just . . . like . . . that. Maeve? Maeve? What are you doing?"

She offered him a sneaky grin as she continued to slide down the length of his body. "I've always wondered what would happen if I—"

His cry of gratification cut off her words. Obviously her experiment was a complete success. "Now then," she panted. "If you would put your hand right here, and I'll just move this way, we can— Oh, yes, Seth."

Mentally, Maeve tried to prepare herself for the pain the romance books had talked about. It was bound to come and bound to be simply awful. She hoped she wouldn't embarrass herself by crying out. Of course the heroines usually bit their lip and bore that pain for the men they loved. But Maeve knew she wasn't quite that brave. She'd never been one to handle pain in any shape, form, or fashion. She soon discovered that her worries were unfounded with such a gentle lover as Seth. For at the same time he tantalized her with his fingers, Seth slowly entered her, at the last moment drawing her attention into receiving a rich, spirited kiss. "Oh, yes, yes, yes!" she cried when he plunged deep. And in giving the part of herself which she'd protected for the man she loved, the pain quickly turned to pleasure. The pleasure turned to an intensity that Maeve could scarcely bear as they met thrust for thrust, stroke for stroke. Maeve ran her hands through his thick, silky hair, reveling in the masculine scent of him, devouring the feel of his body lying atop hers.

Her heartbeat quickened; for a moment, Maeve wondered if she were about to lose consciousness when the intense pleasure she was feeling grew too great and thousands of tingling sensations carried her away on a journey she'd never experienced. A gasp of delight slipped through her parted, trembling lips.

Knowing she'd reached the pinnacle of satisfaction, Seth quickened his pace, thrusting into her wet warmth, delighting in her soft moans of joy. Each sweet moan took him further toward the height of passion until he could hold back no longer. Capturing the silky tendrils of her hair, he lowered his lips to graze the soft lobe of her ear, murmuring tender words of love.

"Any regrets?" Seth whispered much later, stroking her dampened hair.

If she had regretted her actions, those regrets would have disappeared once she gazed into his adoring eyes, for the deep blue orbs contained the words he'd yet to speak aloud. "No," Maeve responded with honesty.

Seth hugged her tenderly and, completely spent, he settled on his side with his arms wrapped around Maeve, her head nestled in the curve of his neck. He smiled as she ran her foot up and down his leg and hugged him tight. What a complete surprise this woman beside him had turned out to be!

Years ago, when he'd worked the mines, he'd often heard discussions about what other women did, but never in his wildest fantasies had he imagined how it could be with the one he loved. And he did love her. How could a man resist her charm, her warmth, her unbridled passion? Her heart was as big as the Montana skies, and she'd held nothing back when giving herself to him, both in body and soul.

She was the type of woman he'd always

hoped to find, hoped to live the rest of his life with, and fate had brought her to him.

The realization filled him with renewed vigor. He trailed his hand up and down the curve of her side. "Next time," Seth murmured, his voice slightly husky, "we'll go slower. I'll kiss each and every part of you. . . . Interrupting his own declaration, Seth captured her nipple in his mouth, laving the tip with his tongue until it hardened.

Maeve moaned.

"And next time," he promised, rolling her onto her back, "I'll kiss right here, and here, and here."

She closed her eyes as his fingers trailed over her stomach, dipping into her navel then down to the entrance of her womanhood. Talented fingers softly parted her folds, stroking her dampness until the spark of desire became a hot, moist need. As he suckled first one breast before turning to the other, she moaned in tormented ecstasy, running her fingers through his thick, jet-black hair.

"Is this next time?" she gasped, barely able to utter the words. Her fingers curled as she dug her nails into his back.

Moving over her, Seth plunged deep. With each intense thrust, he voiced a response, "We'll . . . worry about . . . next time . . . after . . . this time!"

In the wee hours of the morning, as her trembling limbs and racing heart began to calm, Maeve smiled and hugged Seth tightly. The trip the medicine man had sent her on was nothing in comparison to the journey she'd just taken with the man she loved.

Though she wanted nothing more than to stay in Seth's arms forever, a premonition beaded along her spine and ended as a prickle at the top of her head.

Chapter Fifteen

Dear Lord, they were everywhere! Filthy, nasty, bleating balls of cotton with legs. Maeve tried to hide her dismay. The past two months had been such a special time between them all. In sharing their pain, in mourning the loss of Gracie, they had truly come together to mourn as a family. It was a time filled with love and even some laughter and the making of wonderful memories. Looking at the ugly critters roaming over the land, she sighed. "Why sheep, Seth?"

Seth cast a dubious glance at the sight before him. His promised delivery had finally arrived and now, after watching the ignorant creatures, he wanted nothing more than to return them. "Duessa," he replied shortly. "Her family raised sheep for years. Besides, they were all I could afford." He groaned, watching one of the animals butt its head into the side of the smokehouse. "I think I've made a major mistake."

"I think you're right," Maeve agreed. She took pity on his sad expression and wrapped her arm in his. "Don't you worry, Seth. We'll get this all sorted out and it'll be just fine."

Seth shook his head as another of the animals butted against a tree. "I don't know, Maeve, I just don't know."

After ascertaining that the children were nowhere around, Maeve planted a kiss on Seth's cheek. "Together we can do everything, remember?"

A small grin tugged at the corners of his mouth. "If last night was any indication, I believe you!"

"Tsk, tsk, tsk, Seth. Is that all you can think about?"

Sparkling blue eyes met glistening hazel orbs. "That's all I want to think about," Seth admitted with a wide smile.

He reached down and pinched her fanny but Maeve was too puzzled over the sight before her to react the way he would have hoped. "Seth, why are those sheep staggering like that?"

"I don't know," he admitted and reached into his pocket for the receipt. "Maeve, what's that number? I can't see without my reading glasses."

"Fifty."

"Well," he continued, "with fifty of the filthy little creatures, minus the one that died in transport, I'm sure we'll find out all we need to know."

Maeve bit her lip, deep in thought. "Something's not right with these animals. They're acting awfully strange," she commented as one fell to the ground and refused to move. "Come on, Seth, we'd better go see if we can figure out what's wrong."

By mid afternoon, Seth realized they were in trouble. Not only were half of the animals' eyes matted with a thick, green mucus; several of them seemed to labor for each breath.

"We're returning them!" Maeve swore as she stood and arched her aching back.

Seth glanced up to see Jeb coming toward them. "Where's Pea?" he called.

"She took off after one of them baby lambs," Jeb explained. "I can't find her anywhere, Pa. I done checked down by the stream, I checked in the barn, I done looked everywhere for her. She's just up and disappeared."

A niggling sense of worry flooded Maeve. For the past few weeks things had been going far too smoothly, too uneventfully. She knelt down in front of the boy and spoke in a gentle, soothing tone. "She couldn't have disappeared, Jeb. Where did you search?"

Glancing toward Seth, she noted the look of concern in his eyes and spoke with an assurance she didn't feel. Pea was such an adventuresome little girl, there was no telling what she'd gotten herself into this time. "I'm sure she's around here somewhere. We just have to find her, that's all."

Seth ran his hand through his hair. "I don't know, Maeve. If Jeb says—"

"Jeb hasn't looked everywhere, have you, Jeb? She's probably down by the stream—"

"I checked there," Jeb replied softly.

"Then we'll check again and again and again until we find her," Maeve stated adamantly.

When Seth turned toward the cabin, she followed him. "Where are you going?"

"To get my gun," came the curt reply. "The woods are full of wild animals."

"Don't say it." Maeve tried to keep her voice calm and reasonable, yet worry lay heavy on her heart. "We'll find her, Seth. And she's going to be just fine when we do."

"I'll find her," Seth corrected, grabbing his rifle from the shelf. "You stay here in case she returns."

"But—"

He grabbed her arms. "No, Maeve. You're not going with me."

"I—"

"That's final."

The look of determination in his eyes forced her to concede. But she didn't like it. Didn't like it one little bit. "All right, Seth. If you insist."

"Jeb'll stay with you. The last thing I need right now is to worry about what's going on around here." Seth grabbed a jacket and some supplies. When Maeve raised a questioning brow, he paused. "Just in case I'm gone overnight, Maeve. I wish I knew what to tell you to do about those damn sheep, but right now—"

Noting his desperation, she placed her hand on Seth's arm and forced a smile. "Be careful, won't you?"

He gave her a quick hug. "I'll be fine." Placing his rifle on the bed, he tilted her chin with his thumb and searched her troubled eyes. "I love you, Maeve."

It was the first time he'd voiced his feelings toward her and now she didn't have the time to react. Instead, Maeve settled for a deep kiss, then hugged Seth tightly. If anything happened to him, she'd never forgive herself for not insisting she go along. "We'll discuss this when you return with Pea. That way you have to return, right, Seth?"

He wiped a tear from her cheek and smiled. "I'll be back before you know it."

As she watched him ride off, Maeve wrapped her arms around Jeb's shoulders and leaned her chin on his head. He must come back. Simply had to. Fate wouldn't be so cruel as to take him away. Please, God, she prayed inwardly.

"What we gonna do with all these sheep, Maeve?"

"Have mutton stew," she growled, watching the silly animals stagger around like drunken sailors.

As the day slowly gave way to the setting sun, Maeve lit the lanterns. When Seth returned with Pea, she wanted the cabin to be alive with light. With warmth instead of cold darkness. After placing a hastily prepared dinner on the table, she watched Jeb toy with his food instead of eating. She could hardly blame him since she was guilty of doing the same. A few silent moments passed before Maeve picked up both plates and put them beside the washtub.

"I feel sorry for Pa." Jeb sighed as he moved toward the fireplace.

"How so, Jeb?"

"Well, he ain't hardly got over the sickness yet and here he is gone searching for Pea. Then when he gets back, he's gonna have to return them sheep."

A notion, a ridiculous notion, Maeve admitted silently, filled her mind. "Not if we return them for him."

Jeb turned to offer her an incredulous stare. "We can't do that . . . can we?"

By the light of a flickering campfire, One Feather observed the sleeping child. Her even, steady breathing attested to the fact that she was comfortable. He let out a soft whoosh of air. Golden Hair had more energy than an unbroken colt.

As he continued to watch her, he fingered the folds of material lying in his lap. The color of the garment had somehow managed to capture the brilliance of the sun, along with the warmth of Woman Who Walks On Cloud.

When he'd rescued the young child from the high rocks, his intention had been to return her immediately to Good Heart. But as he rode with the child in front of him, his eyes had been drawn to the bright fabric in his pouch. Many Moons To Come had spoken to him then, allowing him to acknowledge this opportunity was his for the taking. What better way to bring Woman Who Walks On Cloud to his side than to keep the young one with him?

But Many Moons hadn't bothered to inform him he would be hard-pressed to keep Golden Hair occupied. She'd shown him the strange ritual of something called a tea party with her cornhusk doll. Then she'd insisted on playing with his war paint, smearing it from the grease pot onto his cheeks and lips. After she'd tired of that oddity, she'd wanted to engage him in the curious game of slapping the palms of their hands together over and over while singing a strange little song about cake.

Oh yes, One Feather was tired. More tired than when he'd rounded up all the wild horses in the region to offer them to Woman Who Walks On Cloud. But the thought made him smile. Soon—sooner than later, he hoped—he could show Woman Who Walks On Cloud his glorious bounty, thus enticing her into a marriage agreement.

Rising, he stirred the dying embers with a stick. The day had been long. The outcome would be worth it.

Maeve rose just as the sun blushed the sky with glorious colors of red, yellow, and orange.

She shivered as she shoved back the heavy quilt covering the bed and forced herself into action.

All night she'd lain awake and pondered the wisdom of her decision. But Jeb had been right. Seth didn't need the additional burden of returning the animals. It was something she could do—she hoped—for the man she loved.

After putting together a hasty pack of biscuits, dried jerky, and cheese, Maeve turned to find Jeb dressed and ready. The excitement of their upcoming adventure showed on his face.

"You ready, Maeve?"

Maeve bit her lip. "Jeb, have you ever done this sort of thing before?"

"Sure. When Pa purchased all them cows I helped herd them out into open pasture. Sheep can't be much different, can they?"

"But we're not herding them out to open pasture, Jeb. We're taking them back to town." A small rush of delight trilled through Maeve. Town. A definite distraction from her worries. There would be stores . . . maybe even something akin to a mall! And she could finally find a pair of jeans. Maybe even buy a new shirt or two. And shoes. Dear Lord, she needed new shoes. These clodhoppers of Duessa's had tripped her more than once, and even if Reeboks hadn't been invented yet, maybe she'd get lucky and find something close to them.

There was no doubt in her mind that Seth would be successful in finding Pea. He was probably on his way home right now with Blossom in tow. Which gave her even more reason to hurry. If Seth found out what she and Jeb were attempting, he'd never agree to it. He was absolutely the most chauvinistic man she'd ever come across, and a lesson in women's liberation was long overdue.

"Quick, fetch me one of your pencils, Jeb. I'll just leave a note for Seth."

Several hours later, after the last of the ornery creatures had been captured, Maeve climbed into the wagon. "Head 'em up and move 'em out," she called, feeling very Western.

Jeb's brows furrowed. "Maeve, have you ever driven a wagon before?"

"I have my driver's license," she snapped. "If I can drive a stick shift, I figure this wagon'll be a snap!"

"What's a stick shift?"

"Never mind, Jeb. Just stay behind me and make sure none of these sheep jump out of this wagon."

"I don't know, Maeve. I ain't never seen a wagon full of sheep before."

She shoved one of the stinking animals out of her lap. Half the pathetic creatures had already succumbed to the strange disorder affecting them, and though it had been a tight squeeze to fit the rest into the small space, she was determined to return the remaining 23 alive. "Do you have a better suggestion? We tried the herding thing and they kept running off."

Somewhat dubious, Jeb nudged his horse forward.

Maeve ignored the bleating of nervous sheep

and flicked the reins exactly as she'd seen in so many Westerns on television. Much to her amazement, it worked quite well.

Seeing a cloud of smoke hovering on the horizon, Seth galloped forward. With every mile he traveled, his hope of finding Pea alive diminished, and now his heart was heavy with grief. How could he bear the loss of another daughter when he'd barely gotten over the pain of losing Gracie?

A shrill war cry sent a shiver of fear down the back of his spine. He'd heard the same sound years ago when traveling to Montana from his home state of Texas. Apaches! But wasn't that impossible? What would they be doing this far north?

Again came the eerie shriek. An icy feeling settled around his heart as Seth tightened his grip on the rifle. He dismounted and crept toward the circling smoke, prepared, if necessary, to shoot on sight.

One Feather heard the soft rustling of twigs being stepped upon and grimaced. Should anyone from his tribe catch him in such a position, he'd never be able to share counsel again. He'd be even more of an outcast than he already was. He cringed as Golden Hair let loose with another of her shrill cries while skipping around the campfire. Suddenly the child stopped and turned to stare, her eyes wide with delight.

"Papa!"

"Blossom!" Kneeling down, Seth allowed his

daughter to rush into his arms. He closed his eyes with undisguised relief and hugged her tight against him. "Pea, where have you been? I've been searching everywhere for you and—"

"Papa, I ain't gotta go home, do I? Me and my friend was playing a game and I—"

As Seth looked over in the direction his daughter pointed, a helpless stream of laughter came bubbling forth. Tied securely to a wide oak tree—and wearing the dress he'd purchased for Maeve—was his old friend, One Feather. The young brave offered him a weak smile of recognition.

"Well, well, Pea. What have we here?" Seth asked, his eyes bright with laughter.

"Me and One Fedder was playing Injun. I pretended he was the lady and I was the Injun. Oh, Papa, One Fedder is soooooo much fun! He played all kinds of games with me and when I missed you the most of all, he sang to me and made me laugh. Kin One Fedder come live with us, Papa? Huh? Kin he?"

One Feather tried to release himself from the twisted knots of rope, becoming more tangled than he'd previously been.

Seth felt a surge of sympathy for his friend and walked over to lend a hand. "I'm sorry about this, One Feather. Where did you find her, anyway?"

"Her too close to edge of mountain. One Feather rescue Golden Hair from danger."

Seth clapped him on the shoulder. "I'm thankful to have such a faithful friend." He

233

turned to face his daughter. "How in tarnation did you get so far away from home, Pea?"

"One Fedder brought me on his pony. You should see his pony, Papa; it's all speckled and white and—"

"I know what the pony looks like, Blossom." Confused, Seth struggled with the remaining knot and, after freeing the brave, stood. His brows furrowed. "Is this true, One Feather? Instead of bringing her back to me you took her further away?"

"Hmph!" One Feather try to take Golden Hair home when sun fly up to meet sky, but Golden Hair make much noise. Golden Hair no want to go home."

"Yes," Seth drawled, "I've been around Blo— er, Golden Hair when she makes much noise. It's called a temper tantrum and it's not a very pretty sight." He eyed One Feather's attire. "That explains part of it, I think, but what about the dre—your outfit?"

"Hmph!" The Indian struggled to free himself from the garment. "One Feather borrow this from Good Heart's wagon. One Feather hope it bring Woman Who Walks On Cloud to him. One Feather no like to put on. Golden Hair face turn ugly like she going to make much noise again when One Feather say no!" He broke the conversation with a huge sigh. "So . . . One Feather do what Golden Hair want."

Trying to remain serious was taking its toll on Seth. He covered his twitching mouth with his hand and looked at the ground. "I see. You said you hoped borrowing the dress would make Woman Who Walks On Cloud come to you. I'm assuming you mean Maeve."

One Feather folded his arms across his chest and beamed with pride while nodding vehemently. "I have many fine horses to offer Woman Who Walks On Cloud. She will become One Feather's wife."

Seth sucked in a thin stream of air through his teeth in an effort not to laugh at such a ridiculous idea. "My good friend, you have indeed shown your faithfulness to me by saving my daughter. But I must ask you to forget this idea about the woman."

"One Feather no forget."

"But you must! The woman is not one of your people, you know that. Your father would never agree."

"One Feather must have Woman Who Walks On Cloud. One Feather want to walk on clouds too."

Sighing, Seth scuffed at the dirt with the toe of his boot. There was no way he could begin to explain the inexplicable, but he'd do his best to try. "Woman Who Walks On Cloud came to me—" No, that was no good. He tried again. "The Great Spirit sent her especially for me," Seth stated, remembering the details of his strange dream. As he continued to describe how their souls had come together, he found himself believing the unbelievable. But would One Feather? From the scowl on his friend's face, Seth seriously doubted it.

Much later, Seth had run out of words, and
Blossom out of energy. The Indian remained
adamant. "One Feather ask Woman Who Walks
On Cloud to marry after I show her many fine
horses."

In exasperation, Seth lay back against the
cold ground and stared up at the early evening
stars. "She's not like that, One Feather. She
doesn't care for fine possessions. She's unlike
any woman I've ever met in that what makes
her happy is life itself."

"Hmph!"

The next morning, Seth, Blossom, and One
Feather left the forest to make the journey
home. Seth could only pray Maeve would use
tact in turning down his friend's proposal. But,
Seth admitted to himself with a grin, horses
were a considerable improvement over sick
sheep!

Chapter Sixteen

Maeve wearily tucked back a stray strand of hair. She gritted her teeth and ripped a long strip of material from the hem of her dress. Fashioning it into a bandanna, she tied the fabric around her nose in an effort to rid herself of the obnoxious smell coming from the back of the wagon. Jeb had stated he could no longer stand to ride behind her and opted to lead the way.

She thought of rotten eggs, ammonia, smelly diapers, curdled milk; none of them came close to describing the odor wafting from the back of this dadblasted wagon!

As they steadily made their way toward town, they came to a neighboring farm. Maeve waved to two men mending their fence before urging the horses forward. She drew back in amazement as the larger of the two cowboys withdrew his gun and aimed it directly at her.

Jeb circled back to join her. "We're in for trouble, Maeve."

Pulling her kerchief away from her mouth, she eyed the angry expression on the man's weathered face. "No joke. What do you think is the problem?" Just then, one of the sheep leapt from the wagon and took off running. Without hesitation, the cowboy whirled around and shot the animal.

Rage filled every part of her being. "What did you do that for!" Maeve screeched.

"Ain't nobody, man or woman, gonna let those varmints ruin our grassland."

"I hardly think one poor little animal is going to do that," she countered.

"Yeah? Tell me something, little lady. You ever seen what sheep can do to prime grazing land?"

"No," Maeve muttered, "but I have a feeling you're going to tell me whether I want to know or not."

She'd assumed correctly. The cowboy continued his tirade, his face growing bright red with anger. "They eat at the grasses until there ain't nothing left except the root. What those damn critters don't eat, the sun kills." He took a deep breath and tightened his grip on his gun. "No'm, ain't no way in hell I'm gonna let you cross our land."

Maeve expelled a loud sigh. "Look, mister, I'm

tired and I'm miserable. I got sheep sh—manure all over me, and a wagon full of the same. I've been kicked, I've been bleated at, I've been pushed to my limit, you understand me?" She took a calming breath. "Now then, suppose I promise you I'll keep these stupid animals inside the wagon until we get across. Would you let me pass?"

The man mulled over her suggestion. He had to admit he'd never seen a sorrier-lookin' sight in all his born days. How she'd managed to keep those sheep inside the wagon was beyond him. And the boy riding with her looked wearier than a three-peckered billy goat trying to mate. His eyes narrowed as he spoke. "All right, I reckon I'll letcha, but if'n the boss catches me, there'll be hell to pay. And he just might figure you're a she-devil, what with that wagon full of sheep. Still, I ain't never been one to refuse a lady in distress. I'll escort you to the boundary line."

Instead of thanking him, Maeve slapped the horses unnecessarily hard, propelling herself backward as they jerked into action. After she'd managed to climb back onto the seat, she gained what dignity she could and offered her escort a haughty look.

The cowboy shook his head in amusement. "What in God's name made you buy sheep? Surely you've heard about the war between the sheepmen and the ranchers around here."

"I-I'm not from around here," Maeve explained. "And as soon as the stupid animals arrived, I knew a mistake had been made. Now I'm trying to rectify the situation. I'm going to demand our money back."

"Where'd you get 'em from?"

"Elkhorn Shipping," Maeve said in a clipped voice. She wished the man would just hush his silly blabbing. She had enough to worry about with keeping the sheep inside the wagon.

"I know the owner personally. Ain't no way he's gonna take them varmints back, ain't no way atall."

"That's where you're wrong," she insisted.

The rider tipped his hat. "No'm, I reckon you're the one that's wrong."

Maeve stopped the wagon and narrowed her eyes, staring the cowboy down. "You ever heard the expression 'Hell hath no fury like a woman scorned'?"

He nodded.

"Well let me tell you something, mister. I've been scorned, you got it? And the owner damn well better take these sheep back because if he doesn't, I'll personally shove each one of them down his throat, filthy fur and all, you understand me?"

As Maeve and Jeb rode past the boundary line of his boss's ranch, the cowboy removed his hat and grinned. He had no doubt the fiesty woman would do exactly as she'd stated. He almost felt sorry for old man Carmichael.

* * *

When the wind began to pick up a bit, swirling the disgusting odors toward Maeve's face, she groaned. To say she was tired would be like saying she'd fallen into a kettle of boiling water and gotten waterlogged. She'd definitely taken on more than she should have. Would Seth be grateful? Even if he got down on bended knee and uttered his undying devotion, that would hardly be enough.

Lord, how her back ached. This had been a foolish idea, one that she just wasn't strong enough to handle. Unshed tears filled her eyes, blurring her vision as she continued to dwell on her misery. After swiping away an escaping tear, she arched her back and ran a filthy hand down her side to reach the sore spot centered in her lower back. As she did so, her fingers trailed over a protruding hip bone. The feeling of defeat quickly disappeared.

After all, a woman with hip bones could accomplish anything!

Riding up beside her, Jeb noted the lines of exhaustion around his companion's eyes. "There's a stream about fifty yards to our right. You wanna let these animals have a drink and stop there for the night?"

"I guess so," Maeve agreed despondently. As they came upon the trickling water, the sheep began to bleat with increasing fortitude. She couldn't suppress a giggle as she glanced at Jeb's astonished face. "You think that means they're thirsty?"

"Reckon so, Maeve. Say, have you thought about how we're gonna keep 'em from running away if we let 'em out to drink?"

She gnawed at her lip, deep in thought. "Well, I guess we could get them down one at a time and then after they've finished, put them back in the wagon."

Jeb looked dubious. "How we gonna tell which ones we've let drink and which ones we ain't? They all look the same to me."

"They do?" Maeve turned to stare at her passengers. "Not to me they don't. See that one over there? That's Dopey. He keeps trying to jump out. The one with the spot on his nose is Sneezy. For every mile we've covered, he's sneezed at least twice that many times. And that one with the fluffiest tail by the sideboard is Doc. He keeps trying to clean his mate. The one with—"

Laughing, Jeb threw up his hands. "I get your point. Let me tether my horse to that tree and I'll help you get 'em out."

But there was no need for assistance. As soon as Maeve stopped, the animals' instinct for survival took over and they leapt from the wagon, crashing, rolling, and bumping into one another in their effort to make it to the stream.

After climbing down from the driver's seat, Maeve crossed her arms and watched their mad dash. Wearily she sank to the ground.

Jeb crouched down beside her. "What if they try to escape?"

"I wouldn't worry about it," Maeve declared wryly, eyeing the shabby state of her companion. "We're not that lucky."

When the evening sun infused the sky with hues of deep crimson, the soft winds turned harsh and the day ended on a bleak note. Maeve snuggled closer to the fire Jeb had built, grateful for his knowledge of outdoor life. This was a first for her, this sleeping under the stars, and she'd much rather be indoors. A Holiday Inn would be nice, she decided. A Holiday Inn with a large swimming pool and hot tub.

Jeb noticed her far-off expression and wondered if she were sorry she'd listened to his suggestion. Both spoke at the same time.

"Jeb, I wonder—"

"Maeve, are you sorry you—"

Draining the last of the hot coffee from her tin cup, Maeve placed it on the hard ground and leaned back against the saddle Jeb had thoughtfully provided as a pillow. "Wonder if Seth has found Pea yet?" There was a certain amount of shame to her question, as this was the first time she'd thought about the circumstances she'd left behind.

Jeb plucked at a nearby weed and placed it in his mouth. In the background he could hear the sheep bleating pathetically. "Probably. Most likely all Pea did was wander a short ways off. I 'spect if we had stayed home like maybe we should have, they'da been back at first light."

A smile crept over Maeve's lips. The boy's tone held wistfulness. "Sorry we took on this project?" she asked quietly.

"Well, I can't say Pa's gonna be too pleased. It ain't right for a woman to be tryin' to do a man's job, and Miss Maeve, I can't help but admit . . . I think we done took on more than we can handle."

She glanced toward the edge of the stream where the sheep were grazing contentedly. Tilting her head upward, Maeve watched the stars twinkle brightly in the velvet skies. A strange sense of well-being washed away the weariness around her heart. "I don't know, Jeb; the sheep are still here, we're halfway there . . . I'm rather proud of us."

Jeb shrugged. "I guess, but Pa's gonna be—"

"Seth's going to be proud of us too. Just you wait and see!"

Visions of his father's reaction filled Jeb's mind. He'd be glad they were alive, and probably even more glad these stupid critters were taken care of, but proud they'd done it? No! Angrier than a nest of hornets was more like it. And not at Miss Maeve, either. At him. Jebediah Caldwell. For ever gettin' Maeve in this predicament. Because even though his partner in crime thought the hard part was nearly over, Jeb knew better. They still had to talk old man Carmichael into accepting them.

He eyed Maeve, watching as her lids grew heavy with sleep. With her face all dirty and grimy and her dress torn in at least a dozen places, she was a sad sight to behold. And though he wasn't in much of a position to be talking about nasty smells since his own coveralls stank to high heaven, the odor of her dress was almost unbearable. They'd probably be run out of town at the first good whiff.

No, Maeve had been wrong in her assumption. They weren't halfway finished; they'd only just begun.

Chapter Seventeen

The night winds howled through the cove of trees overhead. Maeve stirred restlessly. Beside her, the gentle sound of Jeb's even breathing brought a sense of comfort. She closed her eyes again, willing herself to forget the rugged conditions and dream once more.

Now then, where was she? That's right, at the Holiday Inn. The luxury suite. Big king-size bed, the mattress firm, the pillow cushiony soft . . .

Beside her lay the man who'd stolen her heart forever. And from the expression on his face, it wasn't too hard to tell that his feelings had been hurt.

"Are you happy being with us, Maeve?"

When she rolled over to face him, the mattress

*sank with her weight. Maeve winced. She reposi-
tioned herself so that her proportions would
spread out and lay on her back. "Of course I am,
my darling."*

*"Then why are you back in the future? Why did
you bring me to the Holiday Inn?"*

*Why indeed? Hadn't their bed of straw been
just as comfortable? Seth didn't belong in this
place, yet . . . oh, this bed was such a luxury.*

*Not near as sumptuous as the feel of his fingers
stroking her flattened belly, however. An intense
flash of heat claimed her insides and turned her
newly found bones to jelly. As she returned the
favor by stroking his inner thigh, she could feel
the compact muscles produced by years of toil-
some labor. Moving her fingers lightly over his
hips, she trailed her hand in wispy fashion over
his stomach, then all the way up his side, finally
resting her palm against the soft matt of hair
swirling around his nipple. She could feel his
heart beating, steady and strong.*

With desire for her.

*When he moved to support himself on one el-
bow, his voice came as soft as a caress. "You're
such a delight. Where else could I find a woman
so feminine yet determined enough to return my
sheep?"*

*"It's nothing," Maeve murmured. "I'd move
mountains for you if that's what you asked me
to do."*

*His low chuckle warmed her suddenly chilled
body as he continued. "You gave me a whole new
understanding of time. That was enough."*

"I'd like to take the credit, Seth, but something more powerful than the both of us arranged our circumstances."

"Whatever the power, whatever the force, I'm very grateful." He gathered her to him and held her in a fierce embrace. As he did so, he noticed her trembling limbs. "Don't be afraid of me. You never have to be afraid of me."

"I'm not afraid, I'm cold," Maeve admitted. "Very, very cold."

"Perhaps this will warm you," he whispered as he began a bold exploration of her body. When he cupped the delta of her womanhood, he lowered his head to kiss each taut nipple.

Warmth, so sweet and tender, flowed through her.

"Let me cover you with the blanket," Seth offered, breaking away to grab the covers that were a tumbled heap at their feet.

"Cover me with your body instead," Maeve whispered, feeling wanton and womanly.

"I don't want to hurt you. You're already down to skin and bones, my darling. I'm afraid I'll crush you."

His words brought a fire to Maeve's veins. She moved atop him, straddling his hard, pulsing flesh, knowing, finally, his desire was for her . . . and her alone. As he filled her completely, she moaned in sweet agony.

"I must go back," Seth stated gently, brushing the tip of her nose with his finger.

"Go back where, my darling?"

"Go back to the past. I don't belong in a fancy

hotel, Maeve. I'm a rancher. I need the great out-doors like you need the comforts of modern times. Perhaps we were never meant to be together; perhaps all we had were a few stolen moments."

"Don't leave me, Seth. Please don't leave me."

"Oh, Maeve, I thought you were content with your surroundings, but look—the first chance you got, you brought me to the future. Is that the way it'll always be?"

"No! My happiness depends on staying with you, Seth. And if it must be in the past, then that's where I'll be."

"That's what you say. . . . " His words broke off as he offered her a sad smile and rose from the bed. *"I must go now. It's been wonderful."*

"Don't leave me, Seth. Don't leave me! I need you. I want you, and if I have to live in the past, then so be it."

Beside the bed, a clock ticked ominously loudly. Time is running out, the noise seemed to remind her. Make your decision and stick to it.

"Wait, Seth! Wait for me!"

"Maeve, Maeve, wake up!" Jeb cried, shaking the seemingly tormented woman's shoulder.

When she opened her eyes, Maeve struggled into a sitting position, painfully aware of every aching muscle in her body. The temperature had dropped several degrees. Wiping a strand of hair from her face, she was surprised to find her cheeks damp with tears.

"Are you okay, Maeve? You were having a

nightmare or something. You kept crying out for Papa."

Wrapping her arms around her waist, she ignored the crisp air. "We've got to get those sheep returned, Jeb, and get back. We need to hurry . . . we need to go home. I have to tell your father how happy I am."

Home. When had the tiny cabin begun to feel like home? Was it the moment she surrendered her heart to Seth? No, that had brought forth the happiness that had eluded her ever since her parents' deaths.

To hell with the comforts of the Holiday Inn! A king-size bed was nothing in comparison to the comfort she found in Seth's warm and welcoming arms.

The truth hit her harder than the smell of her dress.

Aunt Gladys had been right. Time had indeed healed the dull, empty feeling in her heart and replaced it with the love of a tender, gentle giant. Oh, maybe not in the conventional way . . . but then nothing in her life had ever been conventional.

For the first time since taking on the momentous task at hand, Maeve was glad she had. And Seth would be glad too, once she got his money back. He'd forgive her for being too independent—wouldn't he?

As she looked up at the sky, she could see that the darkness had turned to a shabby semblance of a newborn day. "Are you ready to leave yet, Jeb? We've got to hurry and get our job done,

then go home. Your daddy's gonna be waiting
on us."

"I 'spect we better. I don't like the look of
them clouds. Sure as I'm Jeb Caldwell, there's a
snowstorm comin'."

Indeed, Maeve could feel the heaviness of
cold moisture in the air. "Let's go."

When they reached the outskirts of town, the
sheep, the wagon, and Maeve were all dusted
with a powdery covering of snow. The smell
wafting from the back of the wagon escalated
with the dampness, to say nothing of the odor
coming from her own garments.

Jeb looked back to see Maeve's reaction as the
town slowly took form. Her mouth hung open
and she seemed to be struggling for words.

"Th-this is town?"

"Yes'm."

"These few little buildings? Where's the mall,
where're the restaurants, the Holiday Inn—
well, forget the Holiday Inn—but is this really
it?"

"Yes'm," Jeb muttered, unable to comprehend her obvious disappointment. To him,
town was a wonderful adventure. He clicked the
reins, urging his horse forward. "Where do you
want to go first, Maeve?" he called over his
shoulder.

"Let's get rid of these sheep. Take me to the
shipping company." As she spoke, Maeve maneuvered the wagon to Jeb's side.

One whiff told him she'd chosen wrong. "Uh,
Maeve, don't you think we oughta get cleaned
up a bit first?"

"Forget it. The reason I smell like this is because that damned man sent us sick sheep to begin with! No, Jeb, he can suffer just like we've had to!"

"Yes'm." A feeling of dread washed over Jeb. This was going to be bad, no doubt about it.

Ignoring the stares and guffaws of the townspeople as they made their way down the long, snow-dusted street, Maeve tried to sit a little taller in the seat. The last thing she needed right now was a dose of insecurity, and if she allowed herself to feel those eyes boring into her, she knew she wouldn't have the fortitude to argue with the one person responsible for getting her into this mess—both literally and figuratively.

By the time Jeb stopped in front of a one-story wooden building, the snow had covered much of the roof. The pure white sparkles seemed to hide the dirt of several years gone by. He dismounted with a huge sigh. "This is it, Maeve; this is the shipping company."

"Great," she stated as she climbed down from the wagon and hitched up her smelly skirts. "Look, Jeb, it's liable to get real ugly in there. I may have to say some things that would be harmful to your tender ears. Maybe you'd better stay outside and watch the damn sheep!" The curse word slipped unintentionally from her mouth.

By now Jeb knew Maeve well enough to know that any argument on his part would be futile. He stepped aside to allow her access to the door and gagged when the scent of her clothes lin-

gered just a little too long. Surely he couldn't
smell that bad, could he? One whiff of his jacket
told him the truth. With another large sigh, he
sat down on the steps and waited for the outcome.

Waltzing past a group of elderly men gathered by the potbellied stove for warmth, Maeve
smiled politely. Her greeting turned to a frown
as one of the men pulled a well-used handkerchief from his pocket and tied it around his
face.

"What can I do for you?" the desk manager
questioned as he eyed the pathetic sight before
him.

Maeve raised a warning finger to let him have
it with both barrels, then stopped. A lady
wouldn't act the way she was dying to, not in
this day and time. No sense in drawing undo
attention to herself. But by now the smell of her
garments had drawn all the attention she could
ever want or need.

She bowed her head in what she hoped would
be polite fashion. "I wish to see the owner. I
believe his name is Mr. Carmichael."

"That is impossible. Mr. Carmichael is in
back working on the ledgers. He doesn't want
to be disturbed."

Anger bubbled in the pit of her stomach as
Maeve tried to hold her tongue. "This is a bit of
an emergency." She quirked a brow. "If you
could just fetch him?"

"Impossible. I already told you, he has especially requested that he not be disturbed."

Good grief, what was that awful odor? Maeve inwardly cringed when she realized it came from her. Okay, if that's all God was going to give her to work with, then she'd have to use the smell to her advantage.

"I see," she answered politely. "In that case, I'll just have to wait, won't I? Maybe a spot by the stove would be nice. That way I can dry these disgustingly wet clothes." Maeve moved toward the warmth, where the men were already backing away. To expedite the situation, she fanned her skirts a bit, making sure the odor wafted in their direction.

"Who are you?" the desk clerk questioned when the silence and smell became unbearable.

"I'm Maeve Fredrickson. Er, Seth Caldwell's woman."

"Old Seth musta got purty damned lonely up there in them mountains to resort to the smelly likes of that one," stated the bushy-browed man closest to the door.

Maeve glared at the three men as if they were pieces of lint on the dustpan of life before turning back to the clerk. "I'll have you know I'm prepared to stay here as long as necessary." She ruffled her skirts once more, enjoying their obvious reaction. "Mister, after two days of travelling in the same clothes, I can take the odor if you can."

By the time she'd made the proclamation, however, the odor emanating from her clothes had seeped to the back room where Mr. Carmichael was enjoying a cup of tea instead of working on the ledgers spread before him. He rose from his desk and, with a frown, went to investigate. The sight that greeted him sent a shiver of disgust over his slight, four-foot-three frame. "May I help you?"

Maeve turned toward the shrill voice. The owner's handlebar mustache twitched like a wary cat's tail under her scrutiny.

She narrowed her eyes and placed her hands on her hips to draw strength from the feel of her bones. "Depends. You Carmichael?"

His voice quavered. "I am."

"Did you sell some sheep to Seth Caldwell?"

"I did."

"And when you sold those sheep, did you realize they were in very poor health?"

"That would be impossible, madam. Might I suggest Mr. Caldwell simply didn't know the proper way to care for such delicate animals?"

"No, you may not!" Maeve declared, indignant at such an outlandish accusation. "Those sheep were sick when they arrived and I intend to make you take them back and return his money."

"That is impossible."

The events of the past two days of traveling—something Maeve tried hard to consider an adventure instead of a nightmare—suddenly caught up with her. She marched toward the desk and reached over the counter, grabbing the man's starched shirt. "Look, mister, I just found out that nothing is impossible if you want it bad enough!"

Suddenly, the snickers coming from behind her stopped and she counted the number of men by the varying intakes of breath.

"Now you just listen to me, you old goat! You sold my betrothed"—*There, that was a good old-timey word!* —"damaged goods. And I demand you take them back!"

From his hiding spot beside the window, Jeb's eyes grew wide. Maeve looked as if she were going to kill old man Carmichael. He leaned his ear against the cold glass windowpane to hear the rest of the argument that, by the look of distress on Carmichael's face, had grown even more heated.

"Where I come from, a man is as good as his word, you weasel! You either give us back our money or I'll—"

Carmichael struggled to feel his feet against the floor. He adjusted his shirt as he jerked it from the crazy woman's grasp. "You'll what?"

It didn't take but a moment to size him up. Maeve took a deep breath and exhaled slowly. "Or I'll sit on you and squash those beady little eyes right out of their sockets!"

Mortimer Hawkins cupped his ear as he leaned forward in his chair. His hearing hadn't been the same since Ma Hawkins had taken a skillet to his head when she found he'd used her good washboard to make moonshine. "Eh? Wha'd you say you wuz gonna do?"

Maeve whirled around. "I said I was going to—" She caught herself just in time. "I don't believe that's any of your business, sir."

"Eh? No business? Who ain't got no business? That true, Carmichael? After all these years is you closin' shop on us? Where we gonna go durin' the day if'n you close this here office up?"

Ignoring the babble, Maeve continued to argue until her voice became ragged, but to no avail. The owner remained adamant in his refusal to take the flock of sheep back.

Tears filled her eyes and spilled over to dampen her cheeks as she left the building. Jeb scrambled to his feet, blowing warm air onto his frozen hands.

"No luck, Maeve?"

"No, J-Jeb," she stammered, her voice breaking. "I failed. We came all this way for nothing."

The door to the shipping company opened as Mort walked out to witness the pathetic pair. While his hearing had deteriorated, there was nothing wrong with his eyes. He hadn't missed the young boy's face pressed against the windowpane any more than he'd missed the tears trailing down the young woman's grimy face as she departed the office. Where her tears had trailed, there were two clean streaks left behind. Finally, he addressed her with a grin, revealing a large gap where teeth used to be.

"Lookie here, little lady. Ain't no need to git yer feathers all in a dander. The li'l missus and me, why, we been pondering on gettin' us some of them sheep. How sick is they?"

Maeve swiped at her nose and stood. She refused to lie about the situation, and her shoulders slumped with dejection. "They're pretty sick," she admitted. "They've got this nasty green stuff in their eyes and they stagger around like they're drunk. We lost several of them on our way into town."

"How many you got left over?"

"Just what's in the wagon." She sniffled, her eyes filling once more.

Mort walked down the steps, ignoring the big, fat flakes of snow peppering his bald head. "Ain't never seen a wagon full of sheep afore. They don't look so bad to me. Lookie here, this'un's right friendly."

Maeve watched as the lamb she'd nicknamed Doc licked the stranger's hand. A spark of hope tickled her heavy heart. "They're not bad animals, I suppose, but we have no idea how to cure them. And to tell you the truth, I don't think I have enough energy left in me to take them home again."

Mort turned and stared deeply into the young woman's eyes.

An inexplicable chill ran up her spine. Maeve felt as if he could read her soul. Though the silence between them was brief, there was enough time for an inner voice to tell her something very, very important was about to happen. She listened carefully.

"Here's what I'm about to do, little missy. I got two calves what was born with defects. Now the defects ain't too bad; they just look strange. If'n you're willin' to settle for one gold piece and them calves, I'll consider it a fair trade."

Tugging at her hand, Jeb pulled Maeve aside.

"I don't know about this, Maeve. Seems like we could be trading bad for worse."

She caught her lip between her teeth and sighed. "Jeb, look at it this way. If we don't trade, we've got to take those stupid sheep all the way back." She met his gaze. "I don't think I can. I'm tired, Jeb. I'm tired and I want to go h-home." Her voice broke again. "When you think about it, the worst that can possibly come of my decision is we'll have enough beef to get us through the winter."

A sense of responsibility made Jeb stand taller. "Then let me be the one to agree. That way, if Pa gits mad about it, he can blame me instead of you."

She smiled. "No, Jeb. I got us into this and I'll take full responsibility for the outcome." Pulling her wrap tightly around her, Maeve walked back to the old-timer's side. Something more than a trade was about to take place; she'd stake her existence on it. There'd be plenty of time to figure out this crazy feeling during the long journey home. With sparkling eyes, she spoke. "Mister, you've got yourself a deal!"

Chapter Eighteen

Under the scrutiny of curious eyes, Maeve and Jeb stopped by the nearest watering trough to wash out the back of the wagon. A wisecrack from the gathering group of people made Maeve bite down hard on her tongue to keep from responding.

"How come you ain't puttin' them cows in the back of your wagon, little lady? Them sheep seemed to enjoy the ride!"

Acting as if she were deaf, Maeve climbed up in the seat. "You ready to go home, Jeb?"

"Ready, Maeve."

"Then let's do it!" With a snap of the reins, the horses moved forward and Maeve glanced back to make sure the calves were still securely tied to the wagon. They were odd-looking little creatures, to be certain. The majority of their bodies were a deep reddish color while their faces were completely white. Patches of the same color blended in with the red along their chests, flanks, lower legs, and at the very tip of their tails.

She was in possession of one male, one female. Maeve's hope was that during the journey home they would fall madly in love and procreate when the time came. Why, two cows could easily turn to three or four or five. . . . Her imagination took over and she closed her eyes to envision an entire herd in the years to come. Again, that inexplicable feeling of something wonderful about to happen flooded through her.

She felt as if she were standing on the threshold of a new beginning for Seth. But what about her? Where did she fit in?

The questions lay heavy on her heart. Maybe her purpose for going back in time had been accomplished with the trade. What if she wouldn't be allowed to stay and see the outcome of her exchange?

The snow blew in cold, icy swirls around the wagon and the driver. Glancing back, Maeve could see Jeb was having as much trouble staying warm as she was. The only other covering they had between them was the blankets in the back of the wagon that she'd rinsed out in the horse trough. When she reached back to check their condition, she found the soggy material stiff with ice.

"Jeb, we'd better stop for the night and make

camp. If I don't get warm, I swear my blood's gonna freeze."

Shivering, Jeb nodded his agreement.

Maeve looked up at the gray, murky sky and frowned. She'd been here long enough to know that the clouds she observed held several inches of snow—if not blizzard conditions.

Okay, angel of mercy. Where are you? I've done the very best I can with all these awful, terrible, conditions—a tear slid silently down her cheek—*and yes, I know I'm feeling sorry for myself, but give me a break, will you? Show me some of that good old-fashioned mercy, for Pete's sake!*

Was it her imagination or had that one cloud actually formed the face of a woman? Duessa's face, if the truth be told. But no, Duessa wasn't the angel of mercy, because had she been then she certainly could have saved them all a lot of trouble and made sure the sheep arrived in perfect condition. Now *that* would have been showing mercy at its most merciful!

After Jeb found a spot he felt would suffice for the night, Maeve untied the calves from the wagon and watched as he built a roaring fire. "Do you believe in angels?" Maeve huddled closer to the flames, trying to stop her body from trembling in the cold air.

"I ain't never gave it much thought, Maeve. I reckon when I think of Mama, I think about her bein' an angel and all. Shoot, maybe Gracie is too."

"She is," Maeve mused.

"She is what?"

"An Angel. Oh, well . . . I mean, I guess she is." There was no use trying to explain to Jeb about her strange experiences by the stream. There were still far too many times when she found the entire happening too hard to comprehend, herself.

Glancing toward the shivering, bawling calves, Maeve stood and guided them closer to the fire. In response to Jeb's strange look, she giggled. "After all we went through to get them, there isn't any way I'm gonna let the poor things freeze to death," she explained.

Their rations had dwindled to one chunk of bread and a long strip of jerky. Maeve sipped the last of the coffee, relishing the warmth the watery substance offered as it made its way to her stomach.

Jeb was quiet. Too quiet. Watching him chew the last bit of dried meat, she perched closer to the roaring fire and stared at the orange blaze. The silence between them was broken by an occasional hissing sound as flakes of snow hit the leaping flames.

"Okay, kiddo, out with it. What's on your mind?"

Jeb's brows furrowed. "Maeve, I ain't never seen cows that look like those two. Their coloring is all wrong."

"Mort warned us they looked funny, now didn't he?" She received a grudging nod. "What would you rather be doing, Jeb, taking these home or a wagon full of sheep?"

"The cows, but—"

"No buts. That settles it. We did what we had to do, and although we couldn't get Seth's investment back, we didn't come away empty-handed. I'll tell you the truth. I've never shot an animal in my entire life, but if I had been forced to bring those darn sheep back with us, I'd have shot every one of them. There's only so much a person can take and I must confess, I'd reached my limit."

"Well," Jeb drawled, "I gotta admit they do smell better than them sheep."

"Too bad we don't." Maeve giggled.

Taking the iron skillet from the bundle of supplies, Jeb walked back to the campfire. "I thought I'd go look for some wild root. Fried with a little bacon grease, it ain't too bad."

Barely able to keep her eyes open, Maeve yawned. "Don't bother to fix any for me, Jeb. I'm so tired that I couldn't even stay awake for a piece of my mom's chocolate cake." She took the saddle and laid it on the ground for her pillow. "I'm going to sleep."

Moments later, she sat up. "I stink too bad to go to sleep. I'm gonna have to wash up a bit."

"I'll fetch you some water from that creek over yonder. It ain't very clean, but—"

"It has to be cleaner than I am." When the boy failed to argue, Maeve laughed. Her spirits lifted a little as she washed her face, hands, and neck from the heated water. Afterward, she lay down once more. Was it her overactive imagination or had the wind and snow let up a bit?

"Thanks, angel of mercy," Maeve muttered
. . . just in case. "I'm gonna try to get some
sleep, how 'bout you, Jeb?"

Jeb lay down, giving his makeshift pillow a
solid thump to make it more comfortable.
"Sounds like a good idea to me. Say, Maeve,
why did you ask me about angels?" When he
received no response, Jeb realized the young
woman had already fallen asleep. Casting a
glance at the two cows, he shook his head. "Just
wait'll Pa sees what she's done got us into this
time," he muttered. "He ain't gonna believe it.
He just ain't gonna believe it."

When Maeve first became aware of footsteps,
she tried to reassure herself it was the cattle
stirring about. Moving slowly, she rolled over
and peeped through half-closed lids. If it was,
then they'd learned how to walk on their hind
legs. And since when did cows wear boots?

Her breath caught at the base of her throat as
fear started her heart pounding. The intruder
was creeping toward Jeb. Kneeling over him.
Did he mean to harm them?

Not if she could help it. With catlike motions,
Maeve rose from her makeshift bed, keeping
one eye on the stranger. The skillet was right
where Jeb had left it, beside the now-dying embers. If only she could reach . . . there, she had
it.

Just in time too. The man had peeled back the
jacket Jeb was using as a cover. Creeping up
behind the shadowy stranger, she lifted the pan

high above the man's head and let loose a blood-curdling scream. "Jeb!"

Jeb sat up and bumped heads with the man kneeling over him. Eyes wide, he glanced up. "Maeve, don't!"

The skillet crashed over the intruder's head and she heard a gentle *whuff* as he expelled a rush of air. Using the toe of her boot, Maeve rolled the unconscious man over so that she could see his face.

"Seth!"

Jeb buried his face in his hands. "You just hit Pa," he groaned.

Oh hell! "I-I thought he was an intruder, that he meant you harm," Maeve babbled.

A soft groan from Seth made her drop the weapon, and, kneeling down beside him, she felt for the lump she knew would be there. Sure enough, there it was, right smack in the center of his head. "Oh, Seth," she cried. "What have I done?"

"Knocked the hell out of me, if you'll pardon my language," Seth managed. When he tried to sit up, the earth seemed to spin at a rapid pace. His head pounded as if his brains were trying to escape. "Remind me to give you fair warning the next time I come to check on you."

As he slowly gained his senses, the anger he'd been trying to control came rushing forth. "Where have you two been, anyway? It's been three days since I returned with Pea and imagine my surprise when I found you gone."

"But the note—" Maeve began.

"What note?"

"The note I left lying on the table. Surely it was still there—you found Pea?"

"Of course I did," Seth stated grumpily while rubbing his head. "She was with One Feather."

"The Indian?"

"Yes, the Indian," Seth snapped. "Now then, someone better explain what's going on."

Maeve tried again. "The note told you everything."

"Excuse me, Maeve," Seth interrupted. "But I didn't take time to read a damn note. I was worried sick about you."

His tone was rather chilly, Maeve decided. Too chilly for the hell they'd endured. And for who? Him, of course. Well, if this was the way he showed his gratitude he could damn well keep it to himself.

Hands clenched into tight fists by her sides, Maeve stormed away from him, fighting back tears. When she heard the crunch of his footsteps behind her, she began to run.

"Maeve, wait a minute!" Seth called, his head still throbbing.

"No!" Maeve sobbed. "Y-you just stay away from me you—you ungrateful thing, you!" But her steps slowed.

Catching up, Seth grabbed her arm and turned her around to face him.

"Let go," she demanded. "You're hurting me."

His hands dropped to his sides. "I'm sorry," he uttered softly. For the first time since finding them, Seth took a good look at the woman before him. Her clothes were in tattered shreds. Her hair, normally silken strands, was a mass of tangles, and her big hazel eyes were framed by dark circles. "What in God's name happened to you, Maeve?"

Suddenly the toll of the past few days seemed too much to bear. Sobbing loudly, she threw herself into his arms, allowing him to hold her tight while she cried. "I-It's been a nightmare, Seth. We thought we could do it for you; we thought we were helping—"

"Helping what, honey?" Seth asked, barely able to breathe from the odor her clothes emitted. He stroked her tangled hair.

Maeve placed her hands against his chest and drew back. "Then you really didn't get our note?"

How could he tell her the truth? Seth shook his head.

"Oh Seth, we put the sheep in the wagon and took them to town. Along the way we met up with this terrible man who shot one of them, and then when we got into town everyone stared at us as if we'd lost our minds."

Placing her head against his chest, she continued to speak between giant, racking sobs. "When we got there, the owner refused to take them back and there were these men who made simply horrible comments about our smell and then this one man came out to look at—"

She stopped. Was he laughing? The sound coming from deep inside his chest certainly sounded like laughter. Maeve blinked.

"Go on," Seth managed, trying desperately to control his mirth.

As she drew back, Maeve placed her hands on her hips. "Why . . . you're laughing, aren't you?"

Seth covered his grin by tugging at his mustache. "I'm sorry, Maeve, but the thought of you loading the wagon with sheep and forcing them to stay inside it is just—just—" He couldn't help himself as he collapsed into deep, rich laughter.

Maeve bit her lip. Damn it, what they'd been through was hardly funny. So why, all of a sudden, did she have this crazy desire to giggle?

Wiping the moisture from his eyes, Seth tried to maintain a serious expression. "Tell me, Maeve, how did you m-manage t-to k-keep the sheep in the wagon?" It was no use. The words kept bringing forth a mental picture of the ridiculous notion.

"Well!" she huffed. "When you're all through laughing like a hyena, maybe I'll tell you!"

"Come here," he growled, and despite the smell, despite the circumstances, his love for this crazy woman overflowed.

Her words came muffled against his chest. "I did manage to trade those sheep for two calves."

"Wonderful," Seth remarked, thinking not of her trade, but of how she felt snuggled next to him. Despite the cold temperature, a heady warmth claimed him. As he stroked her back and allowed her to continue the story, his fingers played with the buttons at the back of her dress.

Oops! One button came undone.

Where was Jeb? Would he allow them the privacy Seth wanted? With Maeve still chattering like a madwoman, he turned to look. Jeb had curled up into a small little ball and was fast asleep beside the fire. Good.

Stopping only to remove his blanket from the saddlebag, Seth guided Maeve further away from camp. He wondered if she'd even noticed since she continued to chatter about the damned sheep and someone named Mortimer Hawkins.

When he slid his hand beneath the fabric of her dress to stroke the warmth of her skin, her words faded to a soft moan of sheer delight.

Chapter Nineteen

While allowing Seth to place feathery kisses along her neck, Maeve couldn't help but ask a final question. "Seth, where is Pea?"

"With One Feather."

"But—"

"Shh," he mouthed, feeling the warmth of her lips against his own. This time, unlike their first time, the sense of urgency gave way to tender ministrations. Seth worked the buttons free until he reached the waistline of her dress. Standing back so that he could watch her response, Seth slowly lowered the dress over her shoulders. When her collarbone became exposed to the frigid air, he kissed the pulsing hollow at the base of her throat.

Running her fingers through his thick black hair, Maeve tingled with excitement. Her body seemed to act of its own accord as she leaned into him, feeling the hard swell between his legs against her throbbing delta. He continued to stoke the growing fire inside her veins as he pushed aside the fabric of her dress and caressed her sensitive nipples with his tongue. When he took a hardened peak into his mouth and suckled gently, Maeve moaned with sweet desire.

Seth drew back. He gazed deep into her eyes, seeing the flicker of passion in their hazel depths. Cradling her head between his large, work-roughened palms, he kissed her eyes, her nose, her cheeks until at last Maeve could stand it no longer.

She stood on tiptoe and wrapped her arms around his neck. Parting her lips, she was greedy with the need to taste him, to consume him. When he plunged his tongue into the warmth of her mouth, she eagerly responded.

Their sparring for position matched the unconscious thrust of Seth's hips as he pressed close against her.

The icy-cold sting of the frigid temperature hit Maeve's exposed skin while the fire of passion consumed her raging desire to have him inside her, filling her completely.

Seth slid his hands down the length of her sides, rested them for a moment against her waist, then with maddeningly slow patience, gathered the folds of her skirt in his hands as he pulled the material up to expose her legs.

Fumbling with the drawstring of her pantaloons that refused to give way proved to be his undoing. Seth grabbed her skirt where the buttons were still fastened together and ripped the fabric apart.

His animalistic action spurred a burning, insatiable need inside Maeve. She fumbled with the snaps of his britches until his manhood, now free of the constriction, sprang toward her grasping fingers. Stroking the length of his shaft, she managed to struggle out of the remaining portion of her skirt until nothing came between them but her thin cotton pantaloons.

On bended knee, Seth wrapped his arms around her waist and hugged her before using his teeth to pull the stubborn drawstring apart.

Maeve grabbed a handful of his jet-black hair and closed her eyes.

Sliding the material down to expose her silken nest, Seth kissed her outer thighs, dipped his tongue into the basin of her navel, then gently spread her legs apart.

When his tongue flickered over her sensitive nub, Maeve cried out with erotic pleasure. Seth held her as she collapsed against him.

Again he took her face between his hands and kissed her long and hard and deep. "I love you," he whispered huskily. "I love every part of you."

"Show me," Maeve moaned, writhing beneath his talented fingers. "Show me how much you love me." Her emotions whirled and skidded out of control as Seth lowered his head once more.

When she felt certain she'd die from sheer ecstasy, Seth positioned himself on top of her. And when he kissed her once more, the taste of her desire lingered on his lips. Her fingers curled involuntarily when he entered her wet, slick warmth, and Maeve dug her nails into his back, climbing higher and higher to reach that elusive pinnacle. Unable to express her joy, she felt tears dampen her cheeks. "I love you, Seth. I love you!" she cried as her passion exploded into a million glistening stars.

Seth thrust even deeper inside her, and when she wiggled away, his emotions plummeted back to earth. "Wha—"

"Let me show you how I love you, Seth. Lie still and let me show you." When he'd arranged himself on his back, Maeve hovered just above him, allowing the tips of her nipples to brush against his hair-roughened chest. He reached up to cup her breast, but she pushed his hand away.

As she blew softly against his exposed nipple, her hot breath brought an instant reaction. Again he reached up to touch her.

Again she stilled his hand.

Taking the hard tip of his nipple between her lips, she nipped playfully, then circled the area with her tongue. Ever so gently, she stroked back a lock of hair that had fallen across his forehead. "I love you, Seth. I love you here"— she kissed his lips—"and I love you here"—she nuzzled his neck—"I love you here." She kissed the left side of his chest where his heart pounded loudly.

Wiggling further down, she continued to verbalize her feelings, dipping her tongue into his navel before turning her attention to his muscled thighs. She placed tender kisses on either side of the portion that made him a man. Finally, her mouth mimicked the act their bodies had engaged in only minutes ago.

The pleasure she provided him was pure and explosive. Wrestling to pull her back along the length of his body, Seth nibbled at her lips before forcing them apart with his tongue. When she straddled him and guided his member into the entrance of her womanhood, Seth felt himself instantly cushioned in her heat. The sensation proved too much as he gave in to the hot tide exploding from his body.

Still joined together, Seth rolled over, sheltering her nakedness with his own. "My God, woman!"

As she reached up to stroke his face, Maeve smiled. "I take it that comment means it was good for you too."

He kissed her lightly. "If it were any better my heart would surely burst. You're beautiful, Maeve. Inside and out."

For the first time in her life, Maeve believed the words. She touched his cheek lightly, but felt the warmth of his soul.

Seth glanced up. With a sneaky grin, he quickly rolled over. From above the covering of trees, a mound of snow that had grown too heavy fell atop them.

Maeve let out a squeal a stuck pig would have

envied. After regaining control of her heartbeat, she smacked his shoulder with her fist. "That was cold and heartless, Seth Caldwell."

"I didn't know snow was supposed to have a heart," he teased.

Actually, Maeve was amazed that while the fat flakes had started to fall once more, she'd never even noticed. She'd been as warm in Seth's arms as if she'd been snuggled deep beneath the covers.

Seth brushed away a fleck of snow from her lashes. "I'll get our blanket," he offered as the cold air hit him full force.

"You're better than any old blanket." But Maeve didn't refuse him when he wrapped it around them. Tucking her head beneath his chin, she smiled as she reflected on her desire for him to show his gratitude over the sheep fiasco.

He'd passed the test with flying colors.

The night passed all too quickly for the two weary lovers. When Jeb jostled his father's shoulder to wake him, Seth was glad he'd thought ahead and donned his long johns before succumbing to sleep. Trying hard not to allow the cold air to creep beneath the covers as he rose, Seth motioned for Jeb to be quiet. "We'll let her sleep for a while longer while we fix breakfast."

"Then I hope you brought some vittles, Pa. Me and Maeve ate the remainder of what we brought with us last night."

"Tell you what, boy, you go get us a few more pieces of firewood and I'll see if I can't rustle us up a rabbit."

Jeb paused. "Pa . . . you know how Maeve feels about eating rabbits."

"Trust me, son, I have a feeling she's going to wake up hungry enough to eat a bear," Seth commented with a smile. So why, he wondered half an hour later, was he standing in the middle of an ice-cold stream trying to catch a trout? Just then, he spotted one. A nice-sized one at that. Using lightning-fast reflexes, Seth grabbed the tail and whisked it out of the water.

Success was sweet. Even sweeter when he'd succeeded in his accomplishment for the one he loved.

By the time he returned to the campfire, Jeb had a nice, roaring blaze. "Feels good, boy. You did a mighty fine job," Seth commented as he gutted the fish.

Jeb reached down and covered the entrails with a small mound of dirt. "Least it's not snowing anymore." He cast a sideways glance at his father. "That how come you and Maeve were sleeping together? 'Cause you were cold and all?"

The moment Seth had dreaded all of his son's life had come. But realizing this talk was bound to happen didn't make it any easier. He felt his face grow hot.

"I won't lie to you, son. The reason Maeve and I were sharing a bed was because—because . . . there was only one blanket." Well, it was a partial truth, anyway, Seth conceded.

Silence prevailed between the boy and his father as Jeb watched Seth cut the fish into small portions before lowering them into the hot skillet. He cleared his throat. "You love her, don't you, Papa?" Seeing the look of hesitation on his pa's face, Jeb grinned. "I think that's just dandy. She's something else again, ain't she, Pa?"

Glancing toward one of the odd-looking, bawling calves, Seth sighed. "Yep, son. She sure is at that!"

Jeb settled down on the ground and crossed his legs Indian fashion. "You loved Mama too, didn't you, Pa?"

Seth placed the fork he'd been using on an empty plate. "Yes, Jeb. I did."

Tears filled Jeb's eyes. "Why did she do it, Pa? Why'd she take such a risk? Surely she realized how dangerous it was."

It was hard to keep the bitterness out of his tone. Seth poured a cup of coffee and joined him, ruffling his hair. "Sometimes, boy, no matter what you try to do to please someone, it isn't enough. Your ma was like that. When we lived in town, she'd complain about how filthy that type of life-style was. She loved you kids a lot and didn't want you to grow up around foul-mouthed miners."

"But she didn't love us enough to want to live," Jeb stated quietly, silent tears rolling down his cheeks.

"Son, I don't believe your mama's mind was right. Surely you remember how different she acted after we finally recovered from that big snowstorm, don't you? She just wasn't the same person at all."

Jeb nodded, recollecting his own feelings of torture at having to remain inside for such a long period of time. He'd thought the snow would never end.

"Your mama craved excitement—that was what attracted me to her in the first place," Seth explained gently. "I'm partly to blame for her unhappiness, Jeb, and I'm willing to admit that. See, boy, it takes two to make an unhappy marriage just as it takes two to make a happy one. When I moved her to Sweetbriar, I thought I was protecting her. As it turned out, I ostracized her from the very people she found repulsive. What I didn't realize was that Duessa needed to be with people, needed the excitement of city living just as much as I needed the solitude of our land.

"But instead of talking to me and telling me the truth, she turned bitter. It was easier to find fault with me than it was for her to look inside herself and realize had she told me how she felt, I would have understood." It felt good to finally sort out his feelings aloud. Even better to be sharing such intimate, painful observations with his son.

"Maeve says bitterness is like taking poison."

"Maeve is right," Seth agreed. "Bitterness is what helped drive your mama clean out of her mind."

"So do you love Maeve, Pa?"

Meeting his son's intense gaze, Seth nodded. "Yes I do, Jeb. I love her very much."

"Life sure is a lot more fun with her around, ain't it?" Suddenly, Jeb threw himself into his astonished father's arms. "Don't let her leave us, please, Pa," he pleaded in desperation. "Make her stay. Just make her stay."

Realization brought forth a feeling of grief. "I can't do that, Jeb. I figure what God gives us is his to lay claim to whenever he decides he wants it back."

Seth stroked his son's head, waiting for the tears to stop.

Jeb's next question caught him off guard. "Pa, what's it like to love a woman?"

Thoughts of last night tumbled through his mind, bringing a smile to his lips. "It's the best feeling in the world, Jeb. It's—"

"Oh, Seth!" Maeve called.

He turned.

"Could you come here for a second?"

Seth shrugged at his son. "You tend to the fish; I'll be back in a minute."

A shy expression matched his inquisitive gaze as he knelt down beside her. "Yes, love?"

Oh God, he called me love! Last night wasn't a dream—and it's a good thing too! How else can I explain the absence of my clothes?

"I seem to be in dire need of clothing. If you'll remember last night—"

Seth touched her cheek, trailing his fingers down to caress the base of her throat. "Oh, I remember all about last night. Every single detail."

She giggled softly before cautioning him to be quiet. "Jeb'll hear you," she whispered.

"I think Jeb understands more than I'm willing to give him credit for."

"Well, no sense in completing his education all at once," Maeve countered. "Now then. What am I supposed to do about clothes?"

"Didn't you bring an extra set?"

"Of course not. I'm not exactly experienced in outdoor life, you know—not that I'm complaining or anything."

A smile tipped the corners of his mouth. "Are you saying you'd be willing to camp out again?"

"Depends on who I'm camped out with. Now if it's an experienced fellow like yourself, well, I'd consider it a lesson in learning."

"Hmm, but that doesn't take care of your lack of clothes this morning, now does it?" Seth asked.

Maeve drew the covers even closer. "Nope. Got any suggestions?"

Seth turned and studied Jeb's slight frame. "Hey son," he called. "Did you bring an extra pair of britches with you, by any chance?"

"Sure I did, Pa."

"Would you be willing to loan them to Maeve?"

"What happened to her dress?"

"I, uh, I—" Maeve stammered to come up with an appropriate response.

"The smell was so bad I burned it," Seth interjected. He glanced down at Maeve. "It really did smell, you know. The last time I caught a whiff of something that bad was when I surprised a skunk out by the smokehouse."

"But did you really burn my clothes?"

"Of course not," Seth admitted, while reaching beneath the cover to tweak her breast. "I buried them so the odor wouldn't intrude on our night of passion." He fell silent as Jeb brought over the extra pair of britches and a shirt.

"I'll never be able to fit in these," Maeve moaned. "They're way too small!"

"Jeb and I will turn our backs to allow you privacy. Come along, son."

How embarrassing! Now Seth would surely realize how fat she was! She wouldn't be able to fit her knee into that small opening, let alone her whole leg.

Maeve gaped in disbelief as she pulled the pants up over her knees, her thighs, and finally her hips.

"But I won't be able to button them," she muttered. "I just know I—Oh, my gosh!" She screamed with delight. "Look at this, you guys, would you take a look at this? Why there's room enough for another person—okay, that's a slight exaggeration—but there is a space between the waistband and me, just look!"

With a shake of his head, Seth looked at his son. "Women," he murmured.

"Women," Jeb echoed.

"Speaking of females . . ." Seth grinned. "You

best get those odd-looking calves tied to the back of the wagon, son. I figure it's time we head for home and rescue One Feather from the clutches of your little sister!"

Chapter Twenty

On the way home, Seth tried to explain the details about Blossom's disappearance. Maeve only half listened. The smell of her lover, all woodsy and fresh and clean, kept distracting her. When Jeb lost patience with their slow pace, he ventured ahead. When they were alone at last, she rubbed her hand up and down Seth's thigh, feeling the sinewy muscles twitch as he maneuvered the wagon and horses.

"Stop that, Maeve," Seth said when her caresses caused a painful reaction between his legs. "You're not paying me a bit of attention, are you?"

"Of course I am. I heard every word you said. I'm supposed to be real nice to One Feather and not hurt his feelings when I turn down his proposal."

Susan Collier

"It goes much deeper than that. To hurt an Indian's pride is to invite trouble."

"I can't understand why he wants to marry me." Maeve cuddled closer, squeezing Seth's arm in a passionate love hold. "What on earth can I possibly have that he finds attractive?"

"It's not you," Seth stated. He glanced down at the woman beside him, wondering if he'd hurt her feelings. "Of course," he added quickly, "any man in his right mind would find you attractive, but we both know One Feather isn't the average man." He flicked the reins and guided the horses around a cove of trees. "It's the, uh, gift he's after."

Genuinely perplexed, Maeve frowned. "What gift?"

"The gift of traveling . . . you know, through the clouds?" He couldn't understand why she suddenly seemed pleased and hugged him so fiercely. Lands, the woman was about to cut off his supply of oxygen.

"Then you believe me! You believe what I told you about traveling through time!" Joy had completely taken over her senses. It was so important to her that Seth realize she hadn't been lying. Their relationship could now be based on trust; one of the most important ingredients in making love last forever, Maeve knew.

"I've always believed in you, Maeve. You know that."

"Oh, but this is so different!" She sighed and squeezed his knee. "Now that you know I didn't lie to you about how I came to be here, you'll

288

trust me with everything else."

Just then, one of the calves started bawling loudly. Seth glanced over his shoulder. "Well, not everything." He laughed. "I think from here on, *I'll* be the one to do the trading."

Maeve grabbed his arm, nearly causing him to drop the reins. When he admonished her to be careful, she giggled. "I'm sorry, I just can't keep my hands off you." But she'd noticed his discreet glance at the two animals tied to the wagon. He'd been severely disappointed with her trade, no doubt about it.

"Seth, about the cows. Did you ever have something happen and know that no matter how silly your decision seemed at that moment, the outcome is going to be simply wonderful?"

Trailing his fingers over the rough fabric of her britches, Seth smiled. "I have. From the moment I first saw you, I knew my life would never be the same."

Maeve experienced a thrill of delight at his pronouncement, knowing he wasn't the type of man to say something if he didn't honestly feel it. Still, the insecurities of her past forced her to question him. "Not even when I couldn't make Gracie well?" she asked quietly.

Although the words held sadness, Seth was quick to respond. "Not even then."

As Maeve chattered, Seth contemplated their future together. A niggling in his heart caused the lines of fatigue around his eyes to deepen. The woman beside him reminded him of an elusive butterfly. Beautiful to behold but when kept in captivity, the resplendent creature withered away.

Would the harsh life-style she'd be forced to endure be her ruination? As much as he wanted to keep her by his side for the rest of their lives, if there was any chance her spirit would be destroyed as Duessa's had been, he'd rather her leave. To go back to where she'd come from.

The thought caused a pitiful ache deep in his gut. How could he go on living? How could he survive such a loss? Seth draped an arm around Maeve's waist and hugged her tight.

In response, she snuggled close. "Oh, Seth, it's going to be so nice to get home and have things settle down a bit. I never realized how *active* the 1800s could be!"

"Perhaps my absence will give you time to rest. I promised my new neighbor, John Peck, I'd go help him build a barn before the harsh winter sets in."

Dusting a few stray flakes of snow from his jacket, Maeve grinned. "That sounds like fun! Count me in."

"Um, Maeve, I don't quite know how to say this without hurting your feelings, but it's very unusual for a woman to come along. It puts a burden on the family to provide for extra mouths. Besides, it would be rather hard to explain our relationship, wouldn't it? How could we tell them we're living under the same roof without the benefit of a marriage certificate?"

"Aww, Seth! I don't want to stay all by myself. I'd miss you so much and I—"

"I'm afraid this is the way it's going to have to be, Maeve."

Hmm. The old-fashioned ways of 'woman keeps mouth shut while man makes decision' has finally caught up with me. Running one finger between the fabric of his shirt and chest, Maeve frowned. "Aren't you going to miss me something terrible?" *Please, please tell me you will.*

Seth placed his hand on her knee and smiled. "I will at that! But haven't you heard the expression 'absence makes the heart grow fonder'?"

"My heart can't grow any fonder than it already is!" she exclaimed with a kiss to his cheek.

"I'll be back before you know I'm gone," Seth promised.

His vow was lost to Maeve, who concentrated instead on an odd sound. "Do you hear that, Seth?"

He listened and heard nothing. "What?"

"This is going to seem ridiculous, but I swear I hear the sound of a ticking clock. Listen!" she admonished. "See if you can hear it too."

Though he tried, Seth heard nothing but the sound of melting snow dripping from the trees. "I hear the snow melting; is that what you're talking about?"

"Mmm, I guess so." Although his explanation seemed reasonable enough, Maeve couldn't shake the sudden tremor of apprehension gripping her heart. Why did she get the feeling time had suddenly turned against her? Was it because she wasn't used to feeling this happy?

This satisfied with life? That must be it, she decided. She changed the subject back to their original one. "I just don't understand why I can't go with you."

Seth allowed her to grumble, no longer listening to the words, but instead concentrating on the sound of her voice. Even when unhappy, her tone carried a musical lilt.

Having ridden ahead, Jeb now circled back to meet the wagon. "Guess everything's okay, Pa. I seen smoke rising from the chimney."

"Either that or Pea's set fire to One Feather," Seth stated with a wry grin.

Worry lines creased Maeve's brows. "What exactly am I supposed to tell One Feather?" she questioned.

Seth patted her knee in consoling fashion. "Tell him you're my woman and you plan to stay that way."

"H-he won't kidnap me or anything, will he?"

"Of course not. One Feather is a reasonable man. Just be careful not to wound his pride when turning him down."

After Seth had reined the horses to a halt, Maeve allowed him to help her from the wagon. She was immediately accosted by two small arms wrapping themselves around her legs.

"You home!" Pea squealed with delight. "Oh Maeve, me and One Fedder have had sooooo much fun! I've taught him how to dance like you showed me and now he knows all the words to 'Jailhouse Rock' and everything! I want to keep him, Maeve, please can we keep him?"

Maeve knelt down and picked her up, hugging Blossom tightly. She was overwhelmed by the deep feelings of maternalism this little girl provoked in her heart. "Gosh, I've missed you, kiddo. As soon as I've talked to One Feather in private, you have to promise to tell me all about your adventure."

Pea twisted a lock of Maeve's hair around her fingers. "But can we keep him?"

"I don't think so, baby. I'm sure One Feather has a family of his own who needs him—"

"Huh-uh. He ain't got nobody, Maeve. He told me so himself."

Seth gently removed his daughter from Maeve's embrace. "I've told you before, Pea. You can't *keep* a human being. They're not like a doll or a pet."

Giant tears washed over Blossom's blue eyes. "But Pa," she whined.

"Come help me with the horses; you know how you like to groom them."

"You gonna let me do it all by meself, Pa?"

"All by yourself."

Blossom considered his offer. "Well . . ."

"All by yourself," Seth stated again, trying not to laugh at her serious contemplation.

"Okay, then." She turned to Maeve. "You won't let One Fedder leave before I git back, will you?"

"Of course not," Maeve promised. "Besides, he wouldn't want to go without telling you good-bye."

As she walked into the cabin, however, One

Feather's expression told a different story. He looked as if he'd been involved in a monthlong war party and came out on the losing side of the battle.

His response to the challenges of baby-sitting helped calm Maeve's racing pulse and served to remind her he was a human being with normal feelings and not someone to be feared. "Hello, One Feather. I'd like to thank you for taking such good care of Blossom while we were away."

The Indian nodded and tried to focus his slightly crossed eyes on the woman before him. "One Feather wait many long, long days for the return of Woman Who Walks On Cloud."

"I know you did," Maeve sympathized. She tried to find a diplomatic way to bring up the subject of marriage. "It's hard taking care of children. Somehow, though, when they're a part of your family, the challenge is easier."

"For you this is easy?"

"With Blossom?"

"I call her Golden Hair," the brave corrected.

Maeve strolled over to the rocking chair and sat down. "You know, that's one thing I always did admire about your people. You come up with some of the most colorful names!" She paused for a moment. The fire crackled as a log fell against the back of the fireplace. "But One Feather," Maeve gently insisted, "You named me wrong. I don't walk on clouds. No one can do that."

"Woman Who Walks On Cloud speak with

294

forked tongue. One Feather knows what he sees"—he struck his chest with unnecessary force—"here, in heart. Why your tongue refuse to speak truth?"

Oh hell! Now what do I say? Biting her lip, Maeve struggled for the words to explain. She placed her hand over her own heart. "My heart was empty, One Feather. And I needed someone to fill it with love. The need became so great that I was given a gift for a brief moment in time. That's when I slipped through the boundaries of common understanding and came to be here. But I didn't walk on any cloud to do it. Something greater than us put me here."

"The Great Spirit," One Feather stated.

"Call it what you will. All I know is I'm here and I'm happier than I've ever been in my life." There, it was done. Surely he'd understand that concept.

"Many fine horses make you happier," One Feather insisted.

Okay, she was wrong! "Nothing could make me happier than Seth," she gently explained. "Though I'm honored you wish to offer me such a fine gift, I have all I'll ever need or want as long as I have him."

The hopeful look on the Indian's face was replaced by misery. "One Feather never learn to walk on clouds if Woman Who Walks On Cloud refuses to teach."

"I did not walk on a cloud!" Maeve insisted.

"Did."

"Didn't!" she exploded. "Just what is it that

you saw, One Feather? Was it a vision? Was it a dream? Explain it to me."

"One Feather received instructions from Great Spirit to fast for four days. To do this, I leave family and go high into mountains where no man walk before. I close my eyes and see vision of woman with dark hair. Her eyes make water and she cry out in agony. When God of Sky Fire lift his mighty hand, he carry her into clouds. There she stay until the Great Spirit allow her to come back to earth."

Caught up in the story, Maeve's eyes grew round. "He did?"

One Feather nodded.

As if suddenly becoming aware of what she'd set out to do, Maeve rose and walked toward the sad brave. Placing her hand on his arm, she spoke softly and tenderly. "One Feather, I believe with all my heart that just as the Great Spirit directed me to Seth, he will one day direct you to a woman who will be able to return your feelings. Please try to understand, if I were to leave with you, it would be like telling the Great Spirit he was wrong when he placed me where Seth could find me."

The Indian appeared to be contemplating her words. Finally he spoke. "Great Spirit never wrong."

"That's right," Maeve answered quietly.

One Feather's spirits lifted. "You teach me to walk on cloud without marriage?"

Maeve shook her head. "I'm sorry, One Feather, but I don't know how."

"Oh."

Oh? That was it? After the duress of racking her brain for the right words, his answer was 'oh'? She watched him gather his belongings. He seemed so disappointed. Maeve couldn't let him leave this way. "One Feather, my advice to you is to learn to listen with your heart and not your ears. When the day comes, you'll find the happiness you've been searching for. I just know you will."

"Listen to her, my good and faithful friend," Seth added. "Her words are truth."

Maeve turned. The sight of her lover standing discreetly in the doorway filled her with a bottomless peace and satisfaction.

Oh, Elvis, I've finally found the man that loves me tender, loves me true!

Chapter Twenty-one

As her gaze swept over Seth, Maeve realized his hands were tightly clenched at his sides as if prepared for battle. Only when One Feather brushed past him did his fingers unfurl. "Whew!" she breathed.

Seth smiled. "I'm sorry that was such an ordeal, but he had to hear the rejection from your lips in order to believe you weren't interested in his proposal."

"Rejection hurts, Seth. Do you think he'll be okay?"

Having grown accustomed to her strange dialect, Seth understood completely. His grin widened. "I think he'll be better than okay. I think he'll be just fine."

"I wish I could say the same about me!" Maeve exclaimed. "Every bone in my body is crying out for relief. I've never been so sore in all my life."

Striding toward her with purposeful steps, Seth's eyes darkened with passion. He turned her around and began to massage her shoulder muscles with the pads of his thumbs. When she sighed and arched her neck, he placed a tender kiss on the exposed area. "How would you like a nice hot bath?"

Maeve closed her eyes. "I'd love one," she admitted.

"I'll go fetch the tub." The gentle touch of her hand on his caused Seth to pause.

"Wait." She turned toward him, searching his rugged features, his crystal blue eyes, as if memorizing every detail. "Seth, thank you for everything. Thank you for taking me into your home, thank you for your understanding, your warmth, but most of all, thank you for your love." Maeve placed a tender kiss upon his warm, moist lips. "I never thought I'd find someone like you. Ever. And now that I have, I just want you to know how grateful I am." She nestled her head against his chest.

"What prompted you to such a heartfelt speech?" Seth questioned, stroking her hair.

She shook her head, unable to voice her emotions.

As soon as the last dinner dish was washed, Seth brought in the large tub. "Shall I warm your water?"

"No, thanks. I'll do it. Poor old Jeb nearly fell

asleep at dinner. I sent him to bed. But Pea's been asking for you. I think her adventure has finally caught up with her and she's overtired."

"I'll tell her a story," Seth answered. "That usually calms her down when nothing else will."

After filling the tub full of hot, steaming water, Maeve drew the curtain Seth had thoughtfully provided to allow her privacy. Quickly stripping, she stepped into the water and with a bit of ingenious maneuvering, managed to lie back. Though her legs hung over the edge at an awkward angle, it was well worth it when the heated water began to ease her aching joints.

She closed her eyes and listened to Seth's gravelly tone as he put emotion into the story he read to Pea. Could she be any happier than she was at this very moment? Definitely not. Though contentment had been a long time in coming to her life, the wait had been worth it. The outcome was pure satisfaction, she decided, rubbing the small bar of soap over her body.

Her mind drifted to the conversation she'd had with One Feather. Poor Indian! He deserved to find his own happiness.

Seth's proud features, the look of love in his eyes as he took her in his arms floated to memory. Dear Lord, how she loved this man. How she wanted desperately to make him as happy as he'd made her . . . but how? What could she do to fulfill his every dream, his every desire?

The image of a clock arose . . . ticking . . .

301

ticking. . . . time running out. . . . No, please, God, no.

A soft shudder stole over her body. What was happening to her newfound joy? Her feelings of peace and contentment?

Pea's delighted laughter stole into her chilled heart and Maeve couldn't suppress a smile. The sound brought a much-needed soothing effect to her shattered nerves.

Maeve wanted nothing more than to be out there with them, lying on the straw-ticked bed and watching Seth's facial expressions as he wove a silly tale about a magic garden with animals that talked.

After donning one of Duessa's nightgowns, she drew the curtain aside and watched the blissful scene for a moment before joining in. When she glanced at the small book in Seth's hands, Maeve scooted in beside him, reading words that didn't match his animated story.

Miss Maribell took his hand and placed it on her breast. Her voice low and husky, she invited Barnaby Jacobs to sample the fruit of her garden.

What? Maeve read further.

Barnaby lifted Miss Maribell's skirts and felt her nearly swoon with delight.

Maeve glanced up at Seth. She noticed his eyes weren't focused on the printed words, but instead were concentrating on Pea's reactions.

He hadn't turned a page since she'd joined them. Why would he hold the book as if he were reading from it when he wasn't?

It took every ounce of patience she possessed to wait until Pea had finally fallen asleep before questioning him.

Maeve waited until Seth joined her beside the fire. She held out the novel. "Read this page to me, would you please?"

His hands trembled ever so slightly as he glanced at the book. Seth cleared his throat. "Maeve, I—"

"You what?" she asked softly.

"I-I—"

"Do you know what kind of book this is, Seth?" Maeve questioned, watching him as he took the novel from her hands and studied it without saying a word.

Finally he met her gaze, anguish written in his eyes. "I never learned to read."

"How come?" The concept was something she simply couldn't understand. Why, to read a book was to escape into a fantasy world, to forget for a while her own problems as she concentrated on an imaginary life.

"I don't know," Seth replied, clearly uncomfortable with the issue. "The words never seemed to make sense to me." He cleared his throat, giving voice to painful memories. "It was important to my father that his boys have an education. Somehow I never mastered the art like my brother and sister did. Because of that, I was labeled a simpleton."

Susan Collier

Taking the book from his hand, Maeve flipped through the pages. She opened it wide, feeling the binding crack as she smoothed the paper with her hands. "I want you to try. Do you know any words at all?"

"Some," he admitted. God, why couldn't she leave this alone? Didn't she realize how ashamed he felt?

"Then read this sentence to me," Maeve insisted, pointing to a paragraph with her finger.

"He . . . grobed her . . . brast. . . . "

"He grabbed her breast," Maeve corrected. "Seth, can you write?"

"I can sign my name."

"Do it."

"Why?" he demanded, growing increasingly agitated. "I wish you'd just let this rest. I—"

"Do it," she insisted again as she grabbed one of Jeb's papers and a well-worn pencil. "Here, write it." She watched the muscle of his jaw flicker as he concentrated.

When Seth was finished, he flung it toward her. "Here. Are you satisfied?"

"Not quite. Now then." She pointed to the book. "Copy this word on the paper as your eye sees it."

Barely able to control his rising fury, Seth glared at her a moment before obeying her instruction. "There. Are you satisfied now, Miss Maeve?"

A small tremor of excitement flashed through Maeve's body. "It's just as I suspected. Seth, the reason you can't read the words is because your brain doesn't see them the way mine does."

He slammed his fist against the table, causing Maeve to flinch. "I see! So you're accusing me of being a simpleton too?"

Placing her hand on his arm to quiet his rage, Maeve shook her head. "Oh no, Seth! That's not what I meant at all!" She studied him for a moment, seeing the look of defeat in his eyes, and her heart went out to him. "Oh, Seth, there's no shame in not knowing how to do something. Especially when a person has a learning disability—"

When Seth cringed inwardly, she saw dismay in his expression and rushed to finish her statement. ". . . such as yours," Maeve finished quietly, feeling his arm stiffen beneath her fingers. "The real pity about this situation is that you gave up. You allowed your parents to make you feel like a fool with their harsh judgments against you. In my time, your condition is called dys—"

"I've heard enough," Seth replied, cutting her off with clipped words and a stony look. He jerked his arm away, rubbing the area she'd touched as if she'd burned him with her fingertips. Turning his back to her, he grappled with the words. "All my life I've been pitied. I certainly don't want yours. Save it for someone who does."

Maeve rushed toward him, reaching out to touch his shoulder. Her heart plummeted when he remained unyielding. "You misunderstood, Seth, I—"

"Save it." As he turned to face her, his eyes were filled with fury. "I thought you were different from the rest of them. I thought you honestly cared, but you didn't, did you? You pity me. It's not love you feel for me, is it, Maeve? It's pity."

With a knot the size of a baseball in her throat, Maeve swallowed hard. Tears filled her eyes, blurring her vision. "If you honestly believe that, then you don't know me as well as I thought you did."

"Perhaps I don't," Seth agreed frostily.

The silence was like the sharp end of a knife, stabbing and painful. Finally Maeve turned away, refusing to allow him to see her cry. She stared at the fire, the wood glowing orange. Blinking back hot tears, she wrapped her arms around her waist. When Seth spoke, she jumped.

"Do something about your clothes. I'm tired of seeing you in Duessa's outfits."

"Trust me, I'd like to," she replied. "But I never learned to sew."

"What? Miss Know-it-all is confessing she actually doesn't know how to do something?" Seth retorted, wanting to hurt her, wanting to make her feel his pain. He knew he'd succeeded when her shoulders slumped, and he was almost sorry. Almost.

"I— I'm g-going to bed," Maeve managed brokenly. How could he waste their time together like this? The realization was too much to bear as she inwardly admitted what her mind refused to let her forget—the chilling image of the clock moving forward, forward, tick after tick after tick.

Time was indeed running out.

When Seth announced he'd be sleeping in the barn, Maeve wanted to beg him not to. Her pride stood in the way. "Fine," she responded. And when the door slammed shut, the tears began to fall.

Chapter Twenty-two

Maeve sniffed back her sobs and listened to the sound of the cabin settling. The wind rustled the branches of the trees just outside the door. She heard the soft nicker of a horse, footsteps, then the cabin door creak as it opened.

In the murky darkness, she strained to watch Seth climb up to the loft to awaken Jeb. She heard his soft whisper of instructions and watched him climb back down. Through slitted eyes, she observed him walk toward her, straighten the covers, then pause before turning away.

Distress caused her eyes to fill. So he was going to leave without saying good-bye, huh? Well, so be it then! If he thought for one little minute *she* was going to come crawling on hands and knees to apologize for something *he* misunderstood, he was . . .

Dead right.

Maeve threw back the covers and ran to the door. The chill of the early morning air sent goose flesh tingling over her bare arms. "Seth, wait!"

In the ensuing silence all she could hear was the echo of the horse's hoofs as it faded in the distance.

"Damn." She turned, seeking warmth from the embers of the fireplace. As she stirred the glowing ashes, Seth's expression from last night's argument haunted her memory. "Damn," she softly repeated.

From her trundle bed, Pea raised up. "Maeve? Is you all right?"

"I'm fine, baby. Go back to sleep."

"You was crying last night. I heared you," Pea responded. "How come you was crying?"

Tiny little footsteps padded toward Maeve. She held out her arms and allowed Pea to crawl into her lap. Slowly rocking the sleepy child, Maeve watched the flames lick higher and higher before disappearing up the chimney.

Much like my dreams, she mused. All my hopes of a happy future with Seth have burned to ashes.

No. She wouldn't, couldn't allow this to happen. Okay, so he was prideful. So he was thick-headed and stubborn and headstrong and warm and wonderful—and her perfect mate, she realized, blinking back new tears.

Would he forgive her? Only if he understood.

And how could he do that being God knows where while here she sat, alone?

Maeve tried to remember if he'd actually forbidden her to join him. No, no . . . he hadn't come right out and said no. If food was the problem, she realized she could cook up a storm today and take a sampling of everything the pantry contained with her.

Why, of course she could! That would be the neighborly thing to do! Yes, she'd bake a cake and a ham and anything else she could get her hands on! Once he saw how thoughtful she could be, Seth would be pleased! He'd be . . . angry as hell, Maeve admitted silently. But not any angrier than he'd been last night, she reasoned. So why not? Why not indeed!

Long before the light of day crept across the sky, Maeve had given up on the idea of gaining any more rest. After rocking Pea, she placed her in the bed and lit a lantern, carrying it into the small kitchen.

As she attempted to make biscuits, the decision she'd reached swung back and forth in her mind like a pendulum.

Yes, I should go. . . . No, I shouldn't go.

This is nuts! Maeve thought. I am a woman of the eighties. I'm perfectly capable of reaching a decision on my own and sticking to it. "So I'm going. No, no, I'm not. Oh shoot! Let's face it, I'm a woman of the 1880s. Not that they're not quite capable of making their own decisions, it's just that the men are so different in this time. So dadblasted male."

She glared at the biscuit dough. "I hope you're enjoying having this delightful little conversation with me." Sprinkling a handful of dry flour atop the counter, she stared thoughtfully. "Too bad you can't give me some type of coded message as to what to do."

It was no use wishing. Flour was flour, Maeve realized and swept the small scattering into a pile.

Gathering the many folds of her gown close to her body, Maeve walked over to the fireplace and watched the dying embers. She grabbed a poker and halfheartedly attempted to stoke the fire. "Oh, Duessa . . . where are you when I need to talk to you?" The absurdity hit hard and Maeve laughed. "Well, I doubt very seriously an angel would be found anywhere near fire, now would she? It'd scorch her wings for sure."

After a long while of deliberating and being unable to reach a decision she felt comfortable with, Maeve went back to her baking. Even if she didn't go to visit Seth, Pea might appreciate hot, fresh biscuits for breakfast.

When Pea finally awakened, it was to the smell of burning dough. "Ick, Maeve. Something stinks!"

"I know," Maeve wailed, wiping tears of frustration from her eyes. "This is my fifth attempt at biscuits." She glanced down at her nightshift in dismay. "I have more flour on my clothes than I do in the bowl!"

"I kin help," came the small voice beside her.

Raising her brows, Maeve looked dubious. "Oh yeah?"

"Sure I kin. Mama taught me how." Pea scooted Maeve out of the way and looked at the bowl of flour. "You isn't got enough bacon grease in here."

Somewhat taken aback, she watched as Pea made her way around the kitchen better than Julia Child. And when the little girl's biscuits were finally baking, a wonderful aroma filled the small cabin.

"Blossom, I gotta hand it to you, you're a life-saver!"

"What's that?"

"Never mind," Maeve said with a chuckle. She picked Pea up and held her close. When the child drew back to play with a lock of Maeve's hair, she studied her serious expression. "Why, Pea! You look like you're about to cry!"

"Just my eyes is."

"Why, honey?"

"I want my P-Papa," Pea whimpered.

Maeve drew her in for a hug. "I know how you feel. I want him too! Tell you what let's do. We'll go surprise him with a visit, won't that be fun?"

"That's what the angel told me to tell you."

"Do what?"

"I dreamed about this angel. Ooooo, Maeve, her was sooooo pretty! Her looked just like Mama and her said to go to Daddy and make him happy."

313

"Oh Pea! Whatever are we waiting for, then?"

"You to get dressed?" Pea questioned earnestly. "Maeve?"

"What honey?"

"Papa's gonna be happy we comed to see him, ain't he?"

God, I hope so, Maeve prayed inwardly. A wonderful thought struck her. "You wouldn't happen to know where my yellow dress is, would you? The dress you and One Feather were playing with?"

"Mmm-hmm," Pea said, walking to the closet. "Pa hung it right in here real careful like. Him said it was your weddin' dress."

With knees the consistency of Jello, Maeve blinked. "What did you just say?"

Pea heaved a large sigh. "I *said*, Pa hung it right—"

"No, no," Maeve interrupted. "I mean the part about the wedding dress."

Placing her hands on her waist in exasperation, Pea swung her hips back and forth. "I *said*, Pa said it was your weddin' dress."

She put her hand over her heart and sank into the rocker. "Are you sure that's what he said, Pea?"

"Mmm-hmm."

Hours later, dressed in the beautiful yellow dress, Maeve faced her second crisis when she opened the door to the barn. "They took the wagon!" she screeched.

"They done left us Matilda, though," Pea reasoned.

"Oh, Pea! I've never ridden a horse before! I don't think I can!"

Pea scoffed. "Yes, you can! All you gotta do is saddle her up and git on. It's fun, Maeve. You go bumpity-bump, bumpity-bump," she reasoned in a singsong voice. "It's fun! Really it is!"

The horse turned its head at the sound of Pea's singing. Maeve bit her lip. "I don't suppose you know how to saddle a horse, do you?"

"Nope!" Pea pronounced, busy swinging back and forth on the gate.

Closing her eyes, Maeve tried to replay every Western she'd ever seen on television. The cowboy always sort of swung the saddle over the horse's back. She could do that . . . maybe.

After successfully accomplishing the first step, Maeve stood back. Something was missing, but what? And were those straps really supposed to just dangle from the animal's stomach like that? "Where's the hold-on thingie, Pea?"

Blossom set free a bug that she'd trapped in her fist. "Don't know," she answered. "But ya gotta fasten them straps, else Matilda'll trip and down she'll go," the child advised, twirling round and round until she fell on her bottom with a plop.

Crawling on hands and knees, Maeve maneuvered herself beneath the horse. The animal grew skittish and one hoof came precariously close to her head. Oh, horsefeathers!"

A delighted giggled filled the air. "Horses ain't

got feathers, Maeve. Them's chickens! You want me to go getcha a handful?"

"No, no," Maeve muttered, finally managing to secure the strap around the horse's stomach. She crawled out from under the animal's belly and stood, dusting the dirt off her outfit. At this rate, they'd never reach the Peck farm.

Oh hell! Just where in tarnation is the Peck farm?

She watched Pea skip toward her with a handful of feathers from a poor helpless chicken. "Uh, Blossom, do you know where the Pecks live?"

"Yep!"

It wasn't until they'd circled the same tree six times, had to stop and right the leaning saddle three times, and take care of Blossom's needs twice, that Pea announced it was the forest fairies that had told her how to reach their destination.

Maeve realized the situation was hopeless. She'd never see Seth again. They were doomed, that's what they were, simply doomed. She walked over to a rock and sat down, watching as Pea happily danced among the trees.

As she tried to look on the bright side, Maeve gave thanks for the fairly warm day and cloudless sky. The sound of the silent forest was broken by a *whack-whack-whack* as someone felled a tree.

The sound was sweeter than Elvis suddenly

appearing to sing Maeve's all-time favorite, "Suspicious Minds."

How apropos! she thought with a grin as the words to the song flooded her memory.

Chapter Twenty-three

When they rode through the clearing, Maeve spotted Seth with his back toward her as he chopped wood. All of a sudden the idea that had seemed so wonderful back at the cabin didn't seem like such a good choice anymore. She watched as a petite, brown-haired woman approached the man working beside Seth and placed a hand on his arm.

"Why, look, John, more guests have arrived," Sarah Peck announced softly.

Both men looked up.

Filled with misgivings, Maeve bit her lip and observed Seth's reaction as they rode closer. When she was finally able to get the horse to stop, Pea slid down from the saddle, leaving her to face three sets of curious eyes.

"Come join us, won't you?" Sarah offered.

"I-I—" Oh boy, the look on Seth's face was not a positive sign. No sirree! "Uh, sure," she answered, glancing back at Sarah. As she handed down the picnic basket, Maeve smiled nervously. "I brought some food."

"How kind of you!" Sarah exclaimed.

"Yes," John agreed. "But I can assure you it wasn't really necessary. The Lord has been generous to us this year."

Maeve's smile faltered as she remembered Seth's words. So they'd be a burden to the family, huh? Maybe what he'd meant to say was she would be a burden to him!

By the time he reached her side, Maeve had already managed to dismount. He raised an eyebrow as if to demand explanation.

"Hello, Seth. Pea and I were lonely back at the cabin. We thought, uh, maybe we could lend a hand or something."

Realizing a storm was about to break between the couple, Sarah wisely backed away, murmuring niceties about the food.

As if to defend her decision, Maeve muttered, "I brought food. . . . "

Suddenly Seth's expression changed. He smiled. "I'm glad you came."

Staring at the pebbles on the ground, Maeve found she couldn't speak over the lump in her throat. When Seth reached out and tilted her chin so that she would be forced to make eye contact, she felt a hot blush stain her cheeks.

"You're wearing the dress I purchased for you. You look lovely in it."

"Thanks," she managed as he placed his hand on her shoulder. "Seth . . . about last night . . ."

"Last night I was being foolish."

"You were?"

"I was."

"So you're not angry with me anymore?"

As he drew her close for a hug, Seth smiled. "No, I'm not angry anymore. As a matter of fact, I owe you an apology. I acted like an ass."

He smelled so good! Like wood and earth and sunshine. Closing her eyes, Maeve returned his embrace with fervor. "No, you didn't," she argued. "I should have been more understanding. I—"

Seth interrupted. "I'm just glad you came."

She drew back, her eyes glistening with unshed tears. "You are?"

"Yes." He sighed deeply. "I realized when we rode away without saying good-bye this morning that I would miss you. I thought about waking you, but—"

"I was already awake," Maeve interrupted. "I saw you hesitate; I wanted to say something—as a matter of fact, I ran to the door, hoping to stop you, but you'd already ridden too far. I guess you didn't hear me."

"If I had, I would have gladly circled back," he answered.

"You would?" Suddenly the inches separating them seemed like miles, and Maeve flung her body against his, reveling in the warmth of his solid chest. "Oh, Seth," she blubbered, "I never want to hurt you and I'm sorry if it seemed as

321

though I was offering you pity when all I meant was I can teach you to read and I love you and I don't ever want to fight again!" The words all blended together, tumbling one atop the other. She took a deep breath to try to regain control. "I love you, Seth. I love you with all my heart and soul and . . ." The words to describe her feelings simply weren't to be found.

Seth tried to be helpful. "With all your heart and soul and body?" he whispered huskily, quite aware they weren't alone and wishing like hell they were.

"Oh yes," Maeve breathed, "my body too!"

When John Peck came toward them, Seth drew away. "John, I'd like you to meet my"—he stumbled over the lie—"wife, Maeve."

"I'm mighty pleased to make your acquaintance, ma'am. I 'spect Sarah's even happier! Why, living out here in the wilderness without a neighbor for miles and miles has been awfully hard for her. She'll be happier than a June bug in May to have another lady to chat with. She gets plain lonesome for female companionship."

His kind words put Maeve at ease. "It's nice to meet you too, John."

John snapped his suspenders. "So how long you two been married?"

"Oh, about a year," Seth stated.

"About three months," Maeve blurted.

Seth felt his face flush brilliant red.

Laughing, John cupped Seth's shoulder. "Don't feel too bad; I can't ever remember either. Drives Sarah plain crazy!" He turned back to Maeve. "You feel free to go on up to the house. I expect Sarah's anxious to entertain you. Why, I'll bet she wasted no time at all on getting out her good china so's she could offer you a cup of coffee." He grabbed the ax and, with a grin on his face, announced he'd be chopping wood if anyone needed him.

As soon as he'd walked away, Maeve placed her hand over Seth's chest, feeling the steady beat of his heart. She raised a brow in a teasing manner. "Married, Seth?"

"I could hardly tell them the truth, now could I?"

"We haven't even known each other for a year," Maeve admonished.

"It seems like a lifetime."

She giggled. "I'm going to take that as a compliment."

"As it was intended," Seth said with a grin. "You know, Maeve, you could make a halfway honest man out of me by consenting to marriage."

Momentarily incapable of an answer, Maeve gulped. "Are you proposing to me?"

Seth reached down and brushed back a strand of her hair. His smile faltered as he studied her serious expression. When he brushed his lips lightly over hers, Seth felt her soft moan. As he lifted his head, he noted her beautiful hazel eyes were filled with distress. "I am. Would you be my wife?"

"C-couldn't we just live together?" Maeve stammered.

He traced the outline of her soft, moist lips with his thumb. "That wouldn't be right." Doubt shadowed his attempt to ease her anxiety. *What's going on? Doesn't she want to marry me?* Seth cleared his throat. "Do you find the idea so repulsive? I thought you'd be happy—that you wanted to be my wife. Instead you look as though you've lost your best friend."

Maeve closed her eyes and drew in a deep breath. "Nothing, Seth, absolutely nothing would make me happier than to spend the rest of my life with you. But—" Oh dear, how could she explain? She stroked his cheek lightly. "Oh, Seth, I want to say yes with all my heart, but how can I?" Her voice lowered. "How can I say no?" She pleaded for understanding with her eyes. "You know how much I love you, but I just can't promise you forever. . . . I can't, Seth. I can't promise you forever when I'm not even sure what's gonna happen tomorrow."

His brows furrowed. "I don't understand."

Struggling to find the proper explanation, Maeve faltered. Finally the words came. "Don't forget, Seth, I crossed the boundaries of reality to be here. What happens when reality claims me once more? Will you wake up some morning to find me gone?"

She placed her hand back on the warmth of his chest and, as she felt the steady beat of his heart, wondered if it was hurting as much as her own. "How would you feel about me then?

Would you be sorry? Angry, even? Maybe bitter that I forced my way into your heart, only to leave without saying good-bye?"

Maeve blinked, her eyes sparkling with unshed tears. "Answer me! If I can't promise you tomorrow, how am I supposed to promise you forever?" When he reached out to hold her, she whispered her command. "Don't! If you touch me right now, I'll fall apart."

Ignoring her request, Seth drew her into his embrace, feeling her body stiffen. "If I were to lose you, the very best part of me would die. But at least I'd know you loved me enough to take my name."

Maeve expressed her inner turmoil by pummeling his chest with her fists. "No! Don't say that! Can't you see, Seth? I love you enough to protect you from that kind of hurt. I don't want to hurt you. . . . I never want to hurt you." She broke down and wept softly, allowing him to comfort her. When Pea called her name, Maeve tried desperately to regain a semblance of control as the child, accompanied by Sarah's son, ran forward.

"Maeve, Maeve! Tell him! Tell Matthew that you did too fall off a cloud!"

Maeve looked helplessly at Seth. Managing a weak smile, she glanced down at the little boy who now eyed her curiously. "Uh . . . well . . ."

Seth broke in. "Pea, where are your manners? You haven't even introduced Maeve to your companion and here you are asking all sorts of questions!"

Okay, Maeve thought. That would buy her a little time, anyway. She crouched down and offered her hand. "I'm Maeve."

"I'm Matthew. And don't nobody fall off of clouds. Pea's not telling the truth. She says you're a fairy."

No, kid. If I were a fairy, I'd make myself vanish about now. "In a way she's telling the truth. The way they found me was certainly magical enough."

The simple statement seemed to pacify the boy and he shrugged. Turning toward Pea he hollered, "Race ya to that tree and back!"

When she straightened, Maeve met Seth's burning gaze. "Forgive me, Seth, but I can't marry you. Not now, not until I know for certain this is where I'm supposed to be, where I'll stay for the rest of my life."

Pride being all he had left, Seth gave a curt nod before turning away.

Chapter Twenty-four

After making her way to the small cabin, Maeve entered reluctantly. The last thing she felt like doing was visiting with the woman inside.

"Come in, come in," Sarah hastened her. Noting the look of distress on Maeve's face, she held out her arms.

Maeve gave in to the urge to weep and did so loudly, letting Sarah comfort her.

"There, there," Sarah soothed. "These men can be downright ornery sometimes, can't they? Look at my John! Now he's a fine man, but once he gets an idea in his head, there's no talking to him! That barn, for instance. Whoever heard of trying to raise a barn this late in the season? I told him, I said, 'John, no one is going to be willing to help you with this; why don't you wait

until summer?' But did he listen? Of course not!
He just forged ahead, giving no thought to anything other than accomplishing his task!"

Knowing she had to pull herself together,
Maeve made good use of the woman's soft prat-
tle. When she finally gained control, she drew
back. "Thank you for not asking questions."

Sarah smiled. "Feeling better now? There's
nothing like a good cry, I always say, to clear
one's heart of pain. Land sakes, when I lost my
other three children I thought I'd never stop!"
She moved toward a china teapot and poured
the steaming liquid into two matching cups.

"You lost three children?" Maeve questioned
softly. All of a sudden her problems didn't seem
quite as severe.

"I did." Sarah sighed. "On the way to Montana. The fever claimed them. I tell you, it was
the hardest thing I've ever done to bury them in
the wilderness. But"—she sighed again—"we
had no choice."

Maeve studied her companion. The woman's
face clearly bore traces of a wearisome life.
When Sarah offered her a cup of hot tea, she
gratefully accepted and sat down at the kitchen
table beside her. "Tell me, what brought you to
this part of the country?"

"John's dreams," Sarah answered. "He wants
to build a sawmill. He's hoping to furnish both
ends of the telegraph race with lumber."

"How far did you have to travel?"

Sarah shuddered. "All the way from Califor-
nia!" she exclaimed with a smile. "I thought

we'd never reach Montana."

Glancing around the small enclosure, Maeve's gaze lowered to the cleanly swept floor. "Isn't cabin life the pits? I can clean and clean and clean and when I turn around, the dust is so thick you can write your name in it!"

Confused by her strange choice of words, Sarah sipped at her tea. "It is a bit of a struggle," she admitted with a smile. "But worth it. If John is happy, I'm happy."

"But what about your life? What about your dreams? Surely you don't want to live way out here in the wilderness forever!"

"What makes John happy makes me happy," Sarah explained. "We have a good life together. I have two healthy children left and"—she lowered her voice a notch—"another on the way." Blushing profusely, Sarah switched subjects. "What about you and Seth? How did you come to settle in this area?"

Great! Just when she thought she'd sated the little boy's curiosity, she'd have to figure a way to answer Sarah. Trying to be as honest as she could without sending the woman into heart failure, Maeve answered. "Seth's first wife passed away. He was lonely and I came." Simple enough explanation, she thought, mentally patting herself on the back.

"Did you know him when he was married to his first wife?"

"Uh . . . well, n-not exactly," Maeve stammered.

"But how—"

This time the children's interruption came as a small blessing. Pea tearfully buried her head in Maeve's lap. "Jeb won't let me help," she cried. "He says I'm in the way."

"And Katie told me to come inside," Matthew joined in. "She says I'm too young to help," he whimpered.

"Katie is his older sister," Sarah offered as explanation. She tousled the small boy's hair. "Well, I'm in desperate need of helpers! I have cookie dough all mixed up and no one to help me bake them!"

"We'll help!" both children chimed in unison.

Watching Sarah move gracefully around the kitchen, Maeve envied her ability. Whenever she'd tried to bake something in the old-fashioned oven, it usually burned to a crisp.

What she didn't envy was the woman's life. Though Sarah hadn't gone into great detail, Maeve knew she'd suffered a lot of headache in order to fulfill her husband's dream. Maybe that was what life was all about back here in the 1800s. From the look of joy on Sarah's face as she worked with the children, it was obvious she had no regrets.

But could she say the same? Maeve had to admit she'd give anything for a Sears gas oven. And even more for a real bathroom with indoor plumbing. Those things, however, were just little things. Little wants and wishes she would gladly sacrifice if it meant the difference between staying here and going back.

Going back. Back to that dull, dreary existence where every morning she had been forced to plaster an artificial smile on her face and pretend to be happy. Was she any happier here? The answer surprised her. Even with all the problems she'd experienced, all the hardships she'd endured, all the disasters that kept happening, yes! She was happy.

The reason came quickly. Seth. It was Seth who made her happy, Seth who brought her comfort, Seth who filled her heart with joy.

Resting her chin in the palm of her hand, Maeve heaved a huge, contented sigh. Maybe she'd finally found a space in time she could call her own.

This place that time had somehow managed to thrust her in could most definitely be called home. A smile lit her eyes. For the first time since she could remember, Maeve knew she fit. Fit the circumstances, fit the situation, and most important, fit just right in Seth's arms.

As the day lengthened to the shadows of dusk, Pea curled up in Maeve's lap, her belly full of warm cookies and ice-cold milk. "Tell me a story," she pleaded between sleepy little yawns. "I told Matthew you tell the bestest stories ever. He wants to hear one, don't you, Matt?"

Maeve glanced at the little boy lying in front of the roaring fire. Since Sarah was busy preparing a scrumptious-looking pot roast for dinner, the least she could do was entertain them for a while.

"Once upon a time," she began, "a very, very

long time ago, there lived a fair maiden named—"

"Blossom," Pea suggested.

Maeve grinned. "Okay, Blossom it is! Blossom was very unhappy because she had no one who loved her. One day, an ugly old toad appeared out of nowhere. He asked Princess Blossom why she was crying."

"Oooo," Pea crooned. "What did she say?"

"She explained that she was lonely and would do anything to find someone who would love her so much she'd never be lonely again."

Matthew rolled over on his side and propped his head up with his fist. "Why was she so lonely? Didn't she have a mother and a father?"

"No," Maeve explained. "She lived with her aunt and ugly, fat cousin, Natasha." *Sorry, Natasha.*

"So what did the frog do?" Matthew questioned.

"Well, he made Princess Blossom close her eyes and picture someone. Someone who would love her completely. And when she had, the frog issued his command." Maeve lowered her voice to a deep, gravelly growl. " 'Now you have to kiss me in order to make your dream come true!' the frog commanded."

Pea giggled and Maeve couldn't resist hugging her as she continued the rest of the story. "Well, Princess Blossom didn't want to kiss a frog! Especially one with a wart on its nose. But she was so lonely, she agreed to do it."

"Did she get a wart from the frog?" Matthew asked.

"No," Maeve said with a shake of her head. "Instead, she watched in amazement as the frog, with a flick of his finger—"

"Oh, Maeve." Pea giggled while wrapping a strand of Maeve's hair around her finger. "Frogs don't have fingers!"

Maeve drew back as if offended. "Well, my frogs do! So anyway, with a flick of his froggie finger, her prince appeared."

"What did he look like?"

"He was a handsome thing, he was! He had hair dark as coal and eyes as blue as a cloudless summer sky. And when he saw the princess, he opened his arms, welcoming her into his life." Lost in her own fantasy, Maeve continued, "His mustache tickled the princess when he kissed her but she didn't mind a bit—"

"You're describing Papa!" Pea exclaimed.

Oops, Maeve realized with a guilty grin. Reality had once again reared its head in the face of fantasy.

"Come, children. Wash up for supper," Sarah interrupted. She smiled at Maeve. "You tell wonderful stories even if you did describe your husband!"

"That obvious, huh?"

"That obvious, my dear. And speaking of husbands, I see ours have finally decided to end their work. It's about time too. In the last few hours the temperature has dropped several degrees."

333

When the door flew open, Maeve shivered from the blast of cold air. She grinned as John walked toward his wife with his fingers curled into claws.

Sarah backed away. "John Peck, don't you dare put those cold fingers on me!"

Some things, Maeve realized, withstood the age-old test of time. She stared wistfully at Seth, noting his refusal to look in her direction. If only life were as easy as a fairy tale, she'd gladly go in search of a frog.

Chapter Twenty-five

While the wind whistled and howled night sounds, sending the temperature outside well below freezing, inside the cabin laughter and love warmed the room as well as the occupants.

Maeve smiled as she watched Jeb try to act older than his age in front of Sarah's daughter. Pea and Matthew had found some paper and were busy drawing pictures. Even Sarah stayed busy by darning her husband's socks.

The men were deep in conversation and Maeve sat back in the chair, watching with fascination as Seth's facial expressions changed as rapidly as the words he so adamantly spoke.

Seth spread his fingers across his knees and leaned forward. "I'm telling you, John, Montana will never be admitted to the union! Why, the—"

"Yes, it will," Maeve corrected without thinking. "Montana was admitted on, let's see, November 8th, 1889. It became the forty-first state to gain admittance into the Union."

John's mouth opened and closed. How could she predict something like that when it was merely the first day of November? "How—"

The sock in Sarah's hand slipped to her lap.

Seth's eyes widened.

Maeve nearly died. How could she explain something that hadn't taken place yet? Feeling a deep blush creep up her neck, she stammered, "Well . . . I mean . . . I-I—"

"What you meant to say is you hope it will take place on the eighth of November, right, Maeve?" Seth offered helplessly.

"Uh . . . yeah! And of course it'll be the forty-first state because as we all know South Dakota is the fortieth." She looked down at her lap, not daring to make eye contact with Seth. He would be furious with her, absolutely livid! Hearing a soft cough, Maeve couldn't resist stealing a glance in his direction.

He wasn't livid . . . the rat! He was desperately trying not to laugh aloud! And failing miserably, she noted as a small giggle rose to her throat.

When Sarah broke the silence by suggesting coffee, Maeve breathed a sigh of relief. And when John went to lend a helping hand, she rose from the chair and joined Seth's side. "Oh, boy, did I nearly blow it or what?"

He cocked a brow. "Blow it?"

"Blow it!" she repeated, not bothering to explain. From the smile on his face—his first that evening—she was almost glad she had slipped. "Are you still angry with me?"

"Oh, Maeve, of course not. I'm disappointed, but I'm not angry."

"Do you understand why I can't marry you, Seth?"

"Not really," he murmured, staring into the glowing embers of the fire. "But I trust you, Maeve. I know when you feel the time is right, you'll agree to my proposal."

She traced a finger lightly over his shoulder. "I've missed you."

"I've been right here."

"No, you haven't, Seth. You've been here in body but your mind is far, far away."

"I suppose you're right," he conceded. "I've been trying to think of a way to keep you here. To keep you from vanishing in the middle of the night as you said could happen."

"Then hold me, Seth. Just hold me."

"Gladly." He opened his arms to her, feeling the gentle curves of her body as she melded against him. He drew her hair back to place a kiss along the column of her neck. "Tell me," Seth groaned, burying his face against her soft skin. "Tell me you can see our future. See us together."

Closing her eyes against the pain in his voice, Maeve tried very hard to do just that. And pictured a room full of clocks, all ticking, all reminding her time was running out. A cold chill

337

Susan Collier

traveled through her system. She drew back. "Sarah just called me."

"No, she didn't," Seth argued.

"She did, Seth. I heard her."

"You heard the wind," he insisted. "Just the wind, Maeve."

Though she didn't disagree aloud, Maeve knew she'd heard something or someone calling her name. The voice had a distinctly familiar sound to it.

Maeve.

There! There it was again. "Did you hear it this time, Seth?"

He graced her with a look of confusion. "I heard nothing except the wind."

"But—" She stopped suddenly as the Pecks came back with a tray of cookies and coffee. Turning toward her hostess, Maeve questioned Sarah. "Did you call me a minute ago?"

"No, dear. Here, have some coffee . . . why, Maeve! You look as pale as a ghost. Are you feeling all right?"

"I-I—" Weakly, Maeve allowed Seth to help her back to her chair. "I thought I heard—" And then it dawned on her. The voice had been that of her mother.

"Perhaps you've tried to do too much today," John offered. "It's getting a bit late. Suppose we all turn in?"

"That sounds like a good idea, John," Sarah agreed. "We'd like for you both to take our bed. John and I can sleep by the hearth."

"No," Maeve insisted. "Seth and I will sleep

338

out here; there's no sense in us putting you out."

"We won't be out, my dear! On a night like this, it's not fit for man or beast."

"I mean . . . oh please, Sarah," Maeve moaned. "Don't argue with me about this. Seth and I will sleep out here; you can sleep in your own bed, all right?"

"Well, if you insist . . ." Sarah glanced toward John, who shrugged his shoulders. "If you need anything . . ."

Maeve needed something all right. She needed privacy with Seth. If only he could hold her, she knew this uneasy feeling inside her body would fade away.

After getting the children settled for the night, Sarah blew out the remaining lantern, surrounding them in darkness. Again, she offered, "If you need anything . . ." before disappearing around the corner to her room.

Once settled in the bed beside her husband, Sarah mused over the odd couple. There was something about Maeve that seemed almost—well—strange. Perhaps it was the way she talked, not with an accent of course, but the choice of words . . . oh well, perhaps tomorrow she'd question Maeve once more about where she came from.

Maeve turned to Seth. Words weren't necessary as they gazed into one another's eyes. When Seth began to undo the buttons of her dress, Maeve allowed her actions to speak the volume of her love. And later, when their sweet, unhurried lovemaking session was over, she nestled in Seth's strong arms, trying to resist the urge to sleep. She had an uneasy feeling that if she did close her eyes, Seth would disappear as quickly as her mother's voice had. The warmth of the fire, the welcome embrace of the man she loved, stole the fear from her heart and replaced it with peaceful slumber.

She awoke to an insistent nudging at her shoulder.

"Maeve," Pea whispered, "wake up! God's done painted everything white!"

Realizing that her dress was a hopeless mass of wrinkles from the way she'd hastily discarded it last night, Maeve opted to borrow the extra change of clothing Jeb had brought with him.

After opening the door, she grinned. God had indeed painted everything white, as Pea had so aptly put it. As far as her eyes could see, the earth glistened with purity. The sun shone brilliantly, sending sparks of light in every direction. "It's beautiful," Maeve whispered.

"Lemme go wake up Pa," Pea pleaded.

Maeve grinned as a sneaky, terrible, nasty, wickedly good idea came to mind. She carefully opened the door, wincing when the hinges squeaked, and grabbed a handful of snow. Tiptoeing back to the hearth, she knelt down beside her victim and, without warning, dropped the small mound on Seth's face.

Sputtering, Seth shot up off the floor like he'd been bitten by a snake. "Dear God!" he yelled.

Pea giggled.

Maeve laughed.

Finally Seth managed a grin. "That was colder than a witch's tit—nose. A witch's nose."

Maeve threw her arms around him, rejoicing in the fact that this was a brand-new day and nothing had stolen her away. "Does this warm you?" she growled low, pushing wantonly against his groin with her hip.

"It's doing more than that," Seth uttered shakily. "And if you keep it up, I'll have to drag you out to the woodshed and show you what warm really is!" he teased.

"Mmmm, sounds wonderful, if you ask me!"

"Pa, Pa, can I go out and play in the snow?" Pea tugged at her father's blanket for attention.

"Ummm, what have you got under that blanket, Seth Caldwell?" Maeve murmured against his ear. Her wandering fingers had made contact with his arousal. As footsteps pattered down the hall, she quickly backed away.

Sarah greeted her guests with a sleepy yawn. "Good morning!" She tried not to stare at Maeve's odd choice of clothing.

"Good morning," Seth replied calmly, though his pulse still raced from Maeve's brazen act.

"I trust you slept well?"

"We slept like babies," Maeve announced. She took Sarah's arm. "If you'll show me where you keep your coffee, I'll be happy to help you make some."

When his daughter followed the two women, Seth took advantage of the time alone and quickly donned his clothes. Maybe Sarah hadn't noticed the fact that their garments were scattered everywhere. Seth groaned as he picked up Maeve's chemise. She had to have noticed!

"Looks like we're snowed in for a spell," John announced from the doorway. His lips twitched with mirth as Seth fumbled to hide the feminine garment. He scratched his left shoulder. "Better get that thing back on, Seth. Funny, I never figured you the type of fellow that would wear women's underclothes."

Embarrassed, Seth managed a weak grin in response.

After being pestered throughout breakfast, Seth finally gave in to his daughter's plea. "Go, Pea! But for pity's sake, stay where we can see you or else go find Jeb and stay with him. And watch out for snowdrifts!"

"I will," Pea promised solemnly. She turned to Matthew. "Betcha I kin beat you to the old tree!"

Maeve laughed. "I hope she's bundled up good, Seth. It's bitterly cold out there!" She removed the soiled plates from the table and took them to the washtub. She paused for a moment, listening to the sound of Seth's low rumble as he talked and laughed with John. The timbre of his voice filled her with a warm glow. Looking out the small window located above the washstand, Maeve grimaced when Pea was hit in the face by a flying snowball. Her grimace turned back to a smile as she watched Jeb take Katie's hand before steering her away from the younger children.

Closing her eyes, Maeve knew she had all she'd ever want or need right here, right now, and the feeling was wonderful. "Thanks, God," she whispered. "Thanks for just one more day."

When Seth came up behind her and circled her waist with his arms, Maeve stayed perfectly still, content to feel the solid warmth of his chest against her back.

"Happy?" he asked quietly.

"What gave me away?"

"Maybe that big grin you're wearing has something to do with it." He tucked two fingers between the buttons of her shirt, feeling the warmth of her flesh. "Where are the children?"

Maeve opened her eyes. "They're—Seth, where are they? They were right out there; look, you can see their tracks." She snapped her fingers. "I'll bet those two followed Jeb and Katie. Those little sneaks!"

Seth heaved a large sigh. As he rubbed the back of his neck, he grinned. "You know, somewhere in my ancestry, I feel certain there was an explorer! I'm always having to hunt those children down."

"Hmmm. Well, I can't really say much," Maeve stated with a smile. "After all, look at me—I wandered through time!"

"I hope they're careful." Seth peered warily out the window at the freshly falling snow. "It can be dangerous in certain areas. The snow blows and forms large drifts during the night. If Pea were to step down in the wrong spot, she could be buried alive."

343

"I'm sure Jeb'll watch after her," Maeve murmured, taking a sip of her coffee.

The kitchen door opened, letting in a blast of cold air. As the two older children walked inside, Maeve noted Jeb's cheeks were scarlet. She had an inkling the brilliant color had more to do with his companion than the frigid temperature. "Are you two trying to escape from Pea and Matt?"

Jeb graced her with a look of confusion. "I don't know what you're talking about, Maeve. We haven't seen them for quite some time. I thought maybe they'd gotten too cold and came back inside."

"We haven't seen them," Maeve informed him. "It's too dangerous out there for them to play alone, however, and someone needs to be watching after them."

Seth experienced a sudden twinge of apprehension and tried to hide it with reassuring words. "I'm sure everything is fine. They're probably close by making snow angels or something. I'll just grab my coat and go check."

"Hang on a minute and I'll go with you," Maeve offered, after taking the last sip of coffee from her cup.

Bundled up in coats, gloves, and caps, Seth and Maeve walked outside. The sun shone brilliantly against the pure white snow, and Maeve shielded her eyes from the glare. "Look over there. You can see two sets of prints and they're just about the right size for Pea's and Matt's footprints. Maybe they walked down to the barn to have a look."

Seth shook his head. "Pea knows better than to wander that far off without permission. Maybe you better go alert John and Sarah to the fact they're missing."

"Missing? Oh Seth . . . you don't think anything's happened to them, do you?"

He shrugged. "I'm probably being overcautious, but just in case . . ." The words trailed off.

Watching him walk past the oak tree toward the half-completed barn, Maeve drew her cloak around her tightly. Nothing bad was going to happen; she simply wouldn't allow it.

While purposely keeping the fear that was building inside her from showing, Maeve broke the news to John and Sarah, then joined in the search for the missing children.

Turning in the direction opposite the one Seth had chosen, Maeve cupped her hands to her mouth. "Blossom!" She paused for a moment, observing the winter wonderland surrounding her.

Drops of water had fallen from the snow-flocked trees and frozen in the process. Images of angels lay everywhere upon the ground, followed by the footprints of children.

A tremor of alarm filled her soul. "Oh, Duessa," she whispered, feeling the heat of tears sting her cheeks. "Not Pea. Please. Don't take Pea."

Chapter Twenty-six

"Blossom! Please! If you can hear me, answer me," Maeve cried in desperation.

The mountains echoed the cry, and her own voice came back to mock her.

Seth ran up to join her. "Don't yell! Whatever you do, don't yell! The sound could cause an avalanche."

"Oh, God, I'm so sorry," Maeve whispered, placing her hand against her lips. She kept her voice low and controlled. "Look, Seth, you go that way and I'll go this way. If Sarah and John take the opposite routes, we'll have every direction covered." Without waiting for his response, she began to run.

"Pea!" Her words came softly. "If you can hear me, honey, please, please answer." When a painful catch in her side made her slow down,

Maeve realized she'd been crying and the tears had frozen on her cheeks.

"Pea! Matthew? Can you hear me?" The sound of her voice was strange to her ears.

The solid white of her surroundings began to play havoc with her sense of direction. Had she come through those trees or was it farther to her right?

"Just follow your own footprints, Maeve," she uttered aloud, trying to calm her racing heart. "Think! I've got to think about what I'm doing!" When she backtracked the way she'd come, Maeve realized she'd been walking in circles. But for how long? And how far away was she from the cabin?

There was no way to tell. Where she'd back-tracked before, the prints were already covered by blowing snow. Funny, she thought. The wind wasn't blowing like this when I left.

Calm down, Maeve. Just calm down. Seth'll find you and when he does, he'll have Pea and Matthew beside him.

She shaded her eyes from the harsh rays of the sun bouncing off pure white. When she heard the sound of someone crying for help, the rhythm of her heart increased. "Pea? Is that you?"

Another plaintive whimper caused Maeve to run toward the overhang of a steep embankment. Far below her, Pea clung desperately to a clump of winter grass.

"Ooooo, Maeve," she cried. "Me can't hold on no longer."

"Yes, you can! You just hold on until I reach you, darling." With faltering steps, Maeve realized the only way to get to the child was to slide down the embankment and hope like hell she ended up close by.

"Help me!" Pea screamed before letting go.

Filled with horror as she watched the child fall, Maeve slid down the rocky incline, crying aloud when the jagged edge of a sharp rock gashed into her forehead.

Struggling to remain conscious, she grasped the fact that she'd reached the bottom. Her vision blurred as blood from the cut leaked into her eyes. "Pea? Where are you, Pea?"

"Over here," came a small whimper.

Moving her head caused tremendous pain, and Maeve swallowed back a sob when she rolled to her side. For a moment she thought the darkness hovering just beyond her vision would swallow her completely, but when Pea closed the distance between them, the joy she felt was deep enough to hold back the demons. She wrapped the shivering child in her shawl. "Thank God you're safe," Maeve murmured, rocking Blossom back and forth.

"How we gonna git back up that hill, Maeve? And how come you bleeding?"

It was becoming increasingly harder to concentrate, Maeve realized. Yet she must. Had to keep those demons away. They were closing in on her, trying to rob her of something. But what?

And was her mind playing tricks on her or

had the wind picked up again?

Painfully she stood, aided by Pea's small hand. "See that little hollow spot over there? That's where we're going, Pea. It'll offer some protection from this dreadful wind."

Pea helped Maeve walk toward their destination, then panicked when her companion stumbled. "Pa!" she screamed, "Come quick, Pa! We need you!"

The earth seem to tremble below Maeve's feet. A sixth sense warned her to look up just as the entire side of the mountain above them gave way.

She shoved Pea toward the pathetic little hollow portion of the hill and began to pray for their salvation as she sheltered the child's small body with her own.

Seth breathed a sigh of relief when he spotted Matthew running toward him. He knelt down and gathered the child into his arms. "Where's Pea?"

Racked by chills, the little boy stammered the words. "Y-you have to come q-quick," he gasped. "Pea fell d-down the incline!"

As he rounded the corner, John stopped for a moment and clasped his aching chest when he saw his son in Seth's arms. Hugging Matthew tightly, he warned his friend of the dangers. "We'll have to use caution, Seth. With all this snow, the ground will easily give way. . . . " He shook his head, unable to finish.

When the earth trembled beneath their feet,

both men glanced toward the mountain, gaping with horror.

"Avalanche," Seth whispered. "Dear God, John, hurry!"

Sarah gathered her son and daughter close. Jeb stared helplessly as his father ran toward the dreaded slope. "Let me go, Mrs. Peck. Pa might need me," he pleaded.

Sarah tightened her grip on the young man's shoulder. "No, Jeb. Your father wants you to stay. There's no telling what they're going to find. No telling at all," she repeated sadly.

When he reached the bank, John stared at the mess below. The snow had fallen directly into the valley, almost filling the hole. "If they're down there, Seth, it's going to be impossible to rescue them."

Seth whirled around to face him. "They're down there all right. I can feel it in my heart. And you're wrong, my friend. Neither heaven nor hell will stop me from getting to them."

Silence. Funny how the snow seemed so alive but remained so silent, Maeve thought. She wiggled a bit to make certain no bones had been broken. Beneath her, Pea did the same.

"You're squashing me, Maeve." Pea grunted. "And how come you pushed me like that? I'm gonna tell Pa and he'll get on to you 'cause he says we ain't 'posed to push people."

Maeve rolled to her side, surprised to find they had enough space between them and the roof of snow to actually sit upright. She patted

Pea's knee. "I'm sorry, honey, I didn't mean to push you, but if I hadn't, we might have—" She bit back the ending of her statement. They weren't out of this predicament yet. Not by a long shot. "Come here, sweetie. Let's cuddle close, want to?"

"I'm scairt, Maeve. I'm real scairt."

"I know you are," she soothed. "But soon you're going to see your daddy's hand digging right through that mound of snow, so hang on, okay?"

Pea sniffled, trying to decide whether she should cry. "You sure?"

"I'm sure." If only I were, Maeve thought inwardly, but to expect Seth to find them beneath tons of snow was absolutely absurd. How long would their oxygen last? How long before the cold seeped in and stole the feeling from their bodies? Her toes were already numb. "Let's play a little game, Pea. I'm gonna wiggle my toes, can you?"

"Can't, Maeve. Can't feel my toes no more. Can't feel my fingers too good either," Pea added as an afterthought.

Maeve took the child's tiny hands between her palms and tried to rub the circulation back into them.

Pea jerked away. "Ouch! You're hurting me! First you pushed me and now you hurted me. I want my daddy," she wailed.

The eerie sound of shifting snow caused Maeve to cringe. "Hush, Pea. You mustn't cry or you'll ruin our nice little ice house, okay?"

"Don't like this ol' ice house. I wanna go home!"

"Me too, darlin', me too!" *Hurry, Seth, please hurry.*

Seth clawed at the snow, ignoring the searing pain in his fingertips. "We've got to get to them, John. If they're underneath this mess, time's running out."

Unable to convey that even if they'd managed to survive the avalanche, chances were time had already become their enemy, John remained silent but began to dig with renewed vigor. He felt he owed his friend the satisfaction of trying.

Had minutes or hours passed? Maeve struggled to keep from succumbing to the desire for sleep. She shook Pea gently. "Wake up, honey. Don't go to sleep, okay?"

"Noooo," Blossom whined. "I want to see Mama agin. Ever'time I close my eyes her's standing there smiling at me. Is her smiling at you too, Maeve?"

As the child curled into a ball, Maeve gnawed at her lip, watching Pea. Maybe this was their only option. Just give in to the desire for sleep and let go. Why fight the inevitable?

There was no way Seth was going to rescue them in time, and to keep holding on to that hope was ridiculous. It seemed as if Duessa would win once more.

She closed her eyes and instead of seeing

an angel, pictured a giant clock, tick, tick, ticking. . . .

When she tried to conjure up an image of Seth, Maeve was severely disappointed with the results. All she could see was the face of the medicine man who had healed Seth.

The medicine man's image turned into that of the Great Spirit as words came to mind with haunting clarity.

Though bitter winds shall blow you apart, the tears she sheds will be like a bond between you. And neither rain, nor wind, nor fire from the sky will break this union.

"Oh yeah?" Maeve said, or perhaps she just thought she'd given voice to her inner thoughts. "Well, you didn't include snow in that little tidbit of information, now did you? You should have included the snow, Mr. Great and Mighty Spirit . . . should have included the snow."

Her body seemed to be floating . . . floating . . . yet Maeve could clearly see Seth working diligently to rake away the snow covering her body. Wait! How could her body be beneath the snow if she was floating?

She longed to touch him, to comfort him, yet knew she couldn't. "Oh, Seth," she whispered, "I guess I was wrong. I did too get a chance to say good-bye."

Sensing someone behind him, Seth turned quickly, only to find no one there. The icy chill that fluttered over his heart was far colder than the snow surrounding him. He stopped digging and listened carefully. Far, far away he could hear Maeve tell him good-bye.

His anguish turned to rage. "No! Don't leave me, Maeve, don't leave me!" Weeping bitter tears, Seth fell to his knees just as John announced he'd reached some sort of culvert.

Chapter Twenty-seven

The heat warmed Maeve's body. She opened her eyes and blinked slowly.

Where am I? What's happening?

The warmth was like nothing she'd ever experienced before. All around her, stars twinkled and danced in an endless sky. And the warmth flowed through her, surrounding her with peace and comfort and such a feeling of love, it filled her very soul.

"You weren't supposed to give up," a familiar voice scolded gently. "You were supposed to fight."

Maeve turned around. A brilliant light seemed to encase the woman's form. "Mama? Is it really you?"

"It's me, my darling. Oh, Maeve, I'd hoped you would fight to live and not give up as you have done. It isn't your time, sweetheart. You have so much more living to do and it's all there . . . waiting for your return."

Tears filled Maeve's eyes. "I'm so tired, Mama. I'm tired of trying to stay somewhere where I don't belong, tired of fighting Duessa to keep her from taking back what she supposedly gave me. . . . " The words faded as hot tears of anguish spilled over to dampen Maeve's cheeks. "B-but most of all, I m-miss you, Mama. I miss having someone to tell me what to do."

"But you don't need me to tell you what to do," Janet explained gently. "Your heart has told you all along, isn't that right, Maeve? You see, your daddy and I have been keeping close watch over you ever since we left our earthly bodies."

"Daddy too?"

Janet stroked back a lock of her daughter's hair and tenderly wiped the tears from her cheeks. "Of course your daddy has. We would have continued to do so until you'd settled this matter once and for all."

"It wasn't up to me to settle it, don't you see, Mama? I tried, I really tried—"

"No, dear heart, you only thought you were trying." Placing an arm around her weeping daughter, Janet encouraged Maeve to walk along beside her. "There are things you must realize for yourself," she explained. The woman pushed aside a cloud with her bare toe. "Now look down there and tell me what you see."

Maeve obeyed. Glancing down, she realized

they were observing the day of her parents' funeral. There she stood, weeping pathetically as the pastor spoke words of comfort to the gathered crowd. When Aunt Gladys tried to place an arm around her, Maeve shrugged it away.

"But you don't understand, Mama, I was angry. Hurting. I couldn't understand why I was allowed to live and you and Daddy had to die."

"The anger you felt was a perfectly normal response, Maeve. The shell you protectively placed around your heart wasn't. Watch carefully, darling, and you'll see what I'm talking about."

Scenes whisked by, ever changing, ever swirling. Maeve at the dinner table, refusing to join in on family discussions with her aunt and uncle. Maeve opting to go places alone instead of joining the family she'd been forced to reside with.

"But, Mama, you just don't understand! Natasha was so perfect, so wonderful. And look at me, Mama. There was no way I could compare to her."

"No one, except perhaps yourself, expected you to be like Natasha. She's her own person, Maeve. Just as you are. The only difference between the two of you is that Natasha learned to accept herself—faults and all."

"Humph. Natasha didn't have any faults."

"Watch," her mother said with a smile.

And Maeve did. She watched as Natasha frowned at herself in the mirror, fussing over a small flaw in her complexion. Upset because she couldn't quite fill the pair of jeans she tried on. "You mean Natasha didn't think she was perfect?"

"No one believes they're perfect. The difference is Natasha never let her self-proclaimed flaws stand in the way of her happiness."

"And I did."

"Take a good hard look at the young girl talking to her Elvis poster, Maeve. Tell me, do you honestly believe she had a problem with her weight?"

The young girl was, of course, herself. Maeve stared in disbelief. She'd been a very pretty young woman, not really heavy at all, more what Maeve would consider healthy, if anything. "But, it wasn't like that when I stared in the mirror or compared myself to Natasha. She was so darn skinny! Oh, and if I wasn't fat, then why did Aunt Gladys keep after me about joining weight classes and stuff?"

"Aunt Gladys knew how unhappy you were with yourself. All she was trying to do was get you to a point where you liked *you* again."

"But, Mama, I do like me . . . or at least now I do." She smiled at her mother. "You see, I've met a man—Seth Caldwell—and he seems to think I'm wonderful just the way I am."

"He's not the only one, my dear. Everyone thinks you're wonderful just the way you are, Maeve. That is, everyone except you."

"Okay, so I'm a wonderful person! But how does that help me now? How am I going to get back to Seth?"

"This is what you really want?"

"Oh yes, Mama. With all my heart."

"Fred and Gladys have been very worried about your disappearance, Maeve. Look below."

The small gathering of relatives walked into a church filled with people Maeve's age. Gladys hung on to Fred's shirt, weeping pathetically. Even Natasha was having trouble keeping her tears at bay.

"What is it, Mama? What are they doing?"

"They're holding a memorial service in your honor. You see, my dear, your body was never found after the dreadful accident."

"Of course it wasn't. I mean, I'm in my body, right?" In confusion, Maeve glanced back down at the inside of the small church. "Gee, would you look at all those people!"

"They're your friends, Maeve. Look, there's Jonathan from your high school days. You would have ended up marrying him, you know."

"Jonathan? No way! He was so hung up on Paula he couldn't see the sunshine for the stars in his eyes."

"Ah, but she broke his heart their second year in college. And you were there to pick up the shattered pieces. He fell madly in love with you."

Maeve thought for a moment. "Did we, uh, have any children?"

"Several. Look for yourself."

Looking down, Maeve observed a small backyard filled with all sorts of toys. Five children,

their ages ranging from infancy to—she'd estimate the oldest to be about six, gathered around a picnic table, waiting to be served. "Five kids, Mom? I never wanted five kids!"

"You and Jon couldn't keep your hands off one another, and you weren't very good about keeping up with your birth control pills."

"It's a lovely scene, Mom. But it's not the one I want. Jon's a good man and all, but he isn't Seth. No one can fill my heart with love and happiness like Seth can—besides, I already have two children. I have Pea and Jeb."

"In that case," her mother said with a smile, "I'll see what I can do about having the angel of peace patch things up between Jonathan and Paula."

"What about Aunt Gladys? I hate to be the cause of so much pain," Maeve interjected. "How can I go to Seth and live happily ever after knowing I've hurt them so desperately?"

"They'll get over the pain. Look," Janet said, peeling back the edge of a cloud.

The church was the same. The faces weren't. Smiles everywhere, laughter, tears of happiness. "What is it? What's going on?" Maeve questioned.

"Why, it's Natasha's wedding day."

"Who's she marrying?"

"Who else but Arnie," Janet stated with a smile.

"Ick! Arnie?"

"Arnie. And Maeve, she's as happy about it as you are over the thought of going back to Seth.

In the years to come, Gladys is going to have her hands quite full. Twins run in Arnie's family, and Natasha will have several sets. Trust me, she's going to be very occupied with her grandchildren."

"What about Freddie, Mom? What happens to him?"

"He goes on to become a veterinarian. He works on the rodeo circuit, taking care of their animals."

"Sounds just like him," Maeve stated with a giggle. Suddenly she turned toward her mother, needing an answer to the question that had plagued her since her parents' death's. "Mama, you and Daddy were happy, weren't you?"

"I can honestly say I lived my life to the fullest. There is not a moment I wish to change, not a heartache I wish to forget. All the memories, both good and bad, only served to bring your father and I closer together."

"But that's exactly how it is for me and Seth!" Maeve cried. "I have to go back, Mama. You know that, don't you?"

"I've known it all along," Janet admitted. "But I must caution you, Maeve. When you do go back, all you've seen, all you've experienced, will seem nothing more than a dream."

"Tell me what the future holds for Seth, Mom. Can you do that?"

Walking a few steps away from her daughter, Janet bent and parted a giant fluffy cloud. Peering down, a bright smile lit her face. "I hope you like ranching, Maeve, and you must learn to overcome your fear of riding horses."

"So the trade I made wasn't such an awful mistake after all?" Maeve came running forward in an effort to see.

Janet quickly drew the edges of the cloud together. "No fair peeking into what you don't need to know. The purchase of those two small calves was a wise investment. One day, Seth will be known for raising a breed called the White-faced Hereford. He'll be extremely successful in his venture and—No, that's all I'm going to tell you," Janet stated with a smile.

"I knew it!" Maeve exclaimed. "I just knew it! Tell me, Mama, were you trying to send some type of message to me? It was almost as if I knew I was doing the right thing, do you understand?"

"You can experience the same feeling anytime you wish by simply trusting your heart to lead you, Maeve. There's nothing mystical about it.

"Hurry, my child, you have decisions that must be made before Seth reaches your frozen body."

"Will I ever see you again, Mama?"

"You won't see me again for a long, long time, but remember, Maeve, a mother never truly leaves her children."

For the first time since arriving in this place among the clouds, a frown darkened Maeve's features. "That's exactly what I'm concerned about."

Janet gave a slight shake of her head. "I'm not

sure I understand what you mean."

"It's Duessa, Mom. I don't want her interfering with the way I raise my children."

"Ah, but are you willing to accept the bad times as well as the good, Maeve? All children go through a growing process, and sometimes it can be very painful for their parents."

Maeve whirled around to find Duessa standing behind her. "I'll take the good with the bad. All I know is I love them very, very much. And I need them in my life."

"Now I can turn them over completely to your care," Duessa stated with a smile.

"Does this mean it isn't too late for Pea? We're not going to lose her?"

"Understand, Maeve, children belong to us for a very short period of time. One day you wake up and find they've become their own person and have lives separate from ours.

"It's a parent's responsibility to raise them with all the wisdom we possess, then when the time comes, be wise enough to let them go."

Maeve watched as Janet took Duessa's hand and patted it gently. "I completely agree."

"B-but you keep appearing to her," Maeve argued. "Are you going to deny it?"

"Of course not! I only appeared to her because she was in need of comfort."

"I could have done that," Maeve fussed. "You didn't give me the chance."

"You were in need of your own mother's comfort," Duessa explained. "Now that you've made the decision to stay with them, there'll be no reason for me to interfere." Silence prevailed. "You have made that decision, haven't you?"

"Well, yes, but . . . oh, Mama, I don't want to say good-bye."

"Only for a little while, my child. Only for a while."

"I didn't get to see Daddy, though. I wanted to tell him—"

"That you love him. He knows, Maeve. He also realizes this is a mother-daughter thing. He went to play a round of celestial golf with a fellow angel in an effort to afford us privacy."

Maeve stepped forward to give her mother a farewell embrace and found her feet slipping though the clouds. "I'm falling! Help me, Mama, I'm falling."

"You were never meant to stay. Go back, my darling daughter. Go back to the man you love and have a happy life."

Chapter Twenty-eight

A happy life . . . happy life. The words echoed in the silent cavern of snow. Maeve wondered if she'd dreamed the entire episode.

A soft scratching sound captured her attention.

Oh, Seth, let that be you. Come rescue me; take me home. I need to feel your love warming my heart, my soul.

Seth's heart leapt to his throat as he uncovered Maeve from the mound of snow. One quick look at the odd-shaped little cavern was all he allowed himself before gathering her cold and frozen body to his chest and carrying her up the steep incline toward the Peck home. John followed close behind, carrying Pea.

"Maeve, Maeve! Wake up, sweetheart, wake

up!" Seth held her close once they reached the house, rocking back and forth as he waited for her to regain consciousness. She'd been so still, so pale, when they finally reached her, and if it hadn't been for her courageous act of shielding Blossom with her own body, Seth doubted the child would be alive. "Wake up, sweetheart, please wake up," he pleaded in desperation.

His voice seems so real, Maeve thought. But it can't be that easy. Nothing is ever this easy. Even though she knew she was about to be disappointed, Maeve slowly opened her eyes. Seth's worried expression, though blurred, hovered just above her. Almost hesitantly, she reached up to touch his brow. And felt flesh. His flesh!

"Seth?" Maeve blinked. "Is it really you?"

Tears of joy flawed Seth's vision. "Oh, thank God. I thought you'd never wake up!"

Maeve traced the worry lines creasing his forehead, his bushy brows, and finally, brushed away a single tear from his cheek. "You saved me!"

"I saved you," Seth repeated, nearly choking on the words. He drew her close. "Thank God you're all right."

Struggling to a sitting position, Maeve touched her forehead with her finger and felt a bandage. "What happened?"

"You had a nasty cut," Seth explained. "Sarah had to stitch it with her need—"

Maeve covered his lips with her hand. "No. Don't say it! I don't want to know."

He clasped her hand tightly. "I was so worried about you. I thought that perhaps the future had claimed you back again."

Studying the concern in his eyes, Maeve offered a weak but reassuring smile. "I'm where I'm supposed to be, Seth . . . here, now and forever."

"What happened out there? You seem so sure, so positive—"

"I am." She thought about the dream, still unable to recollect the details. "Does it really matter what took place? All I know is I've never been more certain about my life than I am at this very moment." Their conversation came to an abrupt halt when Pea gave a soft moan.

Maeve struggled to stand and glanced in the direction of the noise. "Pea! Is she all right?"

"Thanks to your courageous act, she is." Seth told her.

"My courageous act? I actually did something courageous?"

"You sheltered her with the warmth of your body," he explained.

"Oh that! Well, it's nothing any other mother wouldn't do for her child, now is it?" She made her way over to the couch where the child lay beneath a mountain of quilts. "Well, hello there, Pea Pot. You still mad at me?"

Two clear blue eyes opened slowly. "Maeve, is that you?"

"It's me, sweetie."

Pea yawned and gave a mighty stretch. "I had a silly dream. Mama told me she had to say good-bye so's she could take care of Gracie, and you know what?"

Blossom pushed away the covers and grabbed Maeve to give her a big hug. "Her told me you is gonna be my mama now. Is you, Maeve? Is you really gonna be my mama?"

Maeve glanced toward an astonished Seth. "I am . . . if your daddy still wants to marry me, that is."

"Always," Seth exclaimed softly. "Always and forever."

"It sounds to me as if a celebration is in order," Sarah exclaimed as she walked into the den.

"Oh my goodness," Maeve murmured, her hand slipping to cover her lips. "You heard?"

"I did and I think it's wonderful."

"I-I'm sorry we lied to you about being married, it's just that—"

"Hush, young lady! I've been observing the two of you and whether you realize it or not, your hearts already belong to one another and a little slip of paper isn't going to make that much difference. However," Sarah added with a smile, "I'll be more than happy to care for Pea and Jeb while you go into town and make it legal."

Maeve's eyes sparkled as she turned back to Seth. "What do you think? Should we?"

"Not today!" Seth laughed. "You need time to regain your strength."

"I'm fine," Maeve interjected.

"No, I agree with Seth. You'll stay here, of

course. Just because you've been living together without the benefit of marriage doesn't make it right for you to continue. And when the decided day comes, Seth can pick you up and carry you into town."

Stay there? Without Seth and the kids? Never! Opening her mouth to disagree, Maeve noted the stubborn set of Sarah's jaw. She offered the man she loved an apprehensive look. "How soon can we do this?"

"As soon as you feel you're able to make the journey."

"In that case, let's leave today."

"No," Sarah argued. "Next week will be soon enough. Haven't you heard? Absence makes the heart grow fonder."

"Yeah, so I heard," Maeve grumbled, recalling those exact words when they came from Seth's lips. She didn't like them any more now than she had then.

Watching Seth and the children drive away in the wagon, Maeve struggled to keep her tears in check. Even though both Seth and Maeve had tried to explain, Pea clung to her as if she'd never see her again. Seth had finally resorted to force in order to remove the child's fingers from around Maeve's neck.

Pea's tearful exclamation had broken her heart.

"You's not 'posed to stay. You's my mama and I needs you to come with me!"

Closing the cabin door, Maeve allowed a gi-

371

ant sigh to escape from her trembling lips. The next few days would surely seem like a lifetime.

"Now, now," Sarah soothed. "You're going to be so busy the time will fly by and you'll be wishing you had more."

"I doubt it," Maeve grumbled.

"Come along," Sarah told her, draping an arm around the unhappy woman's waist. "We need to get started on your wedding trousseau: a few tea gowns, a linsey homespun, a travel dress, bloomers and petticoats . . . my, my, we better get started."

"Oh! I don't sew," Maeve explained. "Tell you what, I can go home and get several of Duessa's gowns—that's Seth's first wife—then all we'll have to do is make alterations."

"Would you honestly be content with an ex-wife's clothing?" Sarah shuddered. "Not me. I wouldn't want my husband remembering what his first wife looked like in my clothing."

"Hmm, you have a point," she conceded, "but like I told you, I can't sew worth a flip." The odd expression on her hostess's face made Maeve realize she'd have to be more careful about using modern expressions.

"Well, you might not be able to now, but when I get through teaching you, you'll be an expert," Sarah informed her with a laugh. "And then there's the small matter of teaching you to cook properly, and clean, and manage a household—"

Maeve's nose crinkled in distaste. "This doesn't sound like fun."

"Why, dear, whoever told you it would be? Nonetheless, these are all things you'll need to know in order to be a successful wife. Tell me, child, where did you say you were from?"

Oh, boy! The next couple of days would prove to be interesting. Mighty interesting indeed!

Chapter Twenty-nine

"Is we really gonna go see Maeve?" Pea asked, watching her papa dress.

Seth fiddled with the unyielding tie. "Yep."

"I missed her. Did you miss her, Papa?"

"Terribly," he stated, knowing the word hardly came close to describing his true feelings. These past few days had been sheer misery for him, and had he not thought Sarah would have a conniption fit, he'd have gone to collect Maeve on the eve of that first day spent without her. "Does this look all right, Pea?" He turned to allow his daughter to see him fully dressed.

"Oooo, Papa, you is handsome!"

Pulling at the sleeves of the jacket which were a little too short for comfort, Seth frowned. "I hope Maeve thinks so."

"Hey, Pa!" Jeb hollered, coming through the

door, "the wagon's ready . . . are you?"

"Just about." Seth ran his finger beneath the stiff collar of his shirt. Lord, he was uncomfortable. "Did you bring extra clothing for you and Pea? You'll be staying with the Pecks for two days, you know."

Jeb's face lit up. "I know. I can hardly wait to see Katie again. Hey, Pa? How do you know if you're in love with a woman?"

Seth would hardly consider Katie a woman, but out of respect for his son's feelings, refrained from saying so. He grabbed his hat. "Come on, boy, I'll explain on the ride over."

While Pea played in the back of the wagon with her doll, Seth and Jeb held a heart-to-heart conversation. "It's like this, son: if you feel sick to your stomach when you're around her, if your hands get all clammy and your heart starts pounding far too fast, then you know it's love."

"How come people say love is so wonderful, Pa? It don't feel too wonderful to me."

"But it will," Seth stated with a laugh. "All those awful feelings of insecurity are soon replaced with a warmth and happiness that can't be described once the newness wears off."

"Is that how you feel with Maeve? All warm and happy?"

"You betcha, boy." Seth hollered at the horses who were suddenly moving far too slow. "Heah! Get on there, you silly animals! I've got a wedding to attend."

* * *

Maeve lifted the yards of white material above her knee in order to place the white satin slippers Sarah had loaned her on her feet. "This is it," she whispered. "I'm about to become Mrs. Seth Caldwell."

As she stared at her reflection in the scratched and scarred mirror, Maeve could swear she saw her mother standing just behind her. "Mama? Is that you?"

A gentle breeze made the curtains billow. Yet how? All the windows were sealed tightly to ward off the cold air, Maeve realized.

Tears of happiness filled her eyes. The one thing that would have made this day even more perfect would have been for her mama to see her all dressed up, and obviously that had just happened.

When she turned back to face the mirror, all she saw was her own glowing image.

"Maeve, Maeve, come quick, Seth is here," Matthew exclaimed, running into the room.

An overwhelming feeling of shyness filled her. What would he think of the 'new and improved' Maeve? Sarah had not only taught her how to sew and cook and clean, she'd also included lessons in how to style her hair and to apply color to her cheeks and lips. A sudden thought caused a wave of apprehension. What if he didn't like the changes? She touched her coiffured hair with trembling fingers.

Suddenly there was no more time for worry; the man she loved with all her heart stood in the doorway, and from the expression on his face, Maeve could tell he was hardly disappointed.

Closing the distance between them, Seth captured her in a long embrace, lifting Maeve off the floor as he twirled her around. "I've missed you terribly," he told her, whispering words of endearment into her ear.

Maeve wrapped her arms around his neck and returned the hug with equal passion. "I love you, Seth. I love you so very much."

Very gently, he placed her back on her feet. "Then let's go get married, shall we?" As his hands encompassed her waist, Seth frowned. "Why, you're nothing but skin and bone. My first duty as your husband will be to fatten you up a bit."

She giggled. "Thanks for the compliment, but I don't think you have much to fear about me starving to death anytime soon. I probably look thinner because of the new clothes."

"Nonsense," Seth scoffed. "Why, I can put both hands around that tiny little waist of yours and touch my thumbs—watch."

Maeve realized she'd just found a small piece of heaven right here on earth. Perhaps the drastic change in life-style which forced her to stay busy was well worth it! Reaching up to kiss his cheek, she smiled. "You look so handsome all dressed up."

"I borrowed the suit from John before we left for home." Seth studied her sparkling hazel eyes. "I must confess, home wasn't much without you there. And I swear Pea has missed you almost as much as I have."

"Where is she?"

"Playing with Matthew, I'd imagine. They seem to have formed quite a bond during the short time they've known one another."

"Let's go see her, shall we?"

"And then we better go. I'm anxious to make you mine."

Wrapping her arms around him for a final hug, Maeve couldn't resist. "And just how do you plan on doing that?"

He kissed the tip of her nose. "It'll be more fun if you'll allow me to show you."

"So what are we waiting for?" she teased, leading him into the den. Both were surprised when they found the room empty. "Sarah? John?"

From just outside the front door, Maeve heard Pea's muffled laughter. She quirked a brow at Seth. "What in the world?"

"Only one way to find out," he said as he opened the door. They were bombarded with a shower of rice.

"Good luck!" Sarah cried, doing her own fair share of throwing.

Maeve's gaze traveled from the excited gathering to the decorated wagon. White ribbons streamed gaily from each side. Now that she had more of an idea what the cost of such an extravagance would be, tears of gratitude filled her eyes. "How can I ever repay you for your kindness, Sarah?"

The woman leaned over to whisper in her ear,

"Just be happy, my dear. Just be happy."

Maeve embraced her warmly. "I am," she assured Sarah, her voice thick with emotion.

When she felt a gentle tug on her gown, Maeve glanced down to find Pea staring up at her with solemn eyes.

"You's gonna go away one more time and then you ain't never leaving me agin', are you, Maeve?"

"That's right, my precious."

Jeb tapped her shoulder. "C-can I give my soon-to-be new Ma a hug?"

"You bet you can!" Maeve gathered the stammering boy in her arms and held on to him for a moment. "I'm so proud of you," she whispered. "I want you to know, Jeb, all the readjusting I had to do, all those terrible days of the sickness . . . well, I couldn't have survived them without your help. You're a wonderful young man and I love you very much." When she pulled away, Jeb's face was scarlet.

"Aww gee, Maeve—I mean Mom."

Nothing could have sounded sweeter.

Chapter Thirty

The trip to Elkhorn was far shorter than the one Maeve and Jeb had taken, as this time it was filled with love, laughter, and excitement about the upcoming wedding.

Though snow still covered much of the ground, Maeve paid little attention to the cold. Her heart was warmed by the man seated beside her. "I can't believe I'm getting married. I wonder if I beat Natasha to the altar?" No sooner had the statement left her lips than Maeve began to wonder why she'd even say such a thing.

Seth drew back and stared at her. "This is the first time you've mentioned your family in a while. Are you missing them, by chance?"

"I suppose with this being such a special day

for me, I'd like them to be here, but I know that's impossible."

He patted her arm in consoling fashion. "Natasha. That's your cousin, right?"

"Mmm-hmm."

"Was she engaged to be married before you . . . er, traveled?"

"No," Maeve admitted, feeling a bit confused.

"So why would she beat you to the altar?"

Maeve turned to face him, recalling the events that happened during the snowstorm. "Have you ever experienced a dream so real that when you awoke, it seemed as if it happened?"

He thought for a moment. "Well, yes, I suppose I have. When I was sick . . . remember? I spoke to you about it. The strange vision I experienced?"

"The Great Spirit. But Seth, somehow, some way, I think that one really did take place. How else can you explain my knowing about what you dreamed?"

"I've thought a lot about it," he admitted. "Maybe somehow we really are connected to one another through our spirits. How else can you explain your presence in my life? Anyone could have found you . . . anyone at all, yet they didn't."

"I know," Maeve said with a sigh of contentment. She grabbed his arm and squeezed. "Let's face it. You and I were just meant to be."

"Friends, lovers, and helpmates," Seth finished, placing one hand on her knee. "If town weren't so close, I'm afraid I'd have to stop this wagon and make love to you right this very minute."

"Town can always wait," Maeve teased.

Seth reined in to allow a wagon to pass. "But travelers won't. We should be there fairly soon. Think you can hold on until tonight?"

Just as she opened her mouth to respond, Maeve heard a loud, boisterous commotion that sent chills up her spine. "What in the world?"

Seth glanced over his shoulder, his brows furrowed with worry. "I think we're in big trouble. That was an Indian war cry if I've ever heard one." He reached beneath the buckboard seat to retrieve his gun.

"Not on our wedding day," Maeve moaned, barely able to contain her dissatisfaction at the intrusion.

"You're taking this too lightly. Here, take my gun and get into the back. Shoot first, ask questions later."

"Well, for Pete's sake!" This living in the 1880s was nothing but the pits. "Just tell whoever it is we're in a hurry to get marri . . ." The words died as something, or someone, came crashing through the brush, kicking up bits of snow in the process.

"One Feather! What in the world are you doing?" Maeve stared at the Blackfoot as if he'd lost his mind. And indeed, it seemed he had.

"Aim your gun!" Seth commanded in a low and gravelly tone.

"Not at One Feather, Seth! He's your friend." She watched in amazement as the Indian rode to the front of the wagon, blocking their way. "Talk to him. Tell him to move."

"You see those black marks on his face?" Seth questioned, his tone a mere whisper.

"Yeah, but so what?"

"War paint," he uttered, barely able to voice the words before having to duck out of the way of a flying arrow. "Stop this, my friend! Speak to me, tell me what's wrong."

"One Feather kidnap Woman Who Walks On Cloud," the Indian stated, his face set in a stubborn expression. Arms folded across his massive chest, he awaited Maeve's response.

"I'm not going with you, One Feather!" Maeve stood and placed both hands on her hips. "Now you just move. This is our wedding day and I won't have you throwing a tantrum because you can't have your way! I've tried to explain to you, I do not know how to walk on the clouds."

"One Feather trade many fine horses for information?" he questioned, somewhat dubiously.

Struggling out of the wagon, Maeve winced as she heard her dress rip on an exposed nail. All those hours of stitching . . . for what? To have them all rip out every time she took a step?

Calmly she handed Seth his shotgun. "Put that thing away before someone gets seriously hurt," she said, walking toward the despondent Indian. "Come on, One Feather, hop on down from your pony so we can talk."

Seth watched in amazement. Was there nothing this wonderful woman feared?

Time Heals

Pouting somewhat, One Feather slid from his pony's back. "You teach One Feather?" When Maeve wrapped one arm in his, it took the Indian by surprise. To have a white woman touch an Indian was unheard of. But then again, this was no ordinary woman. He listened closely to her words.

"One Feather, it doesn't really matter how I got here. Besides, I don't think my heart would allow me to remember the exact details and I'm glad about that. You see, I'm happy here. I have a warm and wonderful man to love and I'm fixing to be married to him, so—"

"Good Heart fine man," One Feather admitted reluctantly. "Will bring you many fine children."

Maeve laughed. "Well, I don't know about many . . . maybe two at the most, huh? But what I'm telling you, One Feather, is that only when you believe in yourself can you perform great and mighty things, do you understand?"

"If One Feather believe he walk on clouds, he can?"

"No, no, no!" she admonished quickly, her head filled with visions of this man who had come to be more than just a friend deciding to walk off a cliff. "It would be very wrong to try."

"Wrong?"

"Wrong. You see, One Feather, Woman Who Walks on Cloud needs you in her life. All these children you insist Seth and I are going to have will need someone to teach them the ways of a

385

Susan Collier

true and gentle warrior. You are just the man to do that."

"Hmmm. Woman Who Walks On Cloud very wise to see One Feather is true warrior. Not many people know these things."

"Oh, One Feather, not many people have looked beyond the color of your skin." She paused. "As a matter of fact, I would be proud if you would accept the role of my brother."

"Blood brother?" One Feather questioned, whipping out his knife.

As Seth observed from the wagon, the Indian's actions threw him into a panic. He jumped down, spooking the horses in the process, and rushed to Maeve's defense. "You are my friend, One Feather, but harm the woman and I'll kill you with my bare hands."

Confused by Seth's sudden verbal attack, the bronze-skinned man tried to explain. "One Feather no harm sister! We share blood, we be blood related."

"Share blood?" Maeve squeaked. "Did he say share blood?"

Taking her by the shoulders, Seth gently led her a few steps away. "What exactly did you tell him?"

She explained and he smiled. "He wants to prick your finger so that your blood will mingle."

"P-Prick my finger?"

"You can't back out now. You'd hurt his pride. Besides, the reason he admires you so much is because you show no fear. It won't hurt

. . . much," Seth consoled.

Walking back to the Indian's side, Maeve stoically held out her hand. "Make it quick, okay?" She closed her eyes as One Feather's knife made contact with her extended finger. One sharp jab and it was over. Opening one eye, she watched as One Feather repeated the process on himself. When their fingers touched and pressed, mingling the drops of blood, Maeve could swear she felt a renewed strength. One that she would need.

Because the horses Seth had spooked were nowhere to be found.

"This is great," she wailed. "Just great!"

"One Feather go in search of missing horses. Sister Who Walks On Cloud have no need to shed water from eyes."

As Maeve watched him depart, Seth removed the blanket from One Feather's pony and placed it on the ground. "Might as well sit a spell. This could take him a while—if he even remembers what he's gone after."

She joined him. "This is going to take a long, *long* while, isn't it?"

"Yep," Seth stated, leaning back on his arms. "Probably so."

"Could we get to town any faster by walking?"

"More than likely, but it's still miles away."

A brilliant idea took shape as Maeve stared dejectedly at the pony. "Couldn't we borrow One Feather's horse?"

"If you want to be scalped, we could."

"One Feather is not going to scalp his own

sister. Half sister," Seth corrected, "and yes he would. You do not, under any circumstances, touch an Indian's horse without his permission."

As the hours passed, the sun began its descent behind the mountain, and soon the travelers leaving Elkhorn became a mere memory. The air that had been crisp yet pleasant all afternoon now turned cold and damp. Maeve shivered. "Do you think he's found them yet?"

"By now, I doubt very seriously that he even remembers what he went after. He's probably found a nice warm shelter for the night and is in the process of cooking a rabbit for dinner."

Her mouth watered. "That sounds wonderful."

Seth drew back in amazement. "It does? You, the protector of all forest critters, would consent to eat one?"

"I'm trying to fit in with the times, Seth. And I'm so hungry," she admitted, "I might be convinced to eat Bambi himself." After a few seconds of silence, she quickly amended her statement. "No, I couldn't."

"I know," Seth stated with a nod and a smile. "But it was a good try."

Snuggling into his arms, Maeve breathed deeply of his scent. "I love you. I love you because you understand me and accept me just as I am."

One quick kiss. That's all she'd give him. That's all she wanted herself, actually. Yet . . . as his tongue darted and plunged, his hands stroked and caressed, a slow, sweet, sensuous fire began to build within.

"Oh, Seth," Maeve moaned, melting into his embrace.

Seth laid her back upon the blanket, working the buttons of her wedding gown free. When he exposed her delicate mounds, he covered them with his hands before taking one ripe bud into his mouth and nipping gently.

"This would have been our wedding night," he observed. "And I would have done this . . . and this . . . and lots of this. . . . " He showed her with his hands and his mouth an unbridled passion.

Hunger took on a new meaning as Maeve returned his caresses. She placed her hand between the warmth of his legs and felt his need for her harden at her touch. Her mouth touched his; her tongue flickered briefly over his lips before moving to his brow, his earlobes, the tender crease of his sun-burnished neck.

When he slipped the bodice of her dress down to her waist, she moaned in sweet expectation.

"Sister Who Walks On Cloud! Sister Who Walks On Cloud! I found him! I have located the shaman!"

Maeve sat up, bumped noses with Seth, then mouthed *Shaman?* to her astonished soon-to-be husband.

The bushes rustled before One Feather finally broke through the thicket and stared proudly down at them. Crossing his arms against his chest, he nodded. "Shaman will perform ceremony."

"And the horses?" Seth asked hopefully.

One Feather frowned. "Horses have no need to attend wedding."

"No, no, of course not," Maeve managed, trying to hold back her laughter.

And in the great universe that had brought her to him, the stars and full winter moon their witnesses, Maeve Fredrickson became, at last and forever, Mrs. Seth Caldwell.

Long after the departure of her newly established blood brother, Maeve stood with her back pressed against Seth's chest, looking up into the magic expanse of sky.

"It was a wonderful ceremony," she observed, craning her neck so that her husband could continue to place kisses along the length of her tender flesh.

Reaching up to remove the pins from her hair, Seth agreed. "Not what I had in mind, but at least we're married." He frowned. "We still don't have a wedding certificate proving our marriage took place to show to Sarah and John."

"We'll tell 'em it's in the mail," Maeve offered with a giggle. She turned to face her husband. "Do you know when I feel our actual wedding ceremony took place, Seth?"

"No. When?"

"During the dream we shared. When the Great Spirit joined us together for all eternity."

"I agree," Seth managed between nibbles to

her ear. "I only went through with this because I thought that's what you wanted."

"What I wanted?" Maeve turned slowly to face him. "Let me show you what I want."

By the time the early morning blush of a newborn day streaked the darkness, Maeve had received all she wanted, and more. Much, much more.

Up in the sky, three remaining stars flickered brightly before disappearing. The angels smiled at one another, then flew home to ring the bells of heaven in joyous celebration.

An Angel's Touch

Where angels go, love is sure to follow.

Don't miss these unforgettable romances that combine the magic of angels and the joy of love.

Daemon's Angel by Sherrilyn Kenyon. Cast to the mortal realm by an evil sorceress, Arina has more than her share of problems. She is trapped in a temptress's body and doomed to lose any man she desires. Yet even as Arina yearns for the safety of the pearly gates, she finds paradise in the arms of a Norman mercenary. But to savor the joys of life with Daemon, she will have to battle demons and risk her very soul for love.

_52026-5 $4.99 US/$5.99 CAN

Forever Angels by Trana Mae Simmons. Thoroughly modern Tess Foster has everything, but when her boyfriend demands she sign a prenuptial agreement Tess thinks she's lost her happiness forever. Then her guardian angel sneezes and sends the woman of the nineties back to the 1890s—and into the arms of an unbelievably handsome cowboy. But before she will surrender to a marriage made in heaven, Tess has to make sure that her guardian angel won't sneeze again—and ruin her second chance at love.

_52021-4 $4.99 US/$5.99 CAN

Dorchester Publishing Co., Inc.
65 Commerce Road
Stamford, CT 06902

Please add $1.75 for shipping and handling for the first book and $.50 for each book thereafter. NY, NYC, PA and CT residents, please add appropriate sales tax. No cash, stamps, or C.O.D.s. All orders shipped within 6 weeks via postal service book rate. Canadian orders require $2.00 extra postage and must be paid in U.S. dollars through a U.S. banking facility.

Name _____

Address _____

City _____ State _____ Zip _____

I have enclosed $_____ in payment for the checked book(s).

Payment <u>must</u> accompany all orders.☐ Please send a free catalog.

DANCE of the FLAME

ELAINE BARBIERI

**Elaine Barbieri's romances are
"powerful...fascinating...storytelling at its best!"**
—Romantic Times

Exiled to a barren wasteland, Sera will do anything to regain the kingdom that is her birthright. But the hard-eyed warrior she saves from death is the last companion she wants for the long journey to her homeland.

To the world he is known as Death's Shadow—as much a beast of battle as the mighty warhorse he rides. But to the flame-haired healer, his forceful arms offer a warm haven, and he swears his throbbing strength will bring her nothing but pleasure.

Sera and Tolin hold in their hands the fate of two feuding houses with an ancient history of bloodshed and betrayal. But no matter what the age-old prophecy foretells, the sparks between them will not be denied, even if their fiery union consumes them both.

_3793-9 $5.99 US/$6.99 CAN

Dorchester Publishing Co., Inc.
65 Commerce Road
Stamford, CT 06902

TIMESWEPT

The Sorcerer's Lady by Debra Dier. Victorian debutante Laura Sullivan can't believe her eyes when Aunt Sophie's ancient spell conjures up the man of Laura's dreams—and deposits a half-naked barbarian in the library of her Boston home. An accomplished sorcerer, Connor has traveled through the ages to reach his soul mate. But his powers are useless if he can't convince Laura that she is destined to become the sorcerer's lady.

_52037-0 $4.99 US/$5.99 CAN

Stardust Time by Marti Jones. Since the Fable Comet streaks across the night skies only once every hundred years, Adrian Sheppard hopes taking pictures of it will start her on a new career. How can she guess that the celestial body will transport her back to the Old West—and into the arms of a handsome farmer with three small children and the key to her heart?

_52031-1 $4.99 US/$5.99 CAN

Dorchester Publishing Co., Inc.
65 Commerce Road
Stamford, CT 06902

Please add $1.75 for shipping and handling for the first book and $.50 for each book thereafter. NY, NYC, PA and CT residents, please add appropriate sales tax. No cash, stamps, or C.O.D.s. All orders shipped within 6 weeks via postal service book rate. Canadian orders require $2.00 extra postage and must be paid in U.S. dollars through a U.S. banking facility.

Name_____

Address_____

City _____ State _____ Zip _____

I have enclosed $_____in payment for the checked book(s).
Payment <u>must</u> accompany all orders.□ Please send a free catalog.

Don't miss these tempestuous romances about modern-day heroines who find their hearts' desires in the arms of men from long-ago eras.

Now And Then by Bobby Hutchinson. Indian legend says that the spirit can overcome all obstacles, even time itself. Yet Dr. Paige Randolph doubts that anything can help her recover from the loss of her child and the breakup of her marriage. But when a mysterious crop circle casts her back one hundred years, her only hope of surviving on the savage Canadian frontier is to open her heart to the love of the one man meant for her and the powerful truth of the spirit world.
_51990-9 $4.99 US/$5.99 CAN

A Love Through Time by Marti Jones. Although tree surgeon Libby Pfifer can explain root rot and Japanese beetles, she can't understand how a fall from the oldest oak in Fort Pickens, Florida, lands her in another century. Yet there she is, face-to-face with the great medicine man Geronimo, and an army captain whose devastating good looks tempt her even while his brusque manner makes her want to wring his neck.
_51991-7 $4.99 US/$5.99 CAN

Dorchester Publishing Co., Inc.
65 Commerce Road
Stamford, CT 06902

Please add $1.75 for shipping and handling for the first book and $.50 for each book thereafter. NY, NYC, PA and CT residents, please add appropriate sales tax. No cash, stamps, or C.O.D.s. All orders shipped within 6 weeks via postal service book rate. Canadian orders require $2.00 extra postage and must be paid in U.S. dollars through a U.S. banking facility.

Name_____
Address_____
City _____ State _____ Zip_____
I have enclosed $_____in payment for the checked book(s).
Payment <u>must</u> accompany all orders.☐ Please send a free catalog.